DARK QUEEN'S QUEST

THE CHILDREN OF THE GODS BOOK 32

I. T. LUCAS

NOTE FROM THE AUTHOR:
Dark Queen's Quest is a work of fiction!
Names, characters, places and incidents are products of the author's
imagination or are used fictitiously and are not to be construed as real. Any
similarity to actual persons, organizations and/or events is purely coincidental.

MEY

"Mey, sweetheart, do you need a few moments to rest?" Derek let his camera hand drop. "You look as lively as a dead fish wearing lipstick."

"Thanks a lot, Derek," Mey huffed and strode toward the cooler, casting a forced smile at the old lady sitting on a bench across from their spot.

The woman had already been there when they'd arrived, and she hadn't budged since, watching the entire thing as if it was live entertainment.

That was the problem with a photo shoot in Central Park. The fresh air was good, the spectators not so much.

Derek lifted his hands. "Not funny? I thought it was. Where is that beautiful smile of yours?"

As always, her photographer's fumbling attempts at humor were more amusing than his jokes, but today even that had failed to lift her mood.

Pulling a bottle of water out of the cooler, she twisted the cap off. "I'm worried about Jin."

"What's wrong?" Derek pulled out another bottle for himself. "The new job not panning out?"

"I don't know." Mey took a few sips, trying not to smear her lipstick but failing. "I haven't heard from her in two days. She sent me a text that she'd arrived and was getting settled in her new place, and that was it. I called and left messages for her to call me back, I texted and asked the same thing, and I even sent her an email. Nothing. No response."

Derek waved a hand. "Give the kid some breathing room. She's probably busy as hell, working hard, making new friends, buying potted plants for her new apartment." He cast her a stern look. "And you, young lady, need to be a professional and look lively for the camera. We have a photo shoot to wrap up."

"Let me fix your lipstick." Julie walked over with her makeup case. "Pucker up." She reached with the lip brush, fixed whatever needed fixing, then checked Mey's eyeliner. "You're good to go."

Derek looked up at the sky. "There is no more than one hour of good light left. We will have to come back tomorrow."

Mey let out a breath. "In that case, how about we call it a day?"

Shaking her head, Julie snorted. "Cruella de Vil is not going to like it."

"Yeah, you're probably right." Mey sighed.

The modeling agency owner was a tough and demanding lady, and she had earned the nickname fair and square. Dalia Cromwell was all smiles and charm as long as everything ran smoothly. Except that was rarely the case in a modeling agency, which meant that most days Dalia was as mellow as a category five hurricane.

Still, Mey had a soft spot in her heart for the dragon lady. When she'd returned to the States three years ago, Dalia had hired her on the spot.

The truth was that they could have lied about cutting their day short, and no one would have been any the wiser, but even though her crew had no problem with that, Mey did. Her life was full of secrets and lies to cover those secrets. So, whenever she could, she stuck to the truth. "Let's do it."

"Think happy thoughts," Derek said.

Julie handed her the tote bag that was the real star of the photo shoot. "Think of taking this beauty home with you." She winked. "It's worth three thousand dollars, and they are letting us keep it."

"You can have it. I like the smaller one."

Julie's eyes widened. "Are you sure?"

"I'm big enough without adding a huge tote to my frame."

"You're tall, not big. There is a difference." With a dismissive gesture, Julie went back to her foldable chair. "You're gorgeous."

"Thanks."

Mey's nearly six-foot-tall willowy frame was great for modeling, and it had played a big role in her winning the beauty pageant that had started her career. But she'd never felt comfortable in her own skin.

Most Asian women were much shorter than her, and Mey didn't like the stares and murmurs that her size provoked.

Her mother had always reassured her that it was her beautiful face people were staring at, not her height, and that she should be thankful for it. But her adoptive mother was an average-sized, average-looking Caucasian lady, who'd never had to deal with stares.

Well, that wasn't entirely true.

A Caucasian couple with two Asian daughters had drawn plenty of attention over the years. Especially after her Jewish parents decided to move to Israel and raise their daughters there.

Mey loved the country, and she loved the people. For the most part, they were warm, real, and welcoming, but unlike Americans, they didn't know the meaning of minding their own business.

People would stop her parents on the street and ask them how they'd gotten their two beautiful girls. School hadn't been easy either. Kids and teachers alike had wanted to know everything. Starting with where Mey and Jin had been adopted from, what had happened to their biological parents, and whether they were ever going back to China to look for them.

The answer to that last question had always been a resolute no.

First of all, because it was an impossible task to get the Chinese authorities to cooperate, and secondly, because Barbara and David Levin were Mey and Jin's parents in every way that mattered. Mey was about twenty months old and Jin a newborn when the Levins had adopted them, and no two girls could have asked for better, more loving parents.

"That's it." Derek snapped away. "That's the mysterious Mona Lisa smile I'm talking about. Give me more, baby."

There was a lot more in Mey's reservoir of good memories. In fact, her life had been great up until about a month ago, but she didn't want to think about that.

To keep on smiling, she had to stay in the past.

Her glory days, so to speak.

"That's it, baby." Derek kept snapping. "If Mona Lisa ever joined the army, she would have looked like you. Confident, strong, and with a sexy smile." He kept up his string of compliments, ensuring that the smile never left Mey's face. "She has nothing on you. Was she declared a beauty queen? No. But you were."

"Stop it. You want me to smile, not laugh."

"But it's true."

After winning the Ms. Teen Israel beauty queen pageant at seventeen, Mey's modeling career had taken off like a rocket. Juggling school and photo shoots hadn't been easy, but she'd felt on top of the world. Then at eighteen, she'd been drafted into the army like most of her age group and had gone through the same basic training as everyone else.

That was an incredibly busy time, but even that had been fun.

Mey had many fond memories from those intense six weeks, and she was still in contact with the friends she'd made there. Fifty girls sleeping in one army barrack and working hard to become soldiers had been a memorable experience. Maybe one day she would write a story about it. Or a script. What most people didn't realize about the Israeli military was that it might be fierce, but it wasn't very formal or strict on the personal level. With every eighteen-year-old drafted, it was an army of the people. There had been a lot of laughs and shenanigans during those intense six weeks.

After basic training was done, her friends had been assigned posts in various military branches, while Mey had been offered a very different kind of job, and her real glory days had begun.

Globetrotting from one on-location photo shoot to another, Mey had become the face of an international fashion label. But even though the label was real, and Mey's pictures had been featured in fashion magazines all around the world, her official job had been only a cover for something much more interesting than posing for the camera.

KIAN

*S*yssi threaded her arm through Kian's. "I'm glad that Annani is staying longer than usual this time. I love these Friday night family dinners. I wish they could continue, but I know she'll be going home soon."

Kian smiled. "Surprisingly, I like them too. We should keep up the tradition even after my mother leaves. It's nice to meet with the family once a week and hear how everyone is doing. It saves me from having to make polite phone calls inquiring about their well-being."

Syssi cast him a sidelong glance. "You're not the one who does the calling. You tell me to do it."

"Actually, I don't. You just do that because you are awesome." He kissed the top of her head.

His mother had been right about Syssi. From the very start, Annani had foreseen that Syssi was going to be the glue that held them all together. At the time Kian had doubted that, mainly because his wife was so shy that picking up the phone was a chore for her, but she was also a strong woman who knew how to work around her quirks.

As they strolled down the meandering path toward his

mother's house, enjoying the late evening breeze, Kian felt the week's tension draining away.

Even though he often worked from home during the weekends, those family dinners had become the delineating mark that signaled the end of his workweek. The effect was more psychological than anything else, but it helped him relax.

Then again, the additional tension he'd been feeling for the past month was gone. The mission to infiltrate the Doomers' island was over, and Carol was safe, or as safe as she could be with Lokan.

She should have come home instead of waiting for her mate's return from his mandatory visit to the island. Especially since Lokan's Washington penthouse was still under surveillance. Those detectives that Turner's guy had discovered were still there, watching the place, and probably eavesdropping too.

But Carol had declined Kian's invitation, claiming that she was still tired and needed the rest. Which was no doubt true. She'd been through a lot.

By now, Lokan should be back, and Kian couldn't wait for his update. Or rather Carol's. Lokan's phone was still suspect. And even though William had flown over and checked the place for bugs, Carol's instructions were to exercise caution until Lokan got rid of the watchers, which he'd promised to take care of as soon as he was back from the island.

Hopefully, Areana's son had kept his mouth shut about where he'd been and with whom. If he had done that, the visit should have passed without incident. After centuries of successfully lying to his father, Lokan was not likely to reveal anything unintentionally, especially now that he had a mate to return to.

Except, Kian didn't trust Lokan, and frankly he didn't trust Areana either.

Not that he was going to share his misgivings with his

mother. Annani was overjoyed at being able to talk with her sister after five thousand years, and she preferred to turn a blind eye to the fact that her sister loved Navuh, and that he was her first priority. Not Annani, and not Annani's clan.

"What happened?" Syssi asked. "Suddenly there is a dark cloud hovering over your head."

"It's nothing." He wrapped his arm around her shoulders. "Just more of the same."

She smiled up at him. "Are you still worried about Lokan's hidden agenda?"

"Of course. And I don't trust Areana either, but don't mention it to my mother."

"I won't. It will only upset her, and it won't change her opinion about her sister."

"Precisely." He sighed. "I'm just afraid that she will tell Areana too much. But then, I tend to be overcautious, especially when the safety of my people is concerned."

Syssi leaned against his side. "Will Annani be able to communicate with Areana once she returns to the sanctuary?"

"William will patch the calls through. They agreed on a specific time every day, so that shouldn't be a problem."

"Good. I thought that maybe that was the reason for her still being here. I'm glad that it's not. I want to believe that she's enjoying herself being with her family."

Kian shrugged. "There are no new babies in the sanctuary, so Annani is in no hurry, but that won't last long. As much as my mother enjoys her temporary lodging in the village, she'll eventually want the comfort and luxury of her Alaskan paradise."

Syssi halted and turned toward him. "What if we build her a mansion here?"

Kian chuckled. "Even if we had the money to splurge, which at the moment we don't, that won't keep her here." Wrapping his arm around Syssi's waist, he kept on walking. "Annani needs her freedom, and she also likes to go on excursions to various places around the world. She knows that I worry when she does that, so she didn't go anywhere while she was here. I'm sure she's already restless and itching to return home."

"How come we are still in a money squeeze? I thought that Ella's fundraiser was going well."

"It is, and maybe in a year or two, it will raise enough money to cover the ongoing living expenses of the rescued girls, but not yet. On top of that, we still have more than seventy Guardians on payroll, and we have financed several super expensive rescue operations." He lifted her hand to his lips. "Don't worry, love. I'm working on a solution. I just need to find ways for the clan to make money faster."

Syssi cupped his cheek. "My poor baby. No matter what you do, it's never enough."

"Ain't that the truth," Kian mimicked Turner's southern accent.

"Here you are, darlings." Amanda opened the door and waited for them to climb the three steps to Annani's front porch. "We are ready to sit down to dinner." She pulled Syssi into a gentle hug and then kissed Kian's cheek.

Andrew and Nathalie were already sitting at the table with their little girl, and Eva was holding Ethan while Bhathian was making funny faces for the baby's delight.

Watching the normally gruff Guardian acting like a clown, Kian wondered if he was going to be as silly when his child was born. Maybe in private, but not in public. After all, he was the leader of this community and had to maintain certain standards of behavior. Clowning around was not part of that.

Once all the kisses and hugs had been exchanged, Annani clapped her hands. "Everyone to the table, please." She smiled at Dalhu. "Come sit next to me. We have not had a chance to chat in a while."

The guy turned a little gray but recovered quickly. "You

honor me, Clan Mother." He dipped his head before taking the seat next to her.

Annani patted his arm. "We are a family. There is no need for formality."

As Annani's servants brought out dinner, Kian thought about Okidu and how different his butler seemed lately.

Something must have gone wrong with Okidu's circuitry during his reboot, but no one dared take a look at his insides for fear of messing things up. William had said that the ocean fall couldn't have caused any serious damage, and that whatever went wrong would repair itself in time.

Supposedly, the Odus were indestructible, but the truth was that this had never been tested. At least as far as Kian knew. Perhaps their resilience had been proven when Annani had been all alone, and they had been her sole companions and defenders.

But what if Okidu's strange behavior had been caused by something other than the reboot?

Maybe the frequent changing of masters he'd had to obey during the mission had messed with his programming. Before the incident, Okidu used to hover over Syssi and Kian until he was dismissed. Now he was slinking away to his room unless ordered otherwise.

"Kian, dear, you are not paying attention."

"My apologies, Mother. Did you ask me something?"

"I said that we need to look for Kalugal. I know that Areana asked Lokan to do that, but he is just one man, and he already has enough on his plate. We need to help him."

Kian lifted a brow. "Why?"

Annani leveled a hard stare at him. "Because my sister asked me to. She does not know whether her son is alright or not, and she worries about him. If our positions were reversed, I would have counted on my sister's aid." She crossed her arms over her chest. "I would have been very disappointed if she did not do everything in her power to help me."

Kian stifled a scoff. Annani was projecting her assertive nature onto Areana, but her sister was nothing like her. She was a follower, not a leader.

Except, Annani probably felt that she owed Areana because of the sacrifice she'd made for her five thousand years ago. The irony was that by taking Annani's place, Areana had found her truelove mate and had him by her side for all those years. Annani, on the other hand, had lost the love of her life and had spent that time alone.

"What's wrong?" Amanda asked, her alarmed tone catching everyone's attention.

Following her worried gaze, Kian turned to look at Syssi just as her eyes rolled back in her head and she started sliding down the chair.

"Call Bridget!" he yelled as he caught his wife before she slid all the way to the floor. Carrying her to the couch, he added, "Call Merlin too!"

"I'm on it," Andrew said.

Adding to the commotion of people getting up and chairs being pushed back, Phoenix started wailing, and then Ethan joined her.

"Take the children out of here," Annani commanded. "They are frightened."

In Kian's arms, Syssi groaned and opened her eyes. "I had a vision."

Except for the little ones, everyone went silent at once, and a moment later, the crying subsided as well.

Kian didn't give a damn about the fucking vision. "How are you feeling?"

She smiled up at him. "I'm fine. It wasn't any worse than the others."

That was why he hated it when she had them. "You weren't pregnant when you had the other visions."

Syssi's smile vanished, replaced by a frown. "Do you think the visions can harm Allegra?"

"I'm not a doctor, love. But in my opinion, the visions themselves are not harmful. It's your body's reaction to them that worries me."

"Bridget is on her way," Andrew said. "I couldn't get ahold of Merlin."

LOKAN

" $\mathcal{L}$ okan!" Carol threw her arms around his neck, jumped up, and wrapped her legs around his hips. "I missed you so much." She covered his face with a barrage of little kisses.

Dropping his suitcase on the floor, Lokan kicked the door closed and carried her to the couch. "I've never had such a joyous welcome home before." He took his time kissing his mate, pouring his love into every leisurely swipe of his tongue and every gentle nip.

After spending a week together, some of it in Arturo Sandoval's estate in Bolivia, and some of it in Washington, leaving her again had been agony.

"I missed you too. Unless I absolutely have to, I'm not going anywhere without you again."

"How did it go?"

Lokan cocked a brow. "Perhaps we should shower first?"

Since their return to Washington, all of his and Carol's conversations involving the clan or the island had been done in the bathroom with the water running.

"It's okay. William was here and gave the place a thorough

scanning with his gadgets. He found no bugs, which was surprising. Just to be safe, though, he left behind a device that interferes with any signals coming out of here. The downside is that we have to go out on the terrace to use our cellphones, and we can't use Wi-Fi."

Lokan let out a breath. "That's a small price to pay for privacy."

"We won't have it for long, though. Didn't your father insist that you take new men with you to replace the others? Because that might be a problem. What if they recognize me?"

"That's why I told him that I don't want any. Besides, I prefer not having men around while you are here."

Carol frowned. "Didn't your father find it odd? And what about your safety? Isn't he worried about that?"

Smiling, Lokan kissed her forehead. "I made a big show of being angry and disappointed with my men and their lack of loyalty. I fumed that after years of service, they had taken the first opportunity to defect and steal my private jet. I told my father that I'm going to hire a couple of humans to take care of my place and that I don't need a permanent security detail. When I go to places I deem unsafe, I'm going to hire human bodyguards."

"Are you?"

"We need a housekeeper. And when I travel, which I have no intention of doing anytime soon, I'll hire a human security firm."

Carol scrunched her nose. "We don't need a housekeeper. I can take care of the apartment."

As if he would ever let his mate do household chores. Carol was going to live like a princess. "I want to pamper you, my angel. I don't want you washing floors or dusting or doing any of those things."

She grimaced as if he was being unreasonable. "Can I at

least cook? I've been going out of my mind with boredom while you were gone."

"Didn't you go shopping like I asked you to?"

One of the first things Lokan had done when he'd returned was to check his safe. Surprisingly, none of the cash had been taken, only his spare phone. He'd given Carol ten thousand before leaving for the island, with instructions to buy herself a new wardrobe and whatever she needed to make the place feel like home.

"I did. But even shopping gets boring after a while. I need something to do while you're schmoozing with politicians."

That was a problem. As a former café manager, Carol was used to being surrounded by people all day, but she knew no one in Washington.

"Maybe you should study something? You're an amazing cook and you love feeding people, so maybe the culinary arts?"

She waved a dismissive hand. "I'll think about it later. Right now I'm still in recuperating mode." She smiled coyly. "While you were gone, I've been reading a hot romance novel every night, which made me even hornier than usual. How about you take me to bed to celebrate your safe return?"

"With pleasure. But there is something I need to do first."

Carol didn't like his answer. "What's so important that it cannot wait?"

"The call I need to make to Losham. I promised Kian to take care of the detectives watching this place as soon as I returned from the island."

"He didn't mean it literally."

"I'd rather not take chances with Kian. He wasn't happy about letting me go. I could feel his mistrust as well as see it in his eyes. Kian caved under pressure. He didn't do it voluntarily, and he's going to jump on the first opportunity to lock me up again."

"You're wrong. Turner convinced him that it was the right

thing to do, and Kian accepted it. That's not pressure. That's a well-informed decision."

"Semantics." He kissed the top of her nose. "I'll make it short."

Just then, his belly rumbled, and Carol's eyes widened. She put her hand over his stomach. "My bad. I prepared a nice dinner for us and then forgot all about it when you came through the door. It's your fault for being so devilishly handsome."

Lokan laughed. "I accept responsibility. How about you heat it up while I make the call?"

"It's a deal." She pushed out of his arms. "Don't forget that you need to go out on the terrace."

Grasping his phone, Lokan got up and walked over to the sliding doors. The drapes were drawn, shielding his living room from the detectives' view. He left them like that, getting behind them and pushing the sliding door open.

He had no proof that Losham was behind the surveillance, but he was the most likely culprit.

Lokan sat on one of the recliners and punched in his brother's number. Not a brother, a stepbrother? Or maybe adopted brother was a better definition?

"Hello, Lokan. I was worried about you. Why haven't you returned my call?"

"I was in South America, and the place was bugged. I didn't want to risk having a conversation with you overheard."

"I see. How was your trip?"

"Eventful, but that's not what I want to talk with you about. I want you to fire the idiots you've hired to spy on me."

"I don't know what you're talking about."

"Come on, Losham. Don't insult my intelligence. Our father would have hired pros, not clowns, and no one else has reason to spy on me."

"Maybe the Secret Service is interested in your activity."

"And that's why they only watch my apartment instead of following me around? I never bring any of my contacts to my place. Just fire the idiots, and I won't mention this fiasco to our father."

"I'll see what I can do about your problem."

It wasn't an admission of guilt, but it was good enough. "How about that lunch you called me about. Are you still in the area and want us to meet?"

"Unfortunately, I'm back in San Francisco, so that's no longer an option. But if you want to visit me in California, I'll gladly meet with you."

"I just came back, and I have a lot of work to do, but once my schedule clears I'll give you a call."

"I'm moving in a couple of weeks, so plan on meeting me in Los Angeles."

That was unexpected. "I thought you enjoyed San Francisco."

"I do. But after the initial seven girls that we shipped to the island, security on campuses in the area has been ramped up. Los Angeles is a much bigger pond with more fish."

"Good luck with that."

"Thank you. We are going to be more careful this time and spread out over a large area. One girl per campus, no more."

"Good strategy. I'll give you a call as soon as I can make time for a visit."

"Excellent. I'm looking forward to seeing you. Goodbye, Lokan." Losham disconnected.

As Lokan got back inside, he wasn't sure if that was good news for the clan or bad. Losham was moving his operation to their backyard, so that would make things easier for them. But on the other hand, he was sure they didn't want a bunch of Doomers hanging around their city either.

Damn, now he also had started using their derogatory nickname for the Brothers.

"I made your favorite dish," Carol said from the kitchen.

He walked over to her and pulled her into his arms. "Thank you. I have news for Kian, which I'm not sure he's going to like. Losham is moving his operation to Los Angeles. You should let him know."

"When is Losham moving?"

"In a couple of weeks."

"Then it can wait until after we have dinner."

4

ANNANI

"You're fine." Bridget patted Syssi's arm. "I just wish I'd been here when it was happening. Whatever was going on is back to normal now."

Annani joined everyone gathered around Syssi in the communal sigh of relief. Truth be told, Kian's reaction had stressed her out more than Syssi's momentary fainting spell. His anxiety for his wife had been so strong that it suffused the room with the unpleasant scent, making every immortal in his vicinity feel as if the fear was emanating from them.

That surely had not been good for mother and baby.

The color returned to Kian's face. "Thank the merciful Fates."

"I don't know why you freaked out like that." Syssi cupped his cheek. "You've seen me having visions before. Pregnancy doesn't make me more vulnerable. I'm a strong immortal, remember?"

He nodded, but his face looked pained.

"Can you tell us what you saw?" Amanda asked. "If you're up to it, that is."

Nathalie handed Syssi a glass of water. "Maybe you are a little dehydrated."

"Thanks." Syssi took a few sips, then handed the glass back to Nathalie. "I think I saw Kalugal."

"Did you recognize him from Dalhu's portrait?" Eva asked.

With her detective skills taking over, the woman did not think about how her mate would react to her mentioning the name of the immortal who had induced her transition.

As Ethan uttered a little whine, Annani cast Bhathian a sidelong glance. Holding his son close to his chest, the Guardian did his best not to show any reaction to Eva's question, but Annani scented his tension.

Kalugal had activated Eva's dormant genes nearly fifty years ago, possibly taking her virginity while she had been drunk. Eva did not remember the details of that night, and it was likely that Kalugal had thralled her to forget the encounter in which she had been a willing participant. Nevertheless, the doubt was enough to anger her mate.

Syssi nodded. "It was weird. One moment I saw him looking exactly like his portrait, and the next his image wavered and turned into someone else. Except, I knew it was still him. Perhaps he was shrouding himself?"

"That's possible," Kian said. "Perhaps Areana was wrong about his compulsion ability, and what he used as a child to sneak into the harem was shrouding."

It was an interesting thought. A strong shrouding ability was not as rare as compulsion.

"Did you see where he was?" Amanda asked.

"Yes. That's the most exciting part." Syssi sat up straight. "He was entering the Stock Exchange building in New York. I recognized the distinctive façade."

Annani's heart leaped in excitement. "We should send Guardians over there to look for him. I know it is a big city, but if he is involved in the stock market, perhaps the Guardians can start with monitoring that building."

Syssi shook her head. "The way my visions work, there is no guarantee that he is still in the New York area. I could have seen the past or the future."

Plopping down on a chair, Annani let out an exasperated sigh. "This is the only clue we have. There must be a way to follow it. Any ideas?" She looked at Kian.

His expression revealed his disinterest. "Even if Kalugal is there now, it will be like looking for a needle in a haystack. Especially if he can shroud himself from immortals as well as from humans."

"What was he wearing?" Amanda asked. "With his ability, I assume that he's making a killing on Wall Street and that he's wearing the latest fashion. His clothing might clue us in as to the timeline of the vision."

Syssi closed her eyes. "He had a navy blazer on. The lapel was slim, so it wasn't too old. But then those are not new."

"No, they are not." Amanda tapped her finger on her lips. "They've been in for the past five years, but that's good. At least we know it wasn't twenty years ago."

"What if we can flush him out?" Annani rose to her feet and started pacing.

"How?" Kian asked.

"He knows what his mother looks like, and I bet he misses her. What if he sees her face on an advertisement?" She turned to Eva. "Alena and Areana share the same build and coloring, and their facial features are similar. Can you work with that? Can you make Alena look like Areana?"

"I will need to see Areana's portrait," Eva said.

"Could you please bring it over?" Annani motioned to Oridu. "It is the one hanging in my bedroom."

He bowed. "Right away, Clan Mother."

Kian rubbed his jaw. "They do look somewhat alike, but it's not as if you could mistake one for the other."

In her usual stoic manner, Alena's only reaction was an amused smile. The resemblance she bore to Areana was only superficial. On the face of it, they both appeared soft and gentle, but their characters could not have been more different.

Alena's softness surrounded a powerful core, while Areana was soft all the way through. Which might have explained how she could stand being mated to someone like Navuh.

Annani still had a hard time accepting that, but she had to tread lightly with Areana.

They were rebuilding their relationship in ten-minute daily increments, and that did not leave room for criticism. Besides, Annani knew that nothing she said was going to change Areana's mind about her mate. The bond between Navuh and Areana had been cemented over five thousand years, and nothing but death was going to break it.

"Should I place the portrait over the mantel, Clan Mother?" Oridu asked.

"Yes, please do."

For the next couple of minutes, everyone in the room gazed at Areana's portrait, then at Alena, and then at the portrait again.

"It can be done," Eva said. "But it would involve elaborate makeup that Alena would have to apply daily. It's not easy to do for an amateur." She glanced at her baby who was sleeping peacefully in Bhathian's arms. "I don't mind going to New York with you, but only if I can take my family with me."

"I still don't get what you want to do, Mother," Kian said.

"I've got it." Amanda walked over to where Kian and Syssi were sitting on the couch and joined them. "We need to make Alena a famous model. We will get her an appointment in one of the major modeling agencies in New York. Brandon can help with that. Yamanu will go with her and thrall whoever needs thralling over there to sign her up for a big gig. Something that will get her face on billboards and buses. Kalugal will see it and he will get curious. He will want to meet his mother's doppelgänger in person."

Annani clapped her hands. "She can even go by Areana's name."

"That's going too far," Syssi said. "How about Ari? Her full name could be Arielle."

"You are all forgetting something," Alena said. "No one asked me if I'm willing to go."

"Oh, dear." Annani walked over to her daughter and took her hands. "I am so sorry. I assumed you would love a little adventure."

Alena smiled. "I'm not you, Mother. I'm not adventurous, and I've spent most of my life by your side. I wouldn't know how to act."

Amanda gave a dismissive wave of her hand. "Easily fixed. Since you will come out of nowhere, you will pretend to be from Slovenia. That will also explain any oddities about your behavior."

"I don't speak Slovene."

"Out of sheer curiosity, why Slovenia?" Kian asked.

Amanda rolled her eyes. "Because Slovenia is a tiny country, and the chances of Alena bumping into any Slovenians are slim. Besides, with her pale skin and blond hair she looks Slavic, but we don't want to make her Russian. We want something obscure."

"Many of the top models are from the Eastern Bloc," Syssi said.

Alena cleared her throat. "As I mentioned a moment ago, I don't speak Slovene."

Annani gave Alena's hands a light squeeze. "If we get you a tutor, how long is it going to take you to learn? A week? Two weeks? That is not really an obstacle. But if you do not wish to go, we can probably find someone else to impersonate Areana. In a pinch, Lucinda might do."

Alena shook her head. "Lucinda is too short to be a model."

"I know, dear. But I do not wish to force you into doing something you are not comfortable with. And cosmetics models do not need to be tall."

Letting out a sigh, Alena nodded. "I'll do it. I've been doing the same thing for thousands of years. I guess it is time I tried something new."

5

KIAN

*A*s everyone around Kian was getting more and more excited about his mother's idea, he wondered whether he should put an end to it or play along.

Sending Alena to New York accompanied by several Guardians was not going to be particularly costly, and his sister could certainly use the change of pace.

Instead of dousing his family's enthusiasm with a cold dose of reality, he could indulge their fantasy at no great cost to the clan.

"I can have Roni create fake social media accounts for Alena," he offered.

And wasn't that magnanimous of him.

"Arielle," Syssi corrected. "Known as Ari."

Kian nodded. "For Arielle." He turned to Alena. "Are you sure about this? We can have Lucinda wear platform shoes."

Lucinda bore only a slight resemblance to his mother's sister, and she was a head shorter than Alena and therefore Areana. So she wasn't going to work, but if Alena refused, he could scrap the idea without risking his mother's wrath.

After all, he'd been helpful. He'd offered an alternative.

Alena spread both hands in a dismissive gesture. "And drag her here from Scotland? I don't think so."

Regrettably, it seemed that Alena was warming up to the idea.

"I can arrange lodging for you and the Guardians in Ragnar's hotel." He turned to Eva. "I can put you, Bhathian and Ethan in one of the suites. Alena will take the presidential suite with Arwel and Yamanu, and two other Guardians will be in a third."

Alena huffed. "I don't need five Guardians. I'm just going to play at being a model. There is nothing risky in that."

Kian cast her a hard look, making it clear that he was not going to budge on that. "Two Guardians accompany me wherever I go, and I'm not doing anything riskier than business negotiations."

She grimaced. "You have a point. I'll also bring Ovidu along. He doesn't really need a bed, and he can take his one-hour rest in a chair."

"That is a splendid idea," Annani said. "You will be safe with him."

Alena frowned. "Do you also expect me to take two Guardians with me anywhere I go?"

"Of course."

"How am I going to explain it?"

"Arwel can be your overprotective boyfriend," Amanda suggested. "And Yamanu can be your manager. Either that or your translator. You can pretend to speak very little English."

"What about the other three Guardians?"

Amanda lifted one shoulder in a dismissive gesture. "They can take turns being your driver, or a visiting family member. I'm sure you can come up with ideas."

Alena glanced at Eva. "You've been a DEA agent. You can come with me to shoots as my makeup artist and watch out for Kalugal."

Eva's eyes started glowing. "I would love to." She turned to Bhathian. "Are you willing to stay with Ethan while I accompany Alena to photo shoots?"

The Guardian shrugged, pretending that he hadn't heard the part about watching out for Kalugal. "Why not? It's a paid vacation for me." He looked at Kian. "Right, boss?"

"Correct. And I will pay Eva for her time as well."

Eva shook her head. "Don't. I'm also looking forward to a change of pace. I promised myself that as long as Ethan is still nursing, I wouldn't do anything dangerous or deal with filth. I don't want any darkness touching him even indirectly. But this seems like a fun assignment, and all I'll be doing is using my makeup skills."

When Kian opened his mouth to argue, she lifted a hand to stop him. "I'm volunteering for this. It's enough that the clan is paying for the flights and the hotel. Not to mention my mate's salary."

Kian was about to voice his opposition, but Eva's glare stopped him. He relented. "Fine. I know better than to argue with you."

She rewarded him with a bright smile. "I always knew that you were a smart guy."

"We need to go shopping." Amanda rubbed her hands with glee. "You need a designer wardrobe, a contemporary haircut, and a manicure and a pedicure." She walked over to Alena and squeezed into the armchair beside her. "We've never done this before. It's about time we did something sisterly."

Alena's horrified expression was comical, but not unwarranted. Amanda was a shopping beast.

Syssi chuckled. "I still remember when Amanda took me to do all that." She looked at Alena. "You're going to have fun. She is a pro at this."

Alena lifted her braid. "What's wrong with my hair? Or with my clothes?"

Kian was wondering the same thing. Alena was wearing a pretty long dress with small pink flowers printed on the soft fabric, and her long blond hair was gathered into a thick braid. She even had a matching pink band on the crown of her head, securing the flyaways. She looked lovely.

"Nothing, it's gorgeous." Amanda wrapped her arm around Alena's shoulders. "But you look like a fairytale princess from a couple of centuries ago. You need a modern makeover."

6

YAMANU

"*D*o you have any idea what this is about?" Yamanu asked as he buttoned up his white dress shirt. "I've never been invited to the goddess's home before." He pushed his feet into a pair of loafers.

When Kian had called, asking Yamanu whether he and Arwel could come over to the Clan Mother's home, he'd said there was a mission he needed to discuss with them, but he hadn't elaborated.

Arwel shook his head. "No clue."

"It must be something about Lokan." Yamanu pulled out his phone. "I'm going to call Carol."

"Why?" Arwel opened their front door and waited for Yamanu to step out.

"Because if the bastard did something to her, I'm going to make him regret he was ever born."

Arwel smiled. "Relax. I spoke with her a couple of hours ago, and her main complaints were about being bored and missing her mate. Lokan is probably back home by now, and the two of them are celebrating his return."

The tension left as quickly as it had seized him. Yamanu

could handle almost anything with calm, except for a friend getting hurt. More so if the friend was a female, and especially one cohabiting with a Doomer.

Lokan seemed okay, but no one really knew what his deal was, and the thing with brainwashing was that it could raise its ugly head unexpectedly and override rational thought.

"Maybe it's news from the island?"

"How about instead of playing twenty questions, we wait until we get there and Kian fills us in?"

"I don't like surprises."

For the next five minutes neither of them spoke, but as they neared Annani's house, Arwel slowed down.

"I sense a lot of excitement."

"Good or bad?" Yamanu asked as they climbed the steps to the goddess's front porch.

"Good."

"Thank the merciful Fates." Yamanu knocked on the Clan Mother's door. "Whatever it is, I hope it doesn't involve another trip in a narco submarine. Once in a lifetime was enough."

Oridu opened up. "Good evening, masters. Please come in."

Inside, the living room was bursting with a lively conversation that for some reason seemed to revolve around Alena. Not only that, but in a rare sisterly display, she was sharing an armchair with Amanda.

The two weren't close.

Whatever was going on, Alena was in the center of it.

Strange. Normally, Annani's eldest liked to blend into the background and observe. She didn't like to attract attention to herself.

Kian rose to his feet and walked over to greet them. "Thank you for coming over. I hope I didn't interrupt your weekend plans."

As if he cared about that. The apology was most likely

meant for Annani's ears, to show his mother that he was polite and treated his people with respect. The second part was true, but the first one not so much. Kian was a pragmatic guy who rarely wasted time on niceties.

Yamanu shook Kian's hand. "Not at all. So, to what do we owe the honor?"

"Grab a couple of chairs and join us," the boss said.

As they took their seats, Yamanu crossed his legs and plastered a smile on his face. He was going to pretend that sitting in Annani's living room, with three out of her four children present and looking at him expectantly, was an everyday event.

"Syssi had a vision," Kian began. "She saw Kalugal entering the Stock Exchange in New York."

While Kian explained the plan, Amanda and Annani added details, and Syssi offered a few suggestions. Everyone was excited about the idea, except for Kian who seemed skeptical, and Alena who looked unsure.

It wasn't like her. Usually she was the picture of serenity and composure.

"What troubles you, Alena?" Yamanu asked.

"It's nothing." She waved a hand. "I'm so used to my quiet and uneventful life that I don't know if I can pull it off. What do I know about being a supermodel?"

Amanda chuckled. "First of all, calling your life uneventful is a joke. You've given birth to thirteen children. In my book, that's huge. And secondly, you live with the queen of mischief. I'm sure our mother provides plenty of excitement. And thirdly, to act like a model, all you need to do is channel Annani."

"Or you." Alena leaned and kissed her sister's cheek. "Maybe you should put on a blond wig and makeup? You're tall, fashionable, and have the proper attitude."

Sighing wistfully, Amanda leaned her head on Alena's

shoulder. "I wish I could. But no amount of makeup is going to make me look like Areana."

Eva cleared her throat. "Don't underestimate what can be done with the proper tools. We can create a face mask that will make you look exactly like Areana, and with me by your side, you'll have no problem transforming into her every morning." She smirked. "It's a pity you've never seen me in one of my disguises. If not for the smell of latex, Jackson and Bhathian wouldn't have figured out that I wasn't who I pretended to be, and I would probably not be here."

Sensing his daddy's agitation, the baby in Bhathian's arms whimpered.

"But I'm so glad that I was unmasked. If I weren't, I wouldn't have my happy ending," Eva added. "I should thank the good Lord every day for my blessings."

She got up and walked over to Bhathian. "Come to Mommy, precious." She took the baby and cradled him in her arms.

Ethan sighed contentedly and went back to sleep.

The woman was full of contradictions. A tough as nails detective but such a devoted and loving mother. Yamanu didn't know much about her past, but Bhathian had let a few things slip. Apparently, the lady had no qualms about taking out evil-doers despite being deeply religious.

"So, who is going to New York?" Kian asked. "Alena, Amanda, or Lucinda?"

"I am," Alena said. "With Yamanu and Arwel keeping me safe, I have nothing to fear. And if I need performance advice, I'm sure Eva can help with that as well as with the makeup."

"I sure can." Eva kissed her baby's forehead. "Wearing a disguise is not enough. To be believable, I acted like the person I was supposed to be. I'm a decent actress."

"Don't be so modest. You are amazing," Nathalie said.

Eva shrugged. "I didn't want to toot my own horn."

"Who else are you sending with us?" Yamanu asked Kian.

"Bhathian is going because of Eva. But I want you to take two additional Guardians, so you can take turns watching over Alena. It's up to you who you want to work with on this mission. I'm putting you in charge of this operation."

"Good deal. But to call it a mission or an operation is an overstatement. It's more like a vacation." Yamanu smirked. "Thank you for rewarding Arwel and me with this little perk. I would like to think it's because of the good job we did with Carol and Lokan."

"It has nothing to do with it," Kian said. "You are needed because of your incredible thralling ability, and Arwel can sense even immortals' emotions. If Kalugal takes the bait, Arwel might sense him snooping around."

Arwel rubbed his jaw. "I wouldn't count on it. I didn't sense Lokan coming, and he snatched Vivian and Ella right from under my nose."

The room went silent. Arwel's remark was a reminder of how easily even the best planned operations could go awry.

"He was using an underground tunnel. That's why you couldn't sense him," Kian said. "There are no tunnels under our hotel in New York."

"What if Navuh sees the advertisements?" Nathalie asked. "He might send Doomers after Alena."

"Not likely." Annani spread her hands in a dismissive gesture. "He never leaves the island, and we are not going to have Alena appear on television commercials. And even if he somehow sees one of those ads, he will dismiss Ari the model as a lookalike. After all, he knows that Areana is safely sequestered in his harem. Kalugal, on the other hand, cannot be sure that his mother is still on the island. He will get curious and investigate."

"When do we leave?" Yamanu asked.

Kian looked at Amanda. "Will one week be enough for the

new wardrobe and everything else you are planning for Alena?"

She huffed. "I can do all that in two days. But Alena needs to learn Slovene, Roni has to create her fake past, and someone needs to go to Alaska and get Ovidu over here or directly to New York."

7

MEY

"We are good." Derek flipped through the photos he'd taken that morning. "The dragon lady will approve."

Mey let out a relieved breath. "I'm glad it's a wrap. I could use a break."

He lifted his eyes from the camera. "Aren't we supposed to start shooting for a new campaign tomorrow?"

Wiping the lipstick off with a napkin, Mey shook her head. "It's a small one-day job, and I'm going to ask Dalia to give the assignment to someone else. I need a couple of days to find out what's going on with my sister."

Julie folded her chair. "Didn't you say that she texted you last night?"

"She did. But I'm still uneasy."

"Well, good luck with your sister and with Dalia." Julie slung the chair's strap over her shoulder and lifted her makeup bag.

"Thanks. Depending on the boss's mood when I talk to her, I'll see you guys either tomorrow or a couple of days after."

"Do you want a ride home?" Derek asked.

"No, thank you. I'm going to Jin's old place to collect a box she's left for me."

"I can take you there."

She patted his arm. "It's okay, Derek. Take Julie home. I want to stay here a couple of minutes."

"Okay. Just be careful."

She rolled her eyes. "It's the middle of the day. I'll be fine."

As Derek and Julie walked away, Mey sat on the bench and pulled out her phone to read the text message again.

Sorry I couldn't get in touch before. We have no reception here, and I've been incredibly busy the entire week. There is just one spot with a barely-there connection, and I'm sending the text from there. Don't worry about me, I'm doing great. Please call Mom and Dad and tell them that I'm okay, and that I can't call them from here. I'll try to send you another message next week. I love you, keep doing what you're doing. Modeling is the best job.

Mey must have read it a hundred times, trying to find a clue between the words to what was going on with her sister.

After the first message that Jin had sent upon arrival, this was the only other communication Mey had gotten from her, and it felt off. Mey knew her sister better than anyone else on the planet, and that didn't sound like Jin.

Well, it did and it didn't.

Jin didn't like using shortcuts and emojis. She always wrote in full sentences, which was rare for someone her age. So that part fit. And yet, something wasn't right.

What kind of business operated in a place without cellular reception? And what about landlines? The internet? Email?

Mey should have suspected something when Jin couldn't tell her any details about the company that had hired her. Her sister had signed a nondisclosure agreement and couldn't even give her the company's location.

There were only two things that she'd been allowed to share

with her family. One was that a furnished apartment was part of her compensation package, and she didn't have to bring anything with her other than clothing. And the other one was the impressive salary and the huge bonus that awaited her at the end of the five-year contract she'd signed. Except, the bonus was contingent on exemplary performance, and that was open to interpretation.

Mey suspected that it was just bait, and that Jin was never going to get it no matter how hard she worked.

In fact, Mey had been uneasy about the entire thing. But Jin had been excited about getting hired right after graduation and the excellent salary and benefits she'd been offered. Naturally, she'd refused to listen to her older sister's misgivings about an offer that was too good to be true.

And that wasn't all that Mey found odd.

Other than the money and the secrecy, she wondered where Jin fit into all of that. Her sister had graduated NYU with a degree in business management, not foreign affairs, not computer engineering, not rocket science, or anything else that qualified her for super confidential work in a place that was shrouded in mystery.

Perhaps Jin was working in Area 51?

Mey chuckled. Unless the government was entering business negotiations with aliens, they had no need for Jin. And even if they were, they would have hired someone with experience and not a fresh college graduate.

She read the message again, pausing at the last sentence. Jin had never thought that modeling was a great job. In fact, she'd preferred working as a part-time bartender to posing in front of a camera. When Mey had offered to hook her up with the agency, her sister had laughed at the idea, saying that it was a mind-numbingly boring job.

On more than one occasion, Jin had said that she couldn't understand how an intelligent woman like Mey could be doing it for so many years, and that she should quit modeling and go to fashion design school.

That would have brought them one step closer toward their dream of one day creating their own fashion line, with Mey in charge of the creative side and Jin of the business.

Was the remark about modeling a clue? Or was that Jin's way of apologizing for hurting Mey's feelings?

Perhaps Mitch would know something.

For no particular reason, Mey didn't like Jin's boyfriend, and normally she wouldn't have called him, but perhaps Jin had sent him a message with another clue.

Pulling out her phone, she called him, but the call went straight to voicemail.

"This is Mitch. Leave me a message."

"Hi, Mitch. It's Mey. Call me when you can."

Perhaps he was at work?

The coffee shop where he worked was only a ten-minute brisk walk away.

Slinging her satchel's strap across her body, Mey started in that direction. If he wasn't there, she would just get a cup of coffee and continue to the dorms.

Mitch and Jin had only been dating for a month or so, and the relationship was not likely to survive the long distance. Especially since communication was so limited.

That was the one good thing about that freaking job. No more Mitch.

She was aware that her dislike for him might have nothing to do with the guy himself but with her general disappointment with men. After all, Jin had started dating Mitch the same week Mey had ended her year-long relationship with Oliver, and it hadn't been an amicable breakup.

She still fumed whenever she thought about it.

When she'd moved out of the studio she'd shared with Oliver, Mey had rented a four-bedroom apartment with two other models. She'd invited Jin to join as the fourth and even offered to pay for her room, but her sister had refused.

The dorms were cheaper and the social life was better.

At the coffee shop, Mey found Mitch working the register.

"Hey, Mitch, do you have a minute?"

"What would you like to order, Mey?" His eyes never reached her face, stopping at her cleavage.

Or rather lack thereof. Since there was nothing to stare at, she had a feeling he was just doing it to annoy her.

Jerk.

"A tall coffee." She pulled out a five-dollar bill and handed it to him. "Now can we talk?"

He poured her a cup and then turned to the other guy behind the counter. "I'm taking a five-minute break."

The guy waved him off. "I got it."

"Let's go outside."

The coffee shop was tiny, with only two tables, which were both taken. Talking on the sidewalk was the only option.

"Did Jin call or text you since she left for her new job?"

He pulled out a cigarette and lit it. "Nope. She broke things off with me before leaving. She said that long-distance relationships never work." He cast Mey a lascivious once-over. "Is that why you're here? To check if I'm still single? Because I am, but not for long."

What had Jin seen in that guy?

"No, that's not why I'm here. I'm worried about her. She doesn't answer my calls, and she's only sent me two text messages since she started her new job. She says there is no reception there, but I don't buy it."

"Why?"

The slight edge in his tone gave Mey a pause, and she decided against sharing with him what she suspected was a clue in Jin's message.

"Because even if that's true, and they have a lousy cellular reception, they must have other forms of communication. She could have called me using a landline or sent me an email. I'm sure she is working on a desktop, not an abacus."

He took another puff on his cigarette. "Some employers are very strict about employees using company time and equipment for their private business. Maybe since Jin is new, she has to follow the rules."

"Yeah, I guess you are right. I'm just used to talking with her every day, and this communication silence makes me uneasy."

Mitch stubbed out his cigarette and flicked the butt into the gutter. "Your baby sister is all grown up. Get used to it." He pulled the coffee shop's door open. "If you do change your mind about hooking up with me, you have my number. And if you don't, feel free to pass it along to your model friends."

"Goodbye, Mitch."

He nodded. "See you around."

As the door closed behind him, Mey let out a breath. Mitch was a dead end. The good news was that Jin had broken up with him. The bad news was that Mey had only one avenue of investigation left, maybe two.

Gabi, Jin's old roommate, might know something. Her sister had left a few things behind that she wanted Mey to pick up, so it was a good excuse for a visit and potentially some snooping around.

Mey pulled out her phone and sent Gabi a message. *I want to stop by and pick up the box that Jin left for me. When is a good time?*

The return message came a few moments later. *I'm in class. Back in an hour. Don't be late. I need to leave for another class.*

Perfect. I'll see you there.

8

YAMANU

*Y*amanu crossed his arms over his chest and put his feet up on the opposite seat. The limousine that Ragnar had sent for them was big enough for ten people, but only Alena, her butler, and he were sharing it to the hotel. The others were arriving by taxis, so it wouldn't be obvious that they were all together.

Kian had insisted on that precaution, but Yamanu saw no reason for it. They could all be part of the entourage following Arielle the famous model around. Nevertheless, Eva and her family had taken one cab, and Uisdean and Ewan another.

With a yawn, Yamanu closed his eyes.

For some reason, he'd been unable to get any shuteye during the flight. Low level excitement had been churning in his gut and keeping him awake, and he was trying to figure out what was causing it.

The mission was more like a vacation, so it wasn't about that, and he'd been to New York many times before, so it wasn't about experiencing a new place either.

It was like a premonition of good things to come.

Perhaps he was looking forward to spending time with

Alena and getting to know her better. She was his favorite out of Annani's four children, mostly because she wasn't as intense as her siblings, and he enjoyed her gentle nature and soft femininity.

Being around Alena wasn't taxing, it was relaxing, and that was a rare quality.

He was also expecting to have fun with Arwel, Uisdean, and Ewan. The four of them could commandeer the executive lounge, not for strategic planning, but to have drinks and play cards.

There wasn't much for them to do, and since it was a fun kind of mission, he'd chosen Guardians who he'd known were easygoing and would get along with everyone.

Next to him, Alena muttered something in Slovene.

He opened his eyes. "How is it going? Getting any better?"

Alena removed her earphones and put them in her lap. "I can speak it but not well enough to pass for a native."

"Can you fake the accent?"

She flipped back her newly styled hair and looked down her nose at him. "Of course, darling. Don't let Ari's fabulous looks fool you. She is a very smart lady."

Yamanu laughed. "I see that you decided to channel Amanda. Good choice. And the accent sounded authentic. You can refuse to answer questions in Slovene, claiming that you are working on improving your English. As long as you can understand what's being said, that's good enough."

"What if someone insists?"

"You are a diva. You do what you please. That's the attitude you need to assume."

"Then I should channel my mother." She waved a hand. "I'll mesh Amanda and Annani's style together. But you know what?" She leaned toward him.

"What?"

"Areana is not like that. She is demure and sweet and

accommodating. You can see it on her face. The haughty attitude doesn't match her."

He wrapped his arm around Alena's shoulders. "Don't overcomplicate it. All you need to do is look like her, and when you smile for the camera, try to look sweet and compassionate. The posters and magazine ads will only show what you want them to see. The moment the shoot is over, you can go back to being a diva. The bitchiest actresses manage to look adorable on the big screen."

"I'm not an actress, but I'll do my best."

As the limo stopped in front of the hotel, a uniformed doorman opened the way for Alena. "Welcome to the Regent Hotel, madam."

"Thank you."

Ragnar was waiting for them in the lobby, contributing to the impression that Alena was a celebrity.

"The beautiful Arielle." He took both of Alena's hands and then kissed both of her cheeks, or rather the air next to them.

She had layers of makeup on, courtesy of Eva's masterful work.

"Let me escort you and your entourage to your suite." Ragnar took her arm.

"Thank you, darling." Alena flashed the hotel manager the supermodel smile she'd been practicing on the plane.

"Let's go," she whispered in his ear. "I can't wait to take this gunk off."

Poor Alena. She hated makeup.

Yamanu nudged Arwel. "You are supposed to be the overprotective boyfriend. Walk over to them and growl at Ragnar."

"There are no photographers here."

"A guest might snatch a picture and sell it to the tabloids. Besides, you need to start practicing."

"Right."

As Arwel caught up to Alena and Ragnar next to the elevators, he tapped the guy's shoulder. "Excuse me."

"Of course." Ragnar let go.

Alena smiled sheepishly. "Oh, baby. I'm so sorry for leaving you behind. Did you get jealous?"

Not bad. Alena had done it just right.

Arwel said, "Yes." And that was it. End of performance.

Yamanu shook his head. Perhaps he should switch places with Arwel who, apparently, sucked at acting. It was easier to play the business manager than the boyfriend.

Except, it was up to Yamanu to get Arielle the model a contract that would put her face on buses, so he had to be the manager. Arwel could probably thrall the modeling agency's owner just as well, but Kian wanted his best guy on the job.

As the elevator arrived, saving the day, Yamanu followed the three inside and waited for the doors to close. "That was the most pitiful performance I've ever seen. You need to do better than that, my friend."

Arwel cocked a brow. "Do you want to be the boyfriend?"

"Maybe I should."

"Nah, ah." Alena shook her head. "You're too good looking. You'd steal the spotlight from me."

Ragnar lifted a finger. "Perhaps I can be the boyfriend."

"Are you an empath?" Arwel asked.

The elevator reached the top floor, and Ragnar held the door open. "Regrettably, I haven't been blessed with any special gifts."

"Be thankful. My so-called gift is more of a curse." Arwel followed them down the hallway. "By the way, is Melanie still in your accounting department?"

Ragnar opened the door to the hotel's presidential suite. "Yes, she is."

"Who is Melanie?" Alena asked.

"Someone that Arwel met the last time we stayed here,"

Yamanu explained. "He snuck out to see her whenever he could. Apparently, accountants have quiet minds."

"Do they?" Alena glanced at Arwel.

"There are exceptions, of course, but compared to other humans, theirs are definitely the quietest."

Ragnar cleared his throat. "What do you think about our presidential suite, Alena?"

"It's very nice."

Ragnar looked disappointed. But what had he expected?

The Regent Hotel was fancy, but Alena lived in Annani's sanctuary, a tropical paradise created under a dome of ice, and when she traveled with the Clan Mother, they stayed in the most luxurious hotels.

"Let me show you your room." Ragnar opened the double doors to the master bedroom. "The two others are down that hallway." He pointed.

"Yamanu and I could have shared one bedroom," Arwel said.

"Speak for yourself." Yamanu clapped him on the back. "I need my quiet space for meditating."

After checking out the bedrooms, the four of them met back in the suite's living room.

Alena sat down on the couch. "Did Eva and Bhathian arrive yet?"

"Not yet," Ragnar said. "But maybe they are down in the lobby. They will be staying in the suite to your left, while Uisdean and Ewan will be in the one to your right."

"Are there any other guests staying on this floor?" Arwel asked.

Ragnar shook his head. "Per Kian's request, the entire floor is at your disposal. But since there is just one more suite here, it's not a big loss. And anyway, this is not a busy time of the year for us. I'm going to program the elevator so only you have access to this floor."

"What about housekeeping?" Yamanu asked.

"There is no need." Alena waved a hand. "Ovidu can take care of it. I don't want to have to put on makeup when I'm here. It's really uncomfortable."

"Then it's settled." Ragnar turned to the butler. "I'll show you where the laundry facilities are, and where you can get fresh supplies."

"Thank you, master." Ovidu bowed.

"What about room service?" Alena asked.

"Ovidu can come down to the kitchen and pick it up. Anything else?"

Alena shook her head. "I think we are good. I just wonder how long we are going to stay here. I don't intend for this to be a permanent move."

"It depends on your mother," Yamanu said. "It's not over until she says it is."

Alena sighed. "Or until we flush Kalugal out. But I doubt that we will. I'm only doing this because it's so important to my mother."

9

MEY

"*A*re you sure that you are not forgetting something?" Mey asked.

Jin's former roommate shook her head. "Jin was very tightlipped about that job."

"Think back. Perhaps you overheard her talking on the phone with someone about it?"

"Nope. She might have gotten text messages or emails, though. If you know her email login, you can check."

"I don't."

Gabi shrugged. "Let me get that box for you." She pulled it out from under the bed. "Jin said that everything in it belongs to you. Clothes that she borrowed and forgot to return." She glanced at her watch. "I really need to run."

Mey smiled. "Forgot is the wrong verb, but never mind. Do you mind if I stay here and go over what's in it? I don't want to schlep the whole thing to my place. I'll only take the things I really want back." She pulled out a designer blouse and fluffed it out. "Like this one. Do you want it? Because it's not really my style."

Mey laid it out on the bed so Gabrielle could get a better

look. "I often get to keep the things I model, but I don't always like them."

The truth was that it was one of her favorites, but given how Gabrielle was salivating over it, the blouse was just the right incentive for the girl to let Mey stay and sift through the box, hoping she would find more things she didn't want.

"I guess it's okay. Just lock things up before you leave. Turn the little knob and slam the door. It will lock it."

"I will. And thank you for letting me stay."

"No problem. Have fun sifting."

When Gabrielle left, Mey did exactly what she'd said she would, sifting through the box, but not to choose what she wanted to take. She was searching for clues. Maybe Jin had left something for her in there? Some breadcrumbs she could follow?

Except she found no surprises. There were no hidden notes tucked into pockets of pants or under the insoles of shoes. And the box itself had nothing other than "For Mey" written on it. She'd even gone as far as fingering the seams and hems, hoping against hope that Jin had sewn a message into one of the garments.

There was nothing. Evidently, Jin had left of her own volition, and she'd felt no need to leave hidden messages for her sister.

There was one more thing Mey could do, and it was the main reason she wanted to stay alone in the room.

Sitting cross-legged on the floor, Mey closed her eyes and started her slow breathing. For her strange past-viewing ability to work, she had to enter a meditative state. The deeper she could go, the better she could witness the echoes of past events.

It was a finicky thing, which sometimes worked and most often didn't. She'd learned from experience that strong emotions left a clearer imprint on the space they'd been felt in, provided that it was enclosed and not too big. It was as if the walls absorbed the echoes of those feelings, saving the imprint they had left and revealing them later to those with the ability to tune into that particular frequency.

Like Mey.

Not that she knew of anyone else who could do that. Jin had a special talent too, but it was both similar and different than Mey's.

Jin could remote view people. Not in the past or in the future, though, only in the present. For it to work, it was enough that she'd met the person once and touched him or her. But again, it didn't work with everyone. Jin's mental tether probably had its own frequency too, and it resonated with some but not with others.

When she did that to Mey, Mey felt as if someone was watching her and got goose bumps all over her arms. But she was the one exception. Others had no clue when Jin was doing it to them.

As teenagers, they'd tested it on their parents and friends, but no one other than Mey had felt Jin's mental spying.

When they'd told their mom about it, she'd laughed it away, thinking that they were playing a game. Nevertheless, she'd warned them not to make up stories like that because people would think they were nuts.

The truth was that it had been hard enough for two tall Asian girls to fit into their mostly Caucasian school without adding weirdness to the mix. So, they had talked it over and had decided to keep it a secret.

They had sworn not to mention it to anyone again.

Besides, even if anyone had believed their story, it would have made people wary of them. No one wanted to be spied on, and that was exactly what both abilities did. So even though what they could do was quite easy to prove, it was better not to. When they got older and realized how their talents could be exploited, the need for secrecy had become even more important.

After long moments of deep breathing, Mey entered the necessary state and the walls started talking. The first echo was naturally the most recent one, and it was of Gabrielle and her boyfriend hooking up. Unfortunately, she couldn't press fast forward and had to suffer through the entire thing.

The next echo was of Gabrielle crying over a bad grade, then another one of her with her boyfriend, and then finally she got to Jin's last day in the dorm room.

Sitting on the bed with her phone clutched in her hand, she was talking with Mitch on Skype, so Mey could hear his side of the conversation as well.

"Don't say things you don't mean. You are not going to wait for me."

"Yes, I am. I love you, pumpkin."

Ugh, what kind of a guy called his girlfriend pumpkin?

Jin sighed and a tear slid down her cheek. "You think that you do. But I know you. You can't be alone. The moment I'm gone, you are going to replace me with someone else. I don't want to think about it while I'm away. My new job is going to be stressful enough. Let's just make it a clean cut and part as friends. Can you do that for me?"

There was a moment of silence, and then Mitch sighed. "I'm going to miss you."

"Me too. But it's for the best. I want to remember the fun times we had together."

"We had a lot of fun. That's why this is so hard."

Jin chuckled. "We are only twenty-two, Mitch. There is still plenty of fun in our future, just with different people."

Mey listened patiently to the back and forth until the final goodbyes had been said, and then Jin disconnected the call, hung her head, and let the tears flow.

It was obvious that it had been difficult for her to break up with Mitch. Why had she done it? Was it really because of the reasons she'd given him?

She'd been right, of course, as Mey could attest. The guy hadn't wasted a moment to try to hook up with the sister of the girl he had claimed to love.

"I had to do that," Jin murmured to herself. "I don't know when I'll be back, and Mitch is not the kind of guy who will wait around." She took in a shuddering breath. "This is worth the sacrifice." She chuckled sadly. "Not that Mitch was such a big one. But we did have fun together." She reached for a box of tissue and blew her nose into one. "There will be others. Hopefully, who are more like me."

The vision wavered and then dissipated.

Mey opened her eyes and frowned. "Others who are more like me?" What had she meant by that?

In the back of Mey's mind, warning bells started ringing, but she didn't want to listen to them. It was probably just a flare of paranoia.

This had nothing to do with Jin's remote spying ability.

It couldn't have.

They had talked about how dangerous revealing it would be for them, and how crucially important it was to keep their abilities hidden. Unscrupulous people of all nationalities and interests would love to get their hands on what she and Jin could do.

10

YAMANU

"Our appointment was for half an hour ago," Arwel said quietly.

"Patience, my friend." Yamanu crossed his legs. "We are not in a hurry."

The truth was that he didn't mind waiting for the modeling agency's owner to be done with her previous appointment. The eye candy milling around was quite entertaining. Too bad that it was probably illegal to even look at some of those girls.

The one sitting across from them and laughing at something on her phone couldn't be more than sixteen. She was tall and leggy, and with makeup she probably looked older. But clean faced, she definitely looked illegal. Not that he was even thinking in that direction, and thankfully, he felt no stirring in his loins.

But being celibate didn't mean that he was blind, and a guy could still appreciate beauty even if it was only to look and not touch.

"Why do you keep your sunglasses on?" Alena whispered in his ear. "You look weird."

"I look even weirder without." He let the glasses slide down his nose and peered at her over their rim.

She waved a hand dismissively. "Don't worry about it. People will think you're wearing contact lenses."

"They tend to stare."

"That's because you are so freaking handsome. Embrace it."

"Is that supposed to be a pep talk?"

"Do you need one?"

"I don't know. Maybe. I'm conflicted."

"You are a strange guy, Yamanu."

"So I've been told."

Alena leaned back and looked at the agency owner's door. "Do you think she is making us wait on purpose? Or does she have someone in there?"

"She is on the phone," Arwel said from Alena's other side. "She's frustrated and angry and harboring murderous thoughts."

Alena gaped at him. "You can feel all that?"

He nodded.

"No wonder you need to drink so much. Perhaps you shouldn't come with me everywhere. I can have either Uisdean or Ewan pretend to be my boyfriend, and you can hole up in the hotel's accounting department."

A smile bloomed over Arwel's face. "It's in the basement. That's why it is so peaceful there. Only accountants, but they also get frustrated from time to time. Just much less than others."

The girl across from them looked up from her phone and smiled at Arwel. "Are you here for an interview?" she asked.

He looked at Alena, but the girl shook her head.

"I meant you." The girl smiled at Alena. "You're obviously a pro."

"How do you know?" She used her fake Slovene accent.

The girl waved a hand in her direction. "Your makeup, your

hair, your clothes. It's obvious that you have a stylist working for you. Your friends are both very handsome, but they lack that professional touch."

Yamanu smiled. *Thank you, Amanda and Eva.*

"I'm Sondra," the girl introduced herself.

"I'm Arielle, and this is Arwel, my boyfriend, and Yamanu, my manager."

Sondra looked impressed. "How come I haven't heard of you? You must be big to come here with your manager."

"I'm famous abroad. I'm new to the United States."

"Oh, I see. I'm not familiar with the scene over there."

Yamanu tuned out the conversation. The door to the waiting room kept opening and closing, with people popping in, leaving messages for the owner with her secretary, and then leaving.

Other than their group, only Sondra and one slightly older model were sitting on the plush chairs and awaiting their turn to meet with the famous Dalia Cromwell.

Everyone else seemed rushed as if this was a hospital emergency room that was dealing with life and death emergencies, and not a modeling agency that was about the more trivial side of life.

But then the door opened once again, and Yamanu's breath caught in his throat.

Now, that was a lady.

Gorgeous, tall, and at least twenty-four, the woman was a stunner, with natural poise and grace that wasn't fake, and a kind, friendly expression that wasn't haughty.

Yamanu had never had a preferred type, but he had one now, and that was her.

Her hair was as long and as dark as his, but she had red highlights added to hers. Big hazel eyes were framed by long lashes, but not the fake ones that every girl and her mother were gluing on these days. In fact, her face was clean of makeup, and she was dressed casually in a pair of faded jeans, a tight T-shirt, and ballet flats.

He had the absurd notion that with him she could wear heels and still feel feminine and delicate. She would like that, wouldn't she?

Tall girls liked tall guys.

Smiling, she walked over to them. "Hi, I'm Mey." She offered her hand to Alena. "Are you here for an interview?"

"Yes, I am."

"Welcome aboard. This is an awesome agency to work for." She bent down and whispered, "Dalia is known as the dragon lady, but that's not necessarily a bad thing. She takes bullshit from no one, and she really cares about her models. You'll be in good hands."

"That's good to know. I'm Arielle, and this is my boyfriend, Arwel, and my business manager, Yamanu."

Arwel remained seated as he shook Mey's hand, but Yamanu felt inclined to show her proper respect and got up, then hurriedly removed his sunglasses and tucked them away in his pocket.

"It's a pleasure to make your acquaintance, ma'am." He took her hand gently in his much bigger one.

As Mey looked up into his eyes, he heard her breath hitch, but she recovered quickly. "You should be a model, Mr. Yamanu. You're much too handsome for a business manager."

"I've retired from the spotlight." He winked. "But thank you for the compliment."

She laughed. "There is something to be said for early retirement. If I could afford it, I would gladly do so as well."

He was still holding on to her hand, but it seemed that neither of them wanted to end the contact. "And what would you have done in your retirement? Traveled the world?"

She shook her head. "Been there done that. My sister and I

want to start our own fashion label. But we need to save up for the seed money first."

Something in her tone had changed when she mentioned her sister. And the smile had left her beautiful hazel eyes.

"I wish you all the luck in the world with your endeavor."

"Thank you." Mey pulled her hand out of his and reached into her back pocket. "Here is my business card." She handed it to Alena. "I've been with the agency for a while. If you need any advice or pointers, don't hesitate to call me. I know how difficult it is to start in a new place."

"That's most kind of you." Alena opened her purse and put the card inside.

"I mean it. It's not the let's-do-lunch kind of lip service. I hate it when people do that."

Yamanu really liked the girl. Poise, grace, delicate femininity, a face to die for, and a no-nonsense attitude that was even rarer than her exotic beauty.

Damn. It would take hours of meditation to get her out of his head.

Celibacy sucked, but he had no choice.

Life was full of compromises. If Arwel could sacrifice his sanity for the clan without complaining, Yamanu could sacrifice his sex life and keep a lid on it as well.

Alena smiled. "I promise to call. I'm sure I can learn a lot from you."

11

MEY

*W*hen Mey had entered the reception room, she'd thought the three new people were models, each waiting for an interview with Dalia.

They were all striking, but only Arielle looked the part. She was dressed to the nines, and her makeup had been done by a professional. It was too much for an interview, but maybe she'd come straight from a photo shoot.

The woman didn't strike Mey as one of those models who wore their public image everywhere they went. She seemed down to earth, and genuinely a nice person, which was why Mey had offered her help, and given her a business card.

No, that was a lie. Or at least partially so. Mey really wanted to befriend the new girl, but more than that she wanted to see Arielle's gorgeous business manager again.

He was the most striking man she'd ever met, and she'd met quite a few throughout her modeling career. But it wasn't only the physical perfection that had evoked such powerful yearning in her.

Yamanu was special. She could sense it the moment he'd opened his mouth and uttered his first words. His voice was hypnotic, soothing. It promised safety and solace, but also wicked things that Mey was embarrassed to think about.

And then he'd taken her hand, and when she'd looked into his pale blue eyes, what she'd sensed before had intensified tenfold.

Like a teenager with her first crush, giddy with excitement because she'd found her perfect guy, Mey wanted him to be hers, but even more than that she wanted to be his.

Totally out of character for her.

Mey was strong, independent, and she had never wished to have a man to lean on. She didn't need that. She'd always thought of relationships as partnerships between like-minded people. True love and the meshing of souls were unachievable ideals, and frankly, such a deep level of closeness seemed suffocating to her.

But maybe she'd been setting her expectations too low?

After her last boyfriend, she'd been willing to settle for someone she could count on not to cheat on her or lie to her.

She was just lonely, that's all. And Yamanu probably wasn't all that she'd imagined.

His strange and beautiful eyes were probably not natural, the effect most likely created by contact lenses. No one other than maybe albinos had eyes that shade.

Except, those strange eyes matched his hypnotic voice, and she'd stood so close to him that she would have noticed the tell-tale rim of contacts. There had been none.

For a brief moment, Mey allowed herself the girly fantasy of being taken care of, protected, and loved by this man.

"I promise to call." Arielle's voice pulled Mey back to reality.

Did she imagine it or had the woman's American accent improved significantly over the course of their conversation?

"I'm sure I can learn a lot from you," Arielle continued. "I'm new not only to the agency but also to the country. I'm from Slovenia." She cast her boyfriend a loving glance. "Arwel convinced me to come to the United States. He said that I'm wasting my talent on Europe."

The heavy Slavic accent was back, and Mey figured she'd imagined the improvement before.

"The United States is the biggest market by far, and this agency is one of the best. Your business manager has chosen wisely for you." She cast a sidelong glance at Yamanu.

Mey wished to draw him back into the conversation, but he didn't pick it up. Instead, he was watching her with unnerving intensity.

"Yes, I agree. And please, call me Ari."

"Ari it is." To avoid getting mesmerized by Yamanu's hypnotic gaze, Mey looked at Dalia's closed door. "Does she have someone in there?"

Arielle's boyfriend shook his head. "She's on the phone."

"Do you mind if I go ahead of you? I just need to ask her a quick question."

"Go ahead," Arielle said. "We are not in a hurry."

Again, her accent had changed, this time sounding more American.

Maybe she wasn't really from Slovenia and was just pretending. A good background story could add to a model's allure.

As Dalia's door opened and she stepped out into the waiting room, Arielle and her companions got up.

The dragon lady was all smiles for Ari and her friends. "Welcome to the Carmichael agency." She offered Ari her perfectly manicured hand. "You are even more beautiful in person." She turned to Yamanu, gave him a once-over, and then did the same for Arwel. "I could use two gorgeous male models like you. Are you available? Because if you are, you're hired."

Yamanu chuckled as he took her hand and brought it up to his lips for a kiss. "I appreciate the offer, but my modeling days are over. I'm here strictly as Arielle's business manager."

"And I'm just the boyfriend and bodyguard." Arwel offered Dalia his hand.

"May I have a quick word with you?" Mey interjected. "I asked Ari's permission to steal a couple of minutes of your time."

Dalia started to shake her head, but Arielle put a hand on her forearm. "We are probably going to take a long time, and Mey only has a quick question. I don't mind waiting a little longer."

Dalia nodded. "That's very kind of you." She motioned for Mey to follow her into the office.

"That was unprofessional," Dalia said as soon as Mey closed the door behind her. "You could have texted me or waited for after the interview."

"It's really a quick question. Can I take the rest of the week off?"

"No, you can't." Dalia lifted a stack of photographs from Mey's last photo shoot. "I just got off the phone with the client, and he's not happy with these. He's sending over a different set of outfits that he wants you to wear, and he wants street shots."

Damn. Clients could be so demanding. "But we did exactly what he wanted."

"I know. He changed his mind, and he wants it done as soon as possible. He's paying us extra to redo the shoot."

Great. Some customers were just a pain in the butt like that. But what choice did she have? To refuse would cost her job.

"When will the outfits get here?"

"He said either later today or tomorrow morning, but I doubt he can have everything ready so quickly. In any case, be ready to start shooting tomorrow."

"Once this is done, can I take a few days off?"

Dalia opened her scheduling software. "I've already given your next assignment to someone else. And the one after that is two weeks away. If you wrap up this one in one week, you can have the next one off."

That was probably better. Maybe a new clue would come up over the next several days, and she would actually know where to start her search.

"Awesome. Thanks, Dalia."

"Make sure he is happy this time." Her boss lifted the photos again. "I didn't tell him so, but this wasn't your best work. The spark is missing, and the mischief in your eyes and the secretive smile that clients love so much are not there either. If they wanted just any pretty face, they wouldn't have chosen you."

Dalia was right. First it had been the breakup with Oliver, and then the concern about Jin. No wonder the spark was missing.

Mey nodded. "I'll do my best."

"On your way out, tell Arielle and her companions that they can come in."

As Mey stepped out into the reception room, she fell straight into Yamanu's gaze. Had he been watching the door the entire time?

"Thank you so much for letting me go in ahead of you. Dalia is ready for you."

Arielle rose to her feet. "Thanks." She smoothed her hand over her short skirt and reached into her purse. "I thought that it was rude of me not to give you my phone number as well." She pulled out a business card. "Call me when you have some free time. We can grab a coffee or something to eat." She smiled. "And I really mean it. It's not the let's-do-lunch thing. I'm new in town and I could use a girlfriend."

Mey took the card and put it in her back pocket. "Thank you. I'm doing an outdoor shoot tomorrow, so I'll probably be free as soon as the sun sets."

YAMANU

*O*n the way back to the hotel, Yamanu left Alena and Arwel to sit in the back of the limo, while he joined Ewan up front.

The two had been smirking knowingly and exchanging glances like a couple of high schoolers, and he had no intention of subjecting himself to their teasing.

That was the trouble with immortals. He could hide his reactions from humans, but not from them. Normally, that wasn't a problem. His meditation and herbal remedies kept him going on neutral, but they hadn't been enough to stifle his attraction to Mey.

"How did it go?" Ewan eased the limo into the traffic.

"Easy." Yamanu crossed his arms over his chest. "I didn't even have to put much pressure on the lady. She loved Alena, or rather Arielle, and the glowing recommendation from Brandon's contact helped a lot. Provided that the client agrees, Alena is going to be the face of *Ravishing*, a luxury cosmetics line from Korea that they are trying to promote in the States. Tomorrow, we're meeting with the photographer for the first test run, and we will have an answer by the end of the week."

"What if the client doesn't like Alena's look?"

"Dalia said that she's exactly what they were looking for."

Ewan cast him a sidelong glance. "How is it going to work with the makeup? Alena already wears plenty to look like Areana. Are they going to add the new stuff on top?"

"I told Dalia that we come with our own makeup artist and hair stylist. aka Eva." He chuckled. "That was the toughest thing for her to accept. I had to push hard past her resistance. She's not an easy lady to thrall."

"You're lucky she is not immune."

"If she was, we would have been forced to seek another agency, and that would have been a mess. It's good that not many humans are immune."

As they got back to their suite, Alena sighed. "I'm going to shower and take this gunk off. Can you guys order dinner? I'm starving."

Arwel headed for the mini bar. "Take a look at the room service menu before you get in the shower and let me know what you want." He opened the leather-bound folder. "In the meantime, I need to do some self-medicating." He pulled out a small bottle of Jack Daniels. "Ragnar must be kidding. What's that? A sample?"

Alena flipped through the offerings. "The roasted chicken with spring potatoes sounds good." She smiled at Arwel. "And you can order yourself a nice big bottle of whiskey, or I can ask Ovidu to get you some from a liquor store."

"I'm sure Ragnar can hook me up." Arwel emptied the little bottle down his throat and reached for another one.

Yamanu took the folder and quickly scanned the menu. "Get me the New York steak. You know how I like it."

Arwel emptied the second bottle and tossed it in the trash. "Where are you going?"

"To my room. I need to meditate."

Arwel snorted. "I bet."

63

"What's that supposed to mean?"

The way Yamanu had explained his meditative routine was that channeling his inner energies into his powerful thralling and shrouding ability required two hours of daily meditation. He hadn't explained the other purpose it served.

Except, Arwel was a smart guy, and he must've figured it out. Good for him, but he wasn't going to get a confirmation.

Plausible deniability was the name of the game.

"Nothing. Just go do your thing. Do you want me to call you when the food gets here?"

"I'll come out when I'm done."

"Suit yourself."

As Yamanu ducked into his room, he heard the suite's front door open, and then he had to listen to Eva and Bhathian asking Arwel a bunch of questions.

Regrettably, the hotel wasn't built for immortals, and the walls and doors had standard soundproofing, which meant that in order to meditate, he would have to put on his noise-canceling headphones.

By the time Yamanu was done, dinner had been delivered and eaten, and everyone was gathered in the living room.

Arwel looked wasted.

Apparently, Ragnar had sent up a proper supply of booze for him.

"Let me warm up your dinner, master." Ovidu rushed over to the dining table and grabbed the plate before Yamanu had the chance to take a bite. "It will only be a minute."

"Don't dry out my steak."

"I won't, master."

Bossy butler.

After spending time with Okidu, Yamanu had started paying attention to the small differences between the Odus. At first glance, they looked identical, but they weren't, and it wasn't only physical. They seemed to have slightly different personalities as well. Perhaps their masters had some influence on the way they acted.

Machine learning and all that.

"How was your meditation?" Arwel slurred.

"Good. Very relaxing." Yamanu glanced at the half-empty whiskey bottle in Arwel's hand. "I see that Ragnar hooked you up."

Arwel shrugged. "We each medicate ourselves in our own way. I drown the bombardment of human emotions in alcohol, and you suppress your sex drive with meditation."

The room fell silent, like in no one breathing kind of silence.

The only one making any sound was little Ethan. Slapping his father's face with his chubby little hands, he was cooing happily.

Denial and redirection or avoidance and redirection were the best strategies in a situation like that. His sex life was nobody's business.

"Instead of drowning in booze, you should go down to the basement and spend time with your accountant. Why are you still here?"

Arwel grimaced. "The other time the hotel was new and there were no guests on the lower floors. That's why it was quiet and peaceful in the basement. Now the place is full, and it's almost as bad down there as it is up here." He took another swig from his bottle. "I need a bunker, or a little house on the prairie."

"Here you are, master." Ovidu placed the heated plate on the dining table.

"Thank you." Yamanu sat down and draped a napkin over his pants. "Or the space station. Imagine how quiet it is up there."

Eva laughed. "Guardians in space. It's a good book title."

That started the conversation going again, and Yamanu let out a relieved breath.

People suspected that he was celibate, but even though they were curious, they had the decency not to ask questions.

Which was the way Yamanu liked it.

His reasons were his own, and the last thing he wanted was for his sex life or lack thereof to become a topic of conversation. As long as his clan members had nothing more than speculation to go on, there was not much to talk about.

Arwel, however, should not have let his mouth flap like that, especially not in front of other people, and Yamanu planned to have a talk with his roomie. Drunkenness was not an excuse, and if Arwel couldn't control himself while boozing, he needed to find a different medicine to numb his pain.

Just to mess with the dude, Yamanu was going to offer to teach him his relaxation meditative rituals.

MEY

*M*ey put a kettle on the stove and sat down at the kitchen table with a French fashion magazine that she'd picked up on the way home.

When her cell phone rang, she hoped it wasn't Dalia telling her that the new outfits for tomorrow's shoot were in. It was after six in the evening, and Mey was in no mood to schlep to the agency to pick them up.

What if she let it go to voicemail?

Maybe at another time she would have, but she was too antsy with worry about Jin to ignore the ringing.

Snatching it off the charger, she looked at the screen and grimaced. "Hi, Dalia. Are you still in the office?"

"Where else would I be? My workday doesn't start at nine and end at five. Being your own boss is the best and worst at the same time. Anyway, I called to tell you that the wardrobe is here and I'm ordering a delivery service to get it to you. Are you going to be home for the next couple of hours?"

"Yes, and thank you. I really wasn't looking forward to dragging myself over there this late."

"I wouldn't have asked you to do that. A beautiful girl like you shouldn't be alone on the streets after dark, and it would have been dark out by the time you headed back."

Mey chuckled. "I'm touched by the concern. But you shouldn't worry about me. I can take care of myself."

"That's why I worry. You think that the self-defense class you took is going to do you any good when someone holds you at knifepoint?"

The answer to that was yes, but Mey couldn't tell Dalia that her self-defense skills hadn't been acquired in a class for suburban ladies. She'd gotten the best training in the world. But the truth was that it had been a while, and she might be a little rusty.

"You're right. But you shouldn't worry. I don't go out much, and when I do, I take a taxi."

"Good. And don't use any of those Uber or LYFT services. I tried it once and the driver was so creepy that I spent the entire ride praying that he would deliver me to my destination in one piece."

Mey stifled a snort. Evidently, the feared and revered dragon lady was a little paranoid.

"Yes, ma'am. Where and when do we shoot tomorrow?"

"Derek is going to pick you up with the van at six in the morning. You're shooting on Fifth Avenue."

"Got it. Thanks, Dalia."

That was the thing about street photography. It required early morning starts.

When the kettle whistled, Mey took it off the burner and put it aside. "Who wants tea?" she yelled in the direction of the bedrooms.

Tatiana poked her head out the door. "I want chamomile."

"Hibiscus for me," Valerie yelled back.

"Not for me." Josephine padded into the kitchen wearing only panties. "I could use some coffee." She pulled out a jar of instant.

"Are you all packed?" Mey asked.

"I'm waiting for the laundry to be done." Josephine put a spoonful of Taster's Choice into a mug and mixed it with water from the kettle. "Are you going to be okay here on your own?"

"Of course. But I'm so jealous of you three. You are going to have so much fun shooting on the beach in Hawaii."

Josephine shrugged. "You could've asked Dalia if you could go with us."

"I couldn't. I was booked, remember?"

"Well, there is always the next time."

That was true, and besides, Mey couldn't have gone with them. First of all because she needed to find out what was going on with Jin. And secondly because she had every intention of giving Arielle a call and inviting herself over. She just had to see Yamanu again.

"What's that mysterious smile about?" Tatiana asked as she walked in.

"A guy."

"Did I hear 'a guy'?" Valerie rushed into the kitchen. "Details, girl." She grabbed her mug off the counter and sat at the table.

"About time," Tatiana said. "You've been moping about Oliver for long enough."

Mey crossed her arms over her chest. "I wasn't moping. I was fuming."

"Whatever." Valerie lifted one shoulder in a dismissive shrug. "You were anti men. Tell us about this new guy."

"There isn't much to tell. He's the business manager of a new model that Dalia was interviewing this morning. We talked a little, I offered the new girl my help to get settled, and we exchanged phone numbers. That's all."

Tatiana rolled her eyes. "What's his name? What does he look like? What did he say to you? Come on, give us something."

"His name is Yamanu, and he is about six feet eight inches of perfection."

"Is he a model?" Josephine asked.

"He said that he is retired, but I've never seen photos of him anywhere. I would've remembered that gorgeous face and those unique eyes."

"Maybe he worked in Europe," Valerie suggested.

"That's possible. Arielle, that's the name of the new girl, is from Slovenia. But Yamanu didn't have an accent."

And neither had Arielle's boyfriend.

Things didn't add up with their story, but it had already occurred to Mey that Ari might be faking her accent to make herself seem more interesting.

Tatiana got up. "Next time you see him, snap a selfie with your guy and send it to me." She rinsed her mug in the sink. "I need to finish packing."

"Yeah, me too." Josephine took her coffee mug with her. "Hopefully, the dryer is done. I need my nightshirt."

"Did you hear anything from Jin?" Valerie asked as she pushed away from the table.

"Just those two text messages."

"It's better than nothing, right? At least you know that she's okay."

Mey sighed. "At this point, I don't know anything. The texts might have been sent by someone else pretending to be Jin." She didn't really believe that, but it was possible. Anyone could send a text using Jin's phone.

"Why would anyone do that?"

Mey shrugged. "Who knows? I won't relax until I hear her voice on the phone."

Valerie patted her shoulder. "I hope you hear from her soon." She walked out.

"Yeah, me too."

Alone in the kitchen, Mey cradled the teacup in her palms and considered her options.

Jin had been so secretive about her new job that she hadn't even told Mey how she was getting there, only that her new employer was taking care of all the travel arrangements.

They'd said their goodbyes the day before.

But that didn't mean that Mey couldn't find out what mode of transportation Jin had used, and where she'd gone, provided that the ticket had been bought in her name and that her employer hadn't given her fake documents.

But that was taking it too far.

Was it, though?

The whole thing was so cloak and dagger that she wouldn't be surprised if Jin had traveled under an assumed name. In any case, there was only one thing she could do while sitting at her kitchen table, and that was to call her old boyfriend from her Mossad days.

They'd remained friends after their breakup, so he might be inclined to help her. Off the record, of course.

Shimon had been her first love and her first lover, but that had ended after their assignment had been done.

Mossad had no more use for Mey, and she'd been decommissioned. Shimon, however, had continued on to better and grander things.

Or so she imagined.

She checked the time, making sure she wasn't calling in the middle of the night, and then selected his number from her list of contacts.

"Mey," he answered right away. "What's wrong?"

She smiled. There was no beating around the bush with Shimi.

"Why do you assume that something is wrong?"

"It's seven in the morning over here. You wouldn't have called this early unless you needed something from me."

"I do. Jin got this new job, and I'm worried." She proceeded to tell him the story. "Can you find out where she traveled to?"

"I'll do what I can. With the level of secrecy you are describing, my bet is that she is working for your government."

"It has crossed my mind. But I can't imagine what they possibly would want her for. She's a business major, not a rocket scientist."

"Maybe they need her for a spying job in China."

A shiver ran through Mey. She'd never told Shimon about Jin and her special abilities, but his shot in the dark was too close to home.

"She doesn't even speak Mandarin." Mey chuckled. "And a six-foot-tall girl can't blend in."

"Give me her phone number."

"I told you. I tried to call and text, and she doesn't answer."

"That's not what I need it for. I'm going to check who she talked to recently and trace the calls."

"You can do that?"

He chuckled. "Are you seriously asking that? Not me personally, but I have friends in high places."

"Thanks, Shimon. You're the best."

14

ANNANI

"*I*t is seven forty-five, Clan Mother." Oridu handed Annani her second cup of coffee of the day. "You wished to be reminded."

"Yes, thank you."

In fifteen minutes Areana's call would come in like it had every day since her sister had been given the communication device, and they would spend ten minutes talking and reminiscing about the past. It wasn't much, and after three weeks of nearly daily calls they were still in the stage of reacquainting themselves with each other, but there was no rush.

Hopefully.

If Navuh found out, all hell was going to break loose, and Annani worried that he would retaliate against Areana. Perhaps not physically, but he might further restrict the already limited freedoms she was allowed.

She rose to her feet and walked out onto the small back-yard. Her house in the village was modest, and some days Annani missed the sanctuary, but she had established a pleasant routine here, and the thought of leaving was becoming just as hard as staying.

Besides, she did not feel like going back without Alena. Up north, her eldest daughter was her only real companion, the only one she could be herself with. Annani loved her people, but she had an image to uphold, and being the Clan Mother twenty-four seven, as the young generation liked to say, was exhausting.

Down here, she could at least let go of the queenly persona with Amanda and Kian, and even Syssi.

So, until Alena's return, Annani was most likely going to stay in the village.

With both her and Alena gone so long, her people were probably feeling neglected, but they were safe in the sanctuary, so unless an emergency came up, there was no real need for her to hurry back.

"You forgot your sunglasses, Clan Mother." Oridu rushed after her.

"Thank you." She took them from him. "But as you can see, the sky is overcast, so I can manage without."

He bowed. "The clouds may part without warning, Clan Mother."

"Yes, you are right. Thank you for your concern."

Oridu bowed again and smiled, then turned on his heel and went back inside.

Annani frowned. Something had changed about her Odus lately. It was subtle, and she could not put her finger on exactly what it was that made them suddenly appear more real, more human-like. She wondered whether it had anything to do with Okidu's reboot.

Since she had received them more than five thousand years ago, none of the seven had suffered an injury severe enough to necessitate a shutdown and then a restart. Could it be that they had been operating on less than their optimal performance level?

Was there a reason to worry?

After all, they had an immense capacity for violence and were indestructible. If something went astray in their programming, they could become incredibly dangerous.

The only way to eliminate them was to eject them into space, or perhaps dismantle them and scatter the pieces around the world.

Annani had no idea what their capacity for self-repair was, and she did not want to test it. She had not even allowed anyone to tinker with them to discover how they worked.

The Odus had become part of her family, and Annani refused to chance losing any of them for the sake of experimentation.

Her phone rang precisely at eight, and as usual, it was William on the line. "Good morning, Clan Mother. I'm patching Lady Areana through."

"Thank you, William."

"How are you this morning, Annani?" Areana opened their conversation with the same greeting she used every day.

"Except for missing Alena, I am fantastic."

"Do you have any news from her?"

"She has not started the advertising campaign yet, so naturally, there is nothing to report."

"I'm not sure your idea is going to work. Kalugal was a little boy the last time he saw me. He might not even remember what I look like."

"I am sure he does. He went to great lengths to see you. I am sure that seeing someone who looks like your twin will pique his curiosity." Annani sighed. "If I saw a picture of someone who looked exactly like Khiann, I would do everything in my power to find him and meet him in person."

"But Kalugal did not lose me. He knows that I am alive and well."

"Perhaps. But I have a good feeling about this."

"I thought about another thing that might be helpful in the

search. Kalugal disappeared together with his entire company. That's about seventy warriors. If they stayed together, that's a lot of immortal males in one place. I don't know if it's significant, but perhaps you can come up with another idea that takes that into account."

Annani chuckled. "With so many warriors, he could have established a base somewhere in South America." She stopped herself before adding that he could have had a successful career as a drug lord.

There was no reason to upset Areana by suggesting such a thing, but it was a possibility.

It was much easier to hide and operate in places where the law had little muscle, especially when illegal activity posed no moral dilemma.

As someone who had grown up in the Doomers' base, Kalugal's idea of right and wrong could certainly be distorted. Even if he did not pursue his father's agenda and did not agree with his methods, his moral compass could have easily been mislaid.

Still, Lokan had undergone essentially the same upbringing as Kalugal and lived with continued exposure to that environment to the present day, and he was a decent man, or as decent as he could be under the circumstances. So, there was really no reason to doubt that Kalugal could be living a perfectly normal life as a stockbroker in New York City.

"You said that your daughter-in-law saw in her vision that Kalugal was in New York. So, he is not in South America."

"That is why we started the search there. I will inform the parties involved that they should open their eyes and ears and look for more than one immortal."

"I really hope you can find him. Talking with Lokan means so much to me. I just wish I could do it more often. Once a week is not enough."

That was a hint the size of an elephant.

"If you wish, I can give up another day for Lokan. Would you like to call him on Wednesdays as well as on Mondays?"

"That would be wonderful. I'm just getting to know him, and it's hard to do in ten-minute conversations once a week."

Annani teared up. Poor Areana. She had so much catching up to do with everyone. And then there were Tula and Wonder. They wanted to talk too, and once a week on Saturday was not enough.

She really should not hog the communication.

"I understand. And if you wish, I can give up another day for Lokan."

Areana chuckled. "No, that's okay. I don't want to overwhelm him. Small steps are better. And besides, you're already giving up three days out of seven."

Annani glanced at her watch and grimaced. "I am afraid that our time is up. I will inform Lokan that he should expect calls from you on Mondays and Wednesdays."

"Thank you."

"You are most welcome, my dear sister. Goodbye until Thursday."

15

MEY

*D*erek lowered the camera and shook his head. "Mey, sweetheart, you were frowning."

She'd been hoping to hear back from Shimon this morning, but it was taking him longer than she'd expected. It was three in the afternoon in New York, which meant ten at night in Israel, so he might still call.

"Sorry about that. I guess I'm getting tired."

Derek shook his head. "Give me twenty more minutes and we will call it a day. Find the happy place in your mind and give me that signature mysterious smile of yours. That's what the clients are paying top dollar for."

He called it her Mona Lisa smile, and Mey had seen it in the pictures Derek had taken of her. But whenever she tried to recreate it in front of the mirror, all she got was a crooked thing that was far from attractive.

Which meant that she couldn't produce it on demand, and the only way to get it was to bring up happy memories that she wasn't allowed to share with anyone.

Not even Jin or her parents had known what international modeling tour had been all about, and why she'd gotten an exemption from the mandatory service to do that. She couldn't tell them that the Mossad had asked for her, and that she'd been basically on loan to the secret service, her time there counting toward the completion of her military obligation.

She'd been merely the prop. The real undercover work had been done by the group of Mossad agents posing as her crew.

During the days they'd shot on location, but during the nights the guys had gone out to do their spying, or at least that was what she'd imagined they had been doing. They might have been assassinating evildoers, but Mey preferred not to know.

Not that she had much choice in the matter. The guys couldn't share details with her because she hadn't had the necessary security clearance.

Mey had been the pretty face, the cover. Still, she'd gone through intense expedited training, and the skills she'd learned were nothing to sneer at. At nineteen, she could shoot a gun with an impressive degree of accuracy and throw an opponent twice her weight over her shoulder.

The guys had been older, but not by much. Shimon had been twenty-three when they'd become an item, and at the time she'd thought he was so much more mature and experienced than her.

A fighter. A real man.

Now that she was older than he had been at the time, her perspective on that had changed, but not by much.

She still respected the hell out of him as well as the other guys on the crew. They had been forced to grow up so much faster than men their age that she was now meeting in the States.

Oliver was almost thirty, and he didn't have half the maturity that Shimi had at twenty-three.

Derek sighed. "And the smile is gone again. But I got a few great shots." He walked over to her. "See that? That's the gold."

"If you say so. I look like I'm plotting something."

He grinned. "And every guy that sees that wants to believe that you have hot kinky sex on your mind."

"Mey the dominatrix," Julie said. "I can totally see that."

"You are both twisted."

She wondered if anyone would have imagined that about her if she was a small woman. Probably not. Because of her size, people assumed she was assertive and dominant.

Assertive, yes, but it had nothing to do with her size. It was just her personality. And dominant? Certainly not.

In fact, Mey often berated herself for being too accommodating, too understanding, and cutting the men in her life too much slack. If she were bitchier, perhaps Oliver would have thought twice about cheating on her.

That betrayal had cut deep, and not because she'd been so in love with him but because of the blatant disrespect.

She'd been good to him, and she hadn't deserved to be treated that way.

"Relax, girl. You look like you're about to kill someone," Julie whispered. "Thinking of Oliver again?"

"How did you know?"

"Most of the time you're nice and mellow. You only shoot daggers from your eyes when you think about him."

"Cheating hurts. If he didn't want to be with me, he should have broken up with me before I left for that shoot. Imagine coming home and discovering that while you were gone, your boyfriend slept with someone else in your bed. That's the worst kind of insult."

"Are you sure he did that? You said that he denied it."

"I smelled another woman all over the bedding that I personally bought and put on that bed."

That wasn't how she'd found out, but it was the only explanation Mey could give without revealing her abilities.

The moment she'd returned home and entered her bedroom, Mey had felt the echoes of what had gone on in there during her absence. And when she'd closed her eyes and meditated for a few moments, she'd gotten way more than she'd wanted to know.

Oliver had denied it, calling her a crazy, paranoid bitch, and that had made it even worse.

Mey had walked out of there without taking a single thing with her and crashed at Tatiana's place. She'd slept on the living room couch until two of Tatiana's other roommates moved out.

Ignoring all of Oliver's phone calls, Mey had gone to collect her stuff when he'd been at work.

A month later she was still fuming every time she thought about it.

Julie patted her arm. "You know how to forget about him, right? Start dating again. I'm sure you have a long list of guys who are just waiting to jump at a crook of your finger."

"Not really, but thank you for saying that."

Most men found her intimidating, and those who didn't were usually too full of themselves and thought that they deserved to be worshiped by the lucky women who they'd bestowed their charms on.

Not Yamanu, though.

He was too tall and good-looking to be intimidated by her, but he wasn't cocky. He'd been polite, respectful, and she'd gotten a good vibe from him, which didn't happen often.

In short, he fascinated her, and she wanted to find out more about him.

"Ready to go home?" Derek asked. "I can drop you off."

"Thanks, but I want to stop by Jin's old dorm room again."

She pulled out a moist towelette from her purse and wiped the bright red lipstick off.

"I can take you there," Derek offered.

"That would be awesome, thank you."

16

KIAN

*K*ian swiveled his chair around and looked out the window, checking whether Onegus was on his way. From his office, he could see all the way to the pavilion, but the chief hadn't arrived yet.

Glancing at his watch, he debated whether the five minutes he had left until the meeting were enough for a quick smoke up on the roof.

Eh, what the hell, why not.

The pavilion was just as visible from the rooftop, and he could head back down when he saw Onegus walking over.

The chief was coming to discuss the Doomers' move to the clan's turf and what they were going to do about it, and smoking helped Kian think things through. Who knew, maybe his brain worked better when he was relaxed.

Opening the drawer, he pulled out the small wooden box containing his cigarillos and put it in his pocket. The lighter was still in his other pocket from his previous break.

Up on the roof, he sat on the lounger, lit up and took a puff.

Oh, yeah. That was it.

He closed his eyes for a moment and concentrated on loosening his shoulder muscles.

After the brainstorming session he'd had with Annani last night, they still hadn't come up with a good idea for utilizing the information Areana had provided.

It wasn't really big news that Kalugal had taken his men with him when he defected, but Areana had given them a more precise number. They had probably stayed together in the beginning and then gradually dispersed over time, but in the unlikely event that they had continued on in the same general location, seventy or so immortal males living together in one place should be easier to find than just one.

The question was how.

If they were indeed based in New York, the city was too big and had too many clubs and bars to search the way the Doomers' had tried to search for clan members in the past. So that was out.

What else would make them stand out?

He'd already asked William and Roni to hack into the state's DMV database and run its driver licenses through the facial recognition software, which they'd been constantly tweaking and improving.

Other than that, there wasn't much else they could do. If they didn't find any suspicious duplicates in New York, they should start working on other states' databases. Not only to find Kalugal and his men, but also potentially other immortals as well.

Like Roni's grandmother, who they still hadn't found.

Glancing at his watch, Kian rose to his feet and looked at the walkway leading from the pavilion to the office building.

As he'd expected, Onegus was on his way.

Stubbing out what was left of his cigarillo, Kian threw it in the trash can and headed back down.

"Good afternoon," Onegus said. "Up on the roof again?"

Kian opened the door and motioned for the chief to go ahead. "Yeah, it's a bad habit."

Onegus pulled out a chair and sat at the conference table. "I've given the situation some thought, and I came up with several ideas, but I don't think that will be enough."

"Let's hear them." Kian pulled out a chair and sat next to Onegus.

"I contacted the chief of police and told him that he needs to watch out. I hinted that whoever is snatching girls up in the bay area is expanding the operation to include L.A."

"There isn't much he can do. They are not going to increase police presence at the campuses until girls start disappearing, and even then they don't have enough officers to spread around."

Onegus lifted his hands. "We have the same problem. There are too many higher learning institutions in the Los Angeles area for us to post Guardians in each one. I thought that we could put up warning posters. We can hire a company to do that for us. Other than that, I can send Guardians to talk to campus security. They can go as undercover agents and thrall a sense of urgency into whoever is in charge."

Kian raked his fingers through his hair. "None of that is going to help. If a Doomer focuses on a particular girl and thralls her into trusting him, no one would know that foul play is involved."

"What do you suggest?"

"We need to find the Doomers' base and take them out."

"They are going to send more."

"Then we will do the same to the next group and the one after that."

Onegus shook his head. "They have thousands of men. They can just keep sending them."

"True, but it will reflect badly on the head Doomer running the operation."

Onegus nodded. "Lokan's so-called brother. Losham."

Kian waved a hand. "Whoever it is will be removed and replaced by someone else. In the meantime, no girls will be taken, and hopefully they will decide to change tactics."

"To what?"

"Voluntary service. Lokan is right about that. There are enough women who are willing to do this for the money."

Onegus shook his head. "The difference isn't that big. Once they get to the island, they will become slaves. It's not a temporary gig."

"I know. But it's the lesser of two evils. Do you have a better suggestion?"

"I wish I did. But unless we conquer the island and topple the despot, we can't stop the import of women. Besides, the island and its Doomers are small fish in the ocean of traffickers. Eliminating them is like swatting one mosquito out of a swarm."

Kian leaned back in his chair and crossed his arms over his chest. "I sometimes wonder whether the gods of old could have done more. If there were a hundred Annanis instead of one, could they have stopped global trafficking?"

"I don't think so." Onegus rubbed his jaw. "And there is more than one. Areana is a goddess too, but she is no more powerful than an average immortal. Our Clan Mother represents the best of the gods. Others were probably not as strong."

"Still, even though there weren't many of them, they managed to keep humans semi-decent."

"That's because the human population was tiny compared to what it is today, and transportation wasn't easy. In places where the gods' influence didn't reach, the same shit and worse was happening." He chuckled. "Sometimes I wonder whether Navuh isn't right about humanity. Is it really worth our efforts?"

Kian sighed. "I wish I knew. But we can't abandon the

cause. We have to believe that a better future is possible. It's just taking so fucking long." He tapped his fingers on the conference table. "But that's enough philosophizing. We need a concrete plan for finding and eliminating the Doomers who are moving into our backyard."

Onegus lifted a finger. "I've got it. They are moving, which means that they've bought or rented a property large enough to house them. We need to check recent real estate transactions of small apartment buildings, hotels, motels, boarding schools, and any other property that can fit a bunch of Doomers who are not too particular about their living conditions."

"Good thinking. I can ask Lokan to find out how many Doomers his brother has with him. If we know how many beds they need, it will narrow our search."

Onegus raised a brow. "How about he finds out the address of their new location and gives it to us?"

"Not a good idea. Firstly, because Losham would become suspicious if Lokan asks too many questions. And secondly, because once the Doomers are eliminated, Lokan would become prime suspect for the intel leak. Keeping his association with us secret is top priority."

"For what? I was wondering what you have in mind for him."

"He can give us advance warning. If Navuh somehow finds out where the village is and decides to send an attack force and take us out, a warning will give us time to move our people, and that's invaluable. If I get that out of him, it would be good enough."

"Right. Just out of curiosity, anything else that you expect from Lokan?"

Kian shrugged. "In the long term, he might be a candidate for taking over command of the island. If we ever find Kalugal, and he is a decent fellow, they could do that together. Kalugal sounds like a very powerful immortal."

17

MEY

"Thanks for the lift." Mey waved as Derek drove off.

Standing in front of Jin's old dorm building, she pulled out her phone and texted Jin's ex-roommate. *Is it okay if I come up? I'm missing a pair of shoes that Jin was supposed to leave behind. They might be under the bed.*

It was just an excuse to get in there again and do another meditative session. Hopefully, Gabi was still in class and the door was easy to open. If not, Mey would have to figure out a way to convince the roommate to let her stay alone in there for a little while.

Perhaps she could invoke a fake Chinese ritual involving the release of house spirits?

She chuckled. That should work. No one would be mean enough to refuse a spiritual cleansing.

Gabi's answer came a minute later. *I'm in class. Just let yourself in. Push the door hard and it will open.*

Mey smiled. That was even better. She would still be breaking and entering, but with permission.

Up on the third floor, she waited until there was no one in

the corridor before putting her shoulder into the door and giving it a strong shove.

Too strong.

The latch gave up easily, and Mey stumbled inside, catching herself on the knob that she was still holding tight.

The room was messy, with Gabi's bed unmade, her clothes strewn over every piece of furniture and some lying on the floor. It hadn't been that bad the last time.

Gabi had probably tidied up before Mey had come over.

Closing the door behind her, she debated what to do. Meditating would be impossible with all that mess distracting her, but Gabi might not appreciate Mey organizing her stuff.

She decided to go with the method she'd often used on her parents. Do first. Apologize later. After all, she came to look for something, and that was a good excuse for moving things around.

Fighting the instinct to fold and stack, she picked up all the clothing and dumped it on Gabi's bed. The shoes went under it.

With that done, Mey sat cross-legged on the floor with her back to the bed and closed her eyes.

After several minutes of deep breathing, the breakup scene from before started playing behind her eyelids again. This time, however, Mey focused on the periphery instead of on what was being said, and she noticed something she hadn't before.

A travel guide. It was on the bed, tilted toward Jin's thigh. Mey could see just part of it, a picture of a waterfall and the logo of the travel guide, but not the name of the place.

Damn. She was willing to bet that Jin had gotten the guide to get familiar with the new place she was moving to. And she'd probably taken it with her.

As her sister started mumbling to herself about the breakup, Mey expected the vision to dissipate like it had the other time, but it kept going.

"There will be others. Hopefully, who are more like me."

Jin's image didn't waver after she'd murmured those words. With a sigh, she pushed to her feet and the travel guide fell down on the floor. She looked at it, but she didn't pick it up.

Instead, she walked over to the square mirror hanging on the back of the door and smoothed her hand over her ponytail. "Who are you, Jin Levine? What defines you? Is it your most unique feature or the most common one? There are more than two billion women in the world with hair exactly like yours. But how many can do what you can? Probably none."

Goosebumps rose on Mey's arms. Jin was referring to her special talent, but was it connected in any way to her new job?

In her imagination, Mey saw an institute like the one in the X-Men movies, complete with a wheelchair-bound, genius director. But instead of mutants, it was home to people like her and Jin.

In fact, she and her sister were mutants of sorts.

Mey shook her head. She was letting her imagination run wild.

Jin's monologue had been most likely about her breakup with Mitch, and not her new job. Perhaps she'd seen something that had upset her.

Like Mey had with her ex.

Normally, Jin would have told her about whatever she'd found out. But her sister might have wanted to spare her feelings and not share with her a similar story.

Had Mitch been unfaithful? Perhaps he'd flirted with someone? Jin would have been upset about that too.

Having the ability to spy on people was a double-edged sword. It was a useful tool, and Mey was thankful for having it, but sometimes the truths it had helped her uncover had hurt. Still, she would take knowledge and pain over blissful ignorance any day.

Where was that travel guide though? Could it have been shoved under the bed?

Activating her phone's flashlight, she looked under Jin's bed, but all she found there were dust bunnies.

Next, she did the same under Gabi's. First, though, she had to clear all the shoes she'd pushed under there before. Besides that, she found a dust-covered towel, a small sleeping bag, and a bunch of books, two of them travel guides.

One was about Virginia, and the other one was about West Virginia.

Flipping through both, Mey looked for earmarked pages or any other indicator that Jin had been interested in a particular location.

She found one page that looked like it had been bent and then straightened. It was about a National Radio Quiet Zone in West Virginia.

Interesting. Mey hadn't known such a place existed.

Was it a clue that Jin had left for her?

Or were those just two old travel guides that had been left over by the previous dorm residents?

Mey shoved both guides back under the bed.

Until Shimon got back to her with some more information, West Virginia was just a possible clue. Regrettably, he wasn't likely to call anytime soon because it was the middle of the night in Israel.

Except, it had crossed her mind that he could have answered her from anywhere in the world. Nevertheless, she shouldn't bug him. He would call whenever he had something for her.

For now, she had no more things to investigate or people to question, but Mey had an idea for how she wanted to spend the rest of the day, and it involved a little chutzpah.

Pulling out the business card Arielle had given her, she punched in the number and waited.

"Hello?"

Mey stifled a chuckle. There was absolutely no Slavic accent in that greeting.

"Hi, Ari. It's Mey. I was wondering if you would like to grab that cup of coffee we talked about. My flat mates are on a shoot in Hawaii, and I don't feel like going back to an empty apartment."

"I would love to," Ari said with an exaggerated Slovenian accent. "I'm staying at the Regent Hotel. I'll text you the address. When you get here, call me, and I'll come down to the lobby."

"Awesome. Is there a café or a restaurant nearby?"

"The hotel has a good restaurant, but we can order room service. I have a very nice suite. Besides, I'm sure you want to say hello to Yamanu as well."

Arielle was no fool, guessing the real reason behind the call, but Mey decided to ignore the suggestive remark. "I can be there in an hour. Is that okay?"

"Perfect. Call me when you get here."

"I will. And thanks for the invitation."

"No, thank you. I'm so happy that you're coming over. See you here in an hour."

As the text with the address came in, Mey was glad that the hotel wasn't very far from her apartment. She was sweaty from the earlier shoot and covered in dust from searching under the beds. A quick shower and a fresh outfit were in order, something casual but flattering. What Mey was going for was effortless elegance that wouldn't look as if she'd been trying too hard.

18

YAMANU

"*A*re you out of your mind?" Yamanu glared at Alena. "Don't bring her up here. Take her to the hotel restaurant."

Alena smiled, but it was a chilly kind of smile. "I'm not asking your permission, Yamanu. If you don't wish to see Mey, you can stay in your room."

"I'm in charge of this operation, and this is a security breach. No one is allowed on this floor. Ragnar is not renting out the remaining suite because of that, and only our keys get the elevator up here. You can't invite a complete stranger just because she is nice."

"I can do as I please, and you'd better adjust your tone. What's gotten into you?"

Damn. Alena wasn't Annani or Kian, and Yamanu treated her as he would Amanda, which was like a friend. But apparently that wasn't going to work. Alena demanded the same type of deference as her mother and brother.

The truth was that Alena had as much right to the title Clan Mother as Annani. If not for the thirteen children that she'd brought into the world, the clan would have been a fraction of the size it was. But she'd always remained in the shadows, acting as Annani's companion and not as a leader in her own right.

Kian and Sari had been appointed regents, Amanda was a council member, but Alena didn't have an official title. Not only that, she'd always been so quiet and mellow that he'd never expected her to act so bossy.

So far, she'd been a good sport, a team player. Why the sudden change? And what was so important about Mey that Alena felt like she had to put her foot down?

Yamanu bowed his head. "My apologies. I didn't think that establishing ground rules was necessary, but evidently I was mistaken. Would you mind taking a seat so we can discuss this like reasonable people and not turn it into a pissing contest?"

"By all means." Alena waved a hand toward the couch. "Let's talk it over."

As Yamanu sat next to her, Arwel opened the door and stepped out of his room. "What's going on? I sensed tension."

"Alena invited Mey over and she wants to bring her up here. I'm trying to explain why it's a bad idea."

"Oh." Arwel smoothed a hand over the back of his neck. "I guess the keep's rules apply here. We weren't allowed to bring outsiders to the clan-occupied floors in the keep. It's a safety precaution that Kian insisted on."

Until he'd broken it himself by bringing Syssi up to his penthouse, but Yamanu wasn't going to mention that.

Alena nodded. "My brother is in charge of the American arm of the clan. I accept that, and I don't intend to undermine his decisions in any way. But I'm not under his jurisdiction. Think of me as Annani's emissary, if you please. I make the decisions here."

Talk about surprises. Alena, who looked like the angel of tranquility, was as assertive and as bossy as her mother.

Arwel glanced at Yamanu. "She has a point."

"I beg to differ. Kian and Sari have a lot of experience safe-guarding the clan. You don't. And as I said before, bringing Mey up here is a security breach."

Alena smiled and put her hand on his thigh. "I take respon-sibility, Yamanu, so you can relax. Worst case scenario, I will thrall her to forget about ever meeting us. But she is just a nice young woman who reached out to a stranger and offered her help. I appreciate it, and I've taken a liking to her. I would like to experience having a friend. Can you understand that?"

Manipulative daughter of a goddess.

Putting things that way was even worse than putting her foot down. How could he refuse her when she looked at him with those big eyes of hers and told him that she craved friendship?

Alena lived in isolation, dedicating her life to her mother and the clan. She deserved to unfurl her wings a bit.

"How good is your thrall?"

"Superb. I'm a very old immortal, and I am my mother's daughter."

He nodded. "Can I ask you not to invite Mey again? I would hate for her to sustain brain damage because of repeated thralls."

"I'm not going to reveal anything I shouldn't, so there will be no need to thrall her. This hotel is our temporary lodging, and we are not going to stay here longer than a month. I really don't think we are risking anything here."

Yamanu looked at her makeup-free face. "What about your disguise? Are you going to have Eva put it on you before Mey comes?"

"No need. Arielle has a look and attitude that are for public consumption, and she is different in private. I'm sure Mey will have no problem with that."

Arwel chuckled. "I'm sure that she caught your accent fluc-tuating as well. You're not very good at keeping it up."

"Oh, well." Alena leaned back and crossed her arms over her chest. "I'm used to short bouts of acting, not keeping up a persona over time. I'll tell Mey that this is part of my public image as well. As you can imagine, I'm good at making up stories." She smiled. "Who do you think cleans up after Annani's messes? She is not very careful, you know. She trusts me to smooth things over."

Yamanu sighed and pushed to his feet. "I'll be in my room, meditating."

This was going to be hell.

There was nothing he wanted more than to spend time with the beautiful and alluring Mey, to get to know her, hear about her life, watch her eyes sparkle, kiss those lush lips of hers...

"Are you sure?" Alena looked up at him. "Both Arwel and I felt the attraction between you two. Why fight it?"

Aha. So that was what it was all about.

It wasn't about Alena wanting a friend, it was about her taking a page out of Amanda's book and playing at matchmaking.

And he was the gullible softie who had bought the bullshit she'd sold him.

Except, it was too late to backtrack now. He'd already agreed. Besides, it seemed that he wasn't in charge of the operation like he'd thought he was, and neither was Kian.

Alena was the boss.

19

LOKAN

*L*okan knocked on the bathroom door. "Are you almost ready, my love?"

"Five more minutes. These damn fake lashes refuse to stay on."

He chuckled. "Why do you bother? You have beautiful eyelashes."

"Frankly, I don't know. They are all over social media and everyone is wearing them, so I had to try. But I think this is going to be the first and last time. Or maybe I'll get lash extensions at a salon."

"Whatever makes you happy. But you really don't need them."

Carol was bored.

Their living room coffee table was covered with fashion and beauty magazines that she was adding to daily. Every morning she went out for a walk around the neighborhood and came back with a new stack.

Lokan had also noticed that her nails were painted a different color every day, and at first it had amused him, but then he'd started thinking about what had prompted her to do that. Carol liked to look pretty, and she took care of her appearance, but this was excessive.

He made a point of taking her out nightly. Plays, movies, restaurants, bars, clubs, Washington had plenty of entertainment options to offer. Tonight, they were going to see an opera. For tomorrow, he'd gotten them tickets to a hockey game.

But that was not enough to keep his mate from getting restless.

He even considered buying a café for her to run. But then he'd discarded the idea because he didn't want her to work that hard. Besides, it wasn't going to solve the problem of her being lonely.

Carol missed her friends and family.

Maybe a visit home would do her good. The problem was that she didn't want to go without him, and he couldn't go. First, because he had lots of catching up to do after his month-long absence, and second, because he wasn't allowed in the clan's base.

Perhaps he should call Kian and ask him what could be done about that. They could stay at a hotel, and Kian could send someone to pick Carol up.

Actually, Lokan was going to do that right now.

After pouring himself a shot of whiskey, he took the glass with him and stepped out onto the balcony. The device William had installed inside the apartment was good at protecting their privacy, but it impacted cellular communication.

No great loss. Carol had ordered a nice bistro set and two loungers for the terrace. They'd arrived yesterday, and this morning he'd had a very pleasant time sitting outside and talking with his mother.

His mother.

It was still a concept he had to wrap his mind around. He

and Areana were just getting to know each other, and the conversations they had during the ten-minute calls were quite formal and a bit strained. Mostly, Areana wanted to hear about his life. So far, Lokan had tried to stick to the nicer parts, creating the illusion that he hadn't done anything she would have found reprehensible.

He'd just found her. He didn't want to lose her.

Pulling out the special clan-issue phone Kian had sent him, Lokan selected the regent's contact.

"Lokan, you must have read my mind. I was just about to call you." There was a slight pause. "Tell me that it is not one of your talents."

"It's not. I wanted to talk to you about arranging a visit. Carol misses her family, but she refuses to go without me. Any way we can arrange for that? Carol and I can stay at a hotel, and you can send one of your guys to pick her up. Or maybe her friends can come over to the hotel. Whatever makes more sense to you and doesn't trigger your paranoia."

"Let me think about it. The hotel idea sounds good, but I need to tweak it. My paranoia whispers in my ear that you might be using Carol to find out where we are."

"On my honor, I am not. But I know that you won't believe me."

Kian's chuckle implied that he didn't think Lokan's honor meant much to him. "Sorry. But I can't take chances with the safety of my people."

Lokan shifted the phone to his other ear. "I understand. What did you want to talk to me about?"

"Losham. When is he moving to Los Angeles?"

"I suppose any day now. When we last talked, he said that they were moving in two weeks. That was twelve days ago."

"Right. Can you find out exactly what day? And while you're at it, can you inquire about how many men he has with him? I don't need an exact count. Just a rough estimate."

Lokan frowned. "Why do you need this information?"

"Don't worry, we are not going to do anything to your so-called brother. I have my people checking out real estate transactions for small apartment buildings. If I know how many men he has, it will narrow the search. We are going to find them and take them out. Not kill them, mind you, just put them in stasis."

Kian's request created a moral dilemma. Even if Losham didn't get hurt or captured during the raid, he would still suffer from the consequences of losing more men. As it was, he had been most likely demoted because of similar failures in the past.

On the other hand, Lokan still had to find out whether Losham knew about the things his adopted son had done to Carol. And if he did, the clan could have him and do whatever they wanted with him.

Hell, he would help torture the information out of the bastard himself.

But it was neither here nor there until he had a talk with the guy.

"Losham will just get more men from the island."

"Maybe yes and maybe no. But it will make him look bad and your father might replace him with someone else. All of that will take time, and in the meantime, female students in the Los Angeles area will be safe."

"What about arousing Losham's suspicions? If I call him asking a bunch of questions and then his base gets attacked, he will connect the dots. Losham is a very smart guy."

"That's why you need to be very circumspect about asking. If you're coming down to Los Angeles anyway, you can call to schedule a meeting with him. That way you'll know exactly when he is moving here. And during that meeting, you can throw in the question about his men in a roundabout way. You are a smart guy too. You'll figure out how to do that."

"Thank you for the compliment."

"You are welcome."

"While I'm meeting with Losham, Carol can see her family."

"True. I'll arrange for the hotel and text you the details."

"I have to pay for the hotel. You can't book it for me and pay for it."

"You are right. I'll text you the details about which hotel to make the reservations at. Are you going to use an alias?"

"Logan Roshmaoni."

"Does it mean anything?"

"No. I made it up."

MEY

*A*s the taxi stopped in front of the Regent Hotel, Mey was relieved to see that it wasn't super fancy. It was one of those new boutique hotels that were popping up everywhere. The trend was about catering to specific tastes and offering a personalized experience.

Still, those were pricey as well. How was Ari affording it? Other than a select few, models didn't make a lot of money, and Arwel didn't look like the billionaire boyfriend who was supporting his girlfriend's career.

But then, with all the stories about tech startups being bought out by the big players, schlumpy computer nerds could become rich overnight.

Except, Arwel didn't look like a nerd either.

Mey had a hard time categorizing him. He was handsome, athletically built, and he didn't slouch like someone who spent his days over a keyboard. But he paid no attention to his appearance. His shoulder-length hair was messy, not in a stylish way, and his clothes looked rumpled as if he hadn't bothered folding them after taking them out of the dryer. Which was the best indicator that Arwel wasn't rich. Wealthy people had housekeepers who did their laundry and either folded their clothes or hung them in the closet.

But the thing that bothered Mey about him the most was the tormented look in his eyes. She wondered if he was suffering from a physical ailment or a mental one. Or maybe he was an artist. She didn't know any personally, but literature often described them as tortured souls.

Yamanu, on the other hand, was well groomed, which she liked. But then he was Ari's business manager, so he had to look more presentable.

With nervous butterflies flapping their wings in her stomach, Mey entered the lobby and looked around. Just as she'd expected, it wasn't big, but it was tastefully done. Grays and light purples were the main colors, giving the lobby a contemporary feel, but the soft carpet and plush couches and chairs ensured that it didn't look cold.

She was about to pull out her phone and call Ari when Arwel stepped out of the elevator.

"Hi, Mey. Arielle sent me to get you." He offered her his hand.

Once again, she was struck by the suffering reflected in his eyes. "Do you have a headache?" she asked as she shook what he offered.

He smiled. "Do I look like I have one?"

"You look in pain. I can massage your temples if you like. It always helps my dad when he has a migraine. He says that I have magic fingers."

"Thank you, but it's not a headache that is bothering me." He walked her over to the elevator. "You seem to have a good relationship with your father." He held the door for her.

"I have a wonderful relationship with both my mom and dad." She sighed. "I miss them so much."

Arwel inserted his key before pressing the top button. "Do they live far from here?"

"The other side of the world."

"China?"

She chuckled. "No, Israel."

He lifted a brow.

"It's a long story."

Arwel didn't press for details, which she appreciated. Telling a stranger her life story in an elevator was not something Mey would do.

In fact, she didn't like to talk about it at all. As soon as she said that she was adopted, the pitying looks would come, and then she felt obliged to say that she'd had a wonderful childhood, but that sounded as if she was being defensive, which she was.

It was better not to say anything.

When they reached the top floor, Arwel led her down the wide but short hallway that had only four sets of double doors.

He opened the second set, and as she walked inside, Arielle rushed toward her with a big smile on a face that looked very different from the one Mey had seen the day before.

"I'm so glad you came." Ari enveloped her in a warm hug as if they had been friends for years.

"Glad to be here." Mey took a step back and gave her a once-over. "You look different."

"Yes, I guess I do. No makeup. That's for Ari the model." Arielle led her to the couch. "She's not really me. It's a persona I assume for the camera."

"You're very beautiful." Mey sat down and turned toward her new friend. "Why do you change your look so dramatically?"

Arielle shrugged. "It's a look that sells. Besides, it allows me to go incognito when I wish to. No one recognizes me."

"There is something to be said for that. I never know if people are looking at me because they think that I'm freakishly tall or because they recognize me from some advertisement I modeled for."

Arielle frowned. "You're not freakish in any way. You're gorgeous. That's why people stare at you."

"Thanks. My mom keeps telling me the same thing."

"She is a smart woman."

The door opened and an older man in a suit came in. "I brought the refreshments, mistress. Where would you like me to serve them?"

"On the coffee table, thank you."

"Yes, mistress." He bowed.

Mey gaped, then leaned closer to whisper in Ari's ear. "Does he come with the hotel or did you bring along your personal butler?"

Ari laughed, the bell-like sound raising goose bumps on Mey's arms. "Ovidu goes wherever I go. I've had him since I was a little girl."

Someone pinch me.

The woman sitting next to her had the face of an angel and a laugh to match, and she had her own butler.

"Who are you, Arielle? And is that even your real name?"

Arielle laughed again. "How are you at keeping secrets?"

"I'm an awesome secret keeper." Mey wasn't exaggerating.

Leaning closer, Ari whispered in her ear. "I'm the daughter of a very important person, and I have to keep my identity secret. That person has enemies who wish me harm." She waved a hand at Arwel. "Arwel is not really my boyfriend. He's my bodyguard."

Well, that explained a lot. Like the money to pay for the expensive hotel suite, the excessive makeup, and the fake accent.

"But if you need to keep your identity secret, why do you model?"

Ari smiled. "I still want to live my life as I please. And I think I'm doing a good job pretending to be someone else."

"Why are you telling me, though? We've just met."

Ari lifted her chin. "I'm an excellent judge of character, and I know that you're trustworthy." She put her hand on Mey's thigh. "And I also know that we are going to be good friends."

"Thank you for that. And you're right, your secret is safe with me. But I don't think you should be so trusting. I worry that you might tell it to someone who will use it against you."

"I appreciate your concern, but I know what I'm doing." She lifted a platter of small sandwiches. "You have to taste these."

Mey took one small triangle. "Carbs are not a model's friend. But these look so good."

"They are. Don't fill up on them, though. I ordered us dinner."

"Thank you, but I don't think I'll be staying that long."

It was the polite thing to say, but the truth was that she didn't want to leave anytime soon. First of all because the man she came to see wasn't there yet, and secondly because she really liked Arielle or whatever her real name was.

"Nonsense." Ari patted her knee. "You're not going anywhere until we have dinner and you tell me all about yourself."

21

YAMANU

$\mathcal{W}$ith a curse, Yamanu yanked his noise-canceling headphones off and dropped them on the floor.

Knowing that Mey was in the next room made meditating impossible. And even though the headphones had done a good job blocking the sounds of conversation that were percolating from the living room, they couldn't stop his mind from imagining what was being said.

Was Mey wondering where he was?

Had she asked Alena about him?

Had she come over because she wanted to see him?

"Nonsense," he heard Alena say. "You're not going anywhere until we have dinner and you tell me all about yourself."

That obliterated the last of his resistance. He couldn't miss out on hearing Mey's story or on having dinner with her either.

His willpower could go only so far.

Pushing up from the floor, Yamanu walked into the bathroom, brushed his teeth, even though he'd already done it after lunch, checked his jaw for whiskers, and combed his long hair. He resisted adding a fresh spray of cologne, though.

No need to give Alena and Arwel more ammunition for their teasing.

As he opened the door, the conversation halted, and everyone's eyes turned to him.

"Look who decided to join us after all." Alena's eyes sparkled with amusement.

"Hi, Yamanu," Mey said. "I thought you weren't here."

"I was meditating." Trying to was more accurate.

She smiled. "We have that in common. I also meditate from time to time. Do you do it every day?"

"He does," Arwel said. "Two hours at least."

"Oh, wow. That's a lot. I usually meditate for ten or fifteen minutes." Her eyes never left him. "How do you manage to hold it for so long?"

He sat on the armchair facing her and crossed his legs at his ankles. "I have many years of practice. But sometimes I get distracted too."

Alena cleared her throat. "Just so you know, I told Mey that I'm the daughter of a prominent person, and that I have to keep my identity secret because there are people who would seek to harm me if they knew who I was. I also told her that Arwel is not really my boyfriend."

Yamanu stifled a groan. Now he would have to thrall Mey for sure. "What did you reveal about me?"

"Nothing, darling. I leave it up to you."

He felt Mey tense up and wondered why. Was she anxious to hear what he was to Ari? Did she fear that he was Arielle's boyfriend?

It shouldn't have gladdened him, but it did.

"I'm not her boyfriend either," he clarified. "Ari is my cousin, and so is Arwel."

Mey looked from him to Alena and then to Arwel. "You must be second or third cousins. There is barely any familial resemblance."

Yeah. Alena was pale, he was dark, and Arwel was somewhere in between.

Yamanu flashed her a bright smile. "You got it."

"Second and third cousins are kosher for marriage," Mey said. "Genetically speaking, that is."

"Not in our family," Alena said.

Like Eva, Mey threw in Yiddish words here and there, but unlike Eva, she didn't have a New Yorker's accent. In fact, he could detect foreign traces in her speech, but even though she was obviously Asian, it wasn't any of those.

It reminded him of Annani's slight accent. But Sumerian was dead, and it had no genealogical relationship with any other language, ancient or contemporary.

"Are the others going to join us for dinner?" Yamanu asked.

Alena shook her head. "Not today. I'm selfish, and I want Mey all to myself." She smiled at Yamanu. "But I'm willing to share her with you and Arwel."

Looking uncomfortable, Mey shifted away from Alena. "Who are the others?"

Alena seemed just as puzzled as Arwel by Mey's discomfort. "My makeup artist, her husband and baby, my driver, and my other bodyguard."

Mey seemed to relax. "That's a lot of people. You travel with a large entourage."

As it suddenly occurred to him that Mey could have misinterpreted Alena's sharing comment, Yamanu stifled a chuckle. A pretty girl like her had probably been propositioned in every conceivable way.

"It's necessary," Alena said.

To change the subject, Yamanu asked, "I detect a slight foreign accent from you, but I can't figure out what it is."

Mey's hand went to the pendant she wore under her blouse. "It's Hebrew. I grew up in Israel. Well, partially in Israel. My parents moved there when I was seven. I've only been back in New York for the last three years."

22

MEY

*E*veryone was looking at Mey, probably trying to figure out why would a Chinese family emigrate to Israel, and now she had no choice but to tell them that she was adopted.

Crap.

Not that there was anything wrong with that, but whenever she told anyone, the pitying look would come. Usually it lasted for only a split second, but still.

"My sister and I were adopted by a Jewish couple from Brooklyn."

There, she had said it.

Surprisingly though, instead of pity, she got three smiling faces.

"Well, that explains it," Arielle said. "I was wondering about the Yiddish words. My makeup artist is from Brooklyn, and she throws them in a lot. I thought it was a New Yorker thing."

Hopefully, no one would ask her about her military service, which those who knew a thing or two about Israel usually did, because she would have to lie about getting an exemption to pursue her modeling career and promote an Israeli fashion label throughout the world. Supposedly, it had been part of a larger campaign designed to improve Israel's image, which had been the official excuse everyone had gotten at the time, including her parents and sister.

In reality, she hadn't been released, only loaned to the Mossad. No one knew that except those she'd met on the inside.

Perhaps the best way to avoid further questions about herself was to turn the spotlight on Ari and her cousins.

"Yamanu is such a unique name. I've never heard of it. Is that the name you were given at birth?"

He chuckled. "You think I would've chosen it for myself?"

"Why not? It sounds exotic, and it kind of suits you. I've never seen anyone who looks like you."

"You mean weird." He laughed.

"No. You're exotic, and I mean it in the best way. It's a shame that you left the modeling life behind." She waved a hand at him. "Women would buy anything you sell."

He put a hand over his chest. "I'm flattered."

"Mistress," the butler said as he bowed to Arielle. "I was informed that dinner is ready. Should I bring it up now?"

"Yes, please," Ari said. "And make sure they don't forget the extra place setting."

He bowed again. "Yes, mistress."

Mey wondered which of the European countries still had monarchies, because Arielle seemed to be royalty. Her butler was acting as if she was a princess.

When he departed, Mey turned to look at Yamanu again and realized that he hadn't answered her question. In fact, he was very good at dodging. Then again, she hadn't asked him directly about the meaning of his name, only if he'd been born with it.

"So, Yamanu, how did you come by your name? Is there a story there?"

Both Arwel and Arielle looked at him expectantly, as if they had been wondering the same thing and had never asked before.

"There isn't much to it," Yamanu said. "My father was Yemenite, and my mother sought to honor him by calling me after his homeland."

That explained some of his unique features. Except, the Yemenites Mey had met in Israel had been mostly skinny and short. Yamanu was practically a giant compared to them. But then she was a nearly six-foot-tall Asian woman, so there was that.

"Where do your parents live now?"

"My father is long gone, and my mother lives in Scotland."

"Is she Scottish?"

"Yes."

That might explain his pale blue eyes. The genetic mix he'd gotten from his parents was truly spectacular.

She caught herself staring at him for too long and looked away. He was just so striking, so compelling, but she had a feeling he wasn't into her as much as she was into him.

Just like in the agency's waiting room, he was polite, charming, and smiled a lot, but his eyes weren't as covetous as those of a man lusting after a woman.

How disappointing.

Was he just good at hiding it? Or was he really not interested in her?

It couldn't be her height because he was at least eight inches taller than her. And he didn't seem intimidated by her looks and size like some men were. Could it be that he had something against Asian girls?

Or maybe it was her lack of cleavage? Perhaps he found her too skinny?

Some guys didn't like the waif look that was a requirement

for fashion models. Ari wasn't as thin as that, but then she was doing makeup ads, so she didn't have to be.

As the door opened and the butler rolled in a cart, her stomach squeezed tight. "Something smells delicious," she said.

Mey was naturally thin, so she didn't have to work too hard to meet the requirements, but she couldn't allow herself to eat whatever she wanted either. Her rule of thumb was to get away from the table before she felt full.

Except, today she was probably going to indulge.

Yamanu's implied rejection hurt, and as irrational as the thought was, it made her feel bad about the sacrifices she was making to stay in the modeling business.

But he was just one guy, right?

There were plenty of men who found her desirable, and she shouldn't doubt her choices just because one gorgeous hunk wasn't attracted to her.

She and Jin had made a deal. They were going to work their butts off for the next five years, saving up as much money as they could, and then start their own business.

Once it was up and running, Mey would model only their own fashion line, and she wouldn't have to stay so skinny.

Except that was irrelevant at the moment. Right now, she was sitting across from a man that she wanted more than any guy she'd ever met, but he didn't want her back and that sucked.

23

YAMANU

*M*ey's disappointment cut through Yamanu's heart, causing as much pain as if she was digging in there with an actual knife.

As dinner had progressed, her mood had kept plummeting, and since all they could talk about were general topics, the conversation had gotten somewhat stilted. All the funny anecdotes they could have told her were clan related and translating them into human terms would have stripped them of their humor.

Mey had also been tight-lipped, not sharing anything about herself unless Alena had pulled it out of her.

He had a feeling that she was hiding secrets, which made him even more curious to find out what they were.

"I should get going," Mey said. "It's late and I have an early shoot tomorrow."

"I can take you home," Yamanu found himself blurting without thinking it through. "The hotel manager is also a cousin of ours, and he lets me borrow the limousine."

Damn, instead of driving Mey home, he should have escorted her downstairs and hailed a cab for her.

"Thank you. I planned on calling a taxi, but if you are up for a walk, I live not far from here." She smiled. "I'm sure no mugger would dare attack me with you by my side."

And hadn't that just made him feel like he had won the lottery. Not only did she trust him to protect her, she trusted him with her address.

Forgetting about his reservations and about why spending time with Mey was a bad idea, Yamanu pushed to his feet and offered her a hand up. "It would be my pleasure to escort you safely to your home."

Alena beamed happily at him. "Make sure to check Mey's apartment for intruders before you leave. Her roommates are gone, and someone might be lurking in there, just waiting for her to come home." She winked at him.

Mey shook her head. "New York has gotten a bad rap, but it's not as dangerous as it's made out to be. This is a good neighborhood, and my building is secure."

"Nevertheless, Yamanu should check. You never know who your neighbors are. What if one of them is a pervert who is just waiting to catch you alone in your apartment?"

"I hadn't thought of that possibility." Mey frowned, but he sensed no fear from her.

She had either dismissed Alena's concerns or was just a fearless type of lady.

Which worried him.

Fear was good. Nonchalance was dangerous.

Alena crossed her arms over her chest. "That's the problem. People naively believe that if they are good, others are good as well. And then they pay dearly for their naïveté. Sharks lurk everywhere."

"True." Mey smiled mysteriously. "But how do you know the bad guys from the good? What if Yamanu has nefarious intentions?" She cast him a glance from under her long lashes.

Damn. She was flirting with him.

He was in so much trouble.

"Yamanu is not a stranger because I can vouch for him. He is a real mensch." She laughed. "Now I sound like a real New Yorker."

"Let's go, my lady Mey." He offered her his arm.

The bright smile that his gallantry had earned him ensured that he was going to keep it up throughout the walk.

Threading her arm through his, Mey turned to Alena and Arwel. "Thank you for inviting me to dinner. It was a pleasure spending time with you."

"Then let's repeat it soon." Alena got up and kissed both of Mey's cheeks. "Are you busy tomorrow?"

"I don't know yet."

It wasn't an excuse. He could sense that she was waiting for something, some news that would determine whether she was free tomorrow evening or not.

The idea that she might be expecting a call from a guy infuriated him for no good reason. He had no right to get jealous over her going on a date with someone else.

He should be glad for her. And for himself.

Mey was proving to be the one temptation he couldn't resist, and the consequences of that could be disastrous.

"Well, call me as soon as you know. I might invite the rest of the gang. You just wait until you see Eva's baby boy. He's adorable."

Mey's face brightened. "I love babies. I'll come if I can."

"Please do."

After another kiss from Alena and a wave goodbye from Arwel, they finally made it out of the apartment.

"I really like Arielle," Mey said. "But she is not fooling me with that fake accent. What's the deal with that?"

Alena wasn't doing a good job of that. Luckily, it wasn't crucial at this point, but she really needed to get better at it.

"She's not originally from Slovenia." Alena had never even visited the country.

"Yeah, I figured out as much. She is not American either. English maybe? Or Scottish?"

He laughed. "I'm not going to tell you. That's Ari's secret."

As they got out into the street, he wrapped his arm around Mey's shoulders, pulling her closer against his side. "I apologize for this. But if we are to walk the streets at night, I prefer you as close to me as possible. It's not about me taking liberties I shouldn't."

She leaned her head against his bicep. "Don't apologize. Do you know how rare it is for me to be able to do this? You make me feel dainty."

"You are dainty. How much do you weigh, a hundred and ten? A hundred fifteen?"

She chuckled. "You either haven't gone out on dates in a long time or have spent a lot of time in Europe. Here, it's considered a great faux pas to ask a woman how much she weighs."

He knew that, but this wasn't a date. "My apologies. Did I offend you?"

"Not at all. I just thought to save you from getting in trouble if you decide to date again."

Aha. Mey was fishing for information.

She wasn't going to get it.

"I'll keep it in mind."

She shook her head. "You're good. But I don't know why you are being so evasive. I just want to know a little more about you."

She was direct, which he appreciated, but regrettably he had no choice. "What about you? You deflect as well as I do. What are you hiding, my lady Mey?"

"Nothing. What you see is what you get."

He cocked an eyebrow. "Right."

"What do you want to know?"

"Did you serve in the army? I heard that in Israel girls also have mandatory service."

"We do. Two years. It's such a tiny country with such a small population that there is no way around it. Mostly, girls are assigned administrative duties, but some want to be fighters, and if they can make it, they are given the chance."

"Were you a fighter?"

She shook her head. "I was too tall for the flight program."

He stopped. "Seriously? You wanted to be a jet fighter pilot?"

Mey burst out laughing. "Got you." She took his hand and kept on walking. "I toyed with the idea for about one day, but I realized that I didn't want it badly enough to put in the tremendous work required to make it through the program. Besides, I won a beauty pageant, and that set me on a modeling path."

"So, you're a beauty queen?"

"Ms. Teen Israel."

"That must've been something. I bet the newspapers had a field day with that."

"Because I'm Chinese?"

He nodded.

"A few years back," Mey said, "an Ethiopian won the title, so my win wasn't such earth-shattering news."

"So, what did you do in the army?"

"I went through basic training like everyone else. And then I was assigned to a clerical position in the intelligence department. Later on I was offered a very lucrative modeling opportunity, promoting an Israeli fashion label and through it Israel's image as an integrated society."

Mey was lying or leaving something out.

Usually, it wasn't easy to detect lies, but she obviously felt guilty about it, and guilt had a very strong and distinctive smell.

Whatever the real story was, she couldn't talk about it because it was a military secret.

But since there was plenty that Yamanu was hiding from her, he had no right to pry, and a change of topic was in order.

"Have you been modeling ever since, or did you take a break for college?"

"Much to my parents' disappointment, I didn't go to college. My sister went for both of us."

"How did that work? Is she your identical twin who changed outfits while hopping between classes?"

Casting him an amused sidelong glance, Mey slapped his arm. "You're funny. Jin is twenty months younger than me, and she recently graduated NYU with a degree in business management. We want to launch our own fashion label one day. I'm going to handle the design part and model our line, while Jin is going to run the business side."

When she'd started talking about her sister, Mey had sounded happy, but towards the end her tone turned a little sad.

"I sense that there is a problem with your plan. Did Jin change her mind?"

"Not that I'm aware of. We knew we had to save up money to start the business, so it wasn't going to happen right after her graduation. She was offered a well-paying job with a large bonus if she stayed on for five years. But she was awfully secretive about it. She said that they had her sign a nondisclosure agreement, and that she couldn't tell me anything about it. She left two weeks ago, and since then I've only gotten two short texts from her, and I'm worried. It's not like her. We used to talk several times a day."

"Did you try to call her?"

"Many times. Phone calls, texts, emails. In her second text

she said that there was no reception over there. From what I understand, she can get to the one spot where there is sporadic reception only once a week."

"That's indeed odd."

Mey seemed relieved that he didn't try to dismiss her fears as irrational.

"That's what I thought. And then she said something about how modeling is a great job, when she used to sneer at it. Do you think she was trying to hint something?"

"Possibly. Any idea what?"

Mey sighed. "I wish I knew. The only thing that comes to mind is that I shouldn't accept any job offers outside of modeling. But why?"

"Maybe her next text will offer another clue."

"Yeah, I had the same thought." She stopped in front of an apartment building. "This is where I live. Do you want to come up and check for intruders?"

She sounded hopeful, and he hated to disappoint her again. "I have to. Otherwise Ari will bite my head off. It will only take a couple of minutes."

Hopefully, she wouldn't try anything because Yamanu wasn't sure he would be able to say no.

He had taken his potion today, adding one more dose to the regular two, but he hadn't meditated. The potion only took care of the physical cravings, but he needed the meditation to get his mind in the right place.

As Mey entered a code to open the front door, he examined the security camera mounted above it and approved. It was a relatively new model.

Once inside, they entered the elevator and Mey pressed the button for the eighth floor.

"It's a nice building," he said just to fill the silence.

"The apartment costs a fortune, but there are four of us. We each pay two grand."

He whistled. "That's pricey."

"I'm sure that the suites you guys are renting at the hotel cost an arm and a leg."

"We get a discount. It's family owned."

"Ah. That explains it. Does it have anything to do with Ari's father?"

The elevator stopped and they got out. "What makes you think it's her father who is the important person?"

"Is it her mother?" She opened the door to her apartment.

"Can't tell you that." He winked.

Flicking the lights on, Mey shrugged. "Whatever. We each have our secrets."

When she made a move to walk in, he put a hand on her arm. "Stay here by the door. It will only take me a couple of minutes."

"Okay."

If anyone was there, Yamanu would have sensed it by now, but after her sister's story, he wasn't taking any chances. Mey was right about it all smelling fishy.

She watched him as he checked the kitchen, opening every cabinet that was big enough for a person to hide in. When he was done with that, Yamanu continued to the bedrooms. First, he opened all the doors and let his senses flare out. No one was there, but he made a show of looking under the beds and inside the closets and bathrooms.

When he finished, he returned to the living room. "All clear. But I want you to have my number." He flashed her a smile. "Just in case you need a big strong guy for any reason at all." He pulled out his phone. "Here is my number. Call me, so you'll have it in your contacts."

She looked at it and frowned. "Is it an international number? I don't recognize the area code."

"It's a private network. Don't worry about the cost. For you, it will be like a local call."

She shook her head as she punched in the numbers. "Ari's mother must be someone really important."

Nice try.

He didn't respond. When his phone rang, he answered it and then hung up.

"Don't hesitate to call me. I mean it. Day or night. If anything seems even slightly suspicious to you, call."

"Why? What are you thinking?"

He leaned and kissed her cheek. "I'm thinking that a beautiful woman like you, alone in an apartment, is not safe."

As her heartbeat sped up, and he scented her arousal, Yamanu knew he had to get out of there as soon as he could.

"Well, I have to run." He pulled the door open. "I hope to see you tomorrow at dinner."

"I'll try to make it."

"Lock the door behind me."

"I will. And thanks for walking me home and checking that everything was okay."

The disappointment in her eyes was killing him.

"Anytime. Goodnight, Mey."

M E Y

"*P*lease tell me that we are done." Mey plopped onto Julie's folding chair and let her arms hang down.

She was tired of forcing herself to think positive thoughts and smiling at the camera. All she wanted was to get to the nearest coffee shop and get herself a gallon-sized cappuccino, made from whole milk, sweetened with brown sugar, and screw the calorie count.

She was so sick of it all.

Jin was wrong about modeling being a mindless job. Other than acting, it was probably the only profession that required mental gymnastics to keep up the right mood. Right now, Mey could've rocked the bitchy, angry one, but that was not what the client wanted. He wanted happy, cheerful, mischievous, sexy, none of which Mey was feeling.

Where was an M-16 and a practice target when she needed one?

Derek scrolled through the thousand or so pictures he'd taken. "For today it seems that we are. Good job, Mey. You really gave it your all. No wonder you are exhausted."

"Here." Julie handed her a bottle of water.

"Thanks."

"Do you want me to take you home?" Derek asked.

"No, drop me at the nearest Starbucks. I'm in the mood for a venti cappuccino."

Julie shook her head. "Even with skim milk, do you know how many calories that thing has?"

"I don't care. Not today."

"Rough date last night?" Julie asked.

"No date."

"Ah, so that's the problem." Julie cast her a knowing look.

"I really don't want to talk about it. Can you hand me a bunch of makeup wipes? I don't want to walk into Starbucks looking like this."

"I'll do it." Julie made quick work of cleaning her face. "Do you want me to put a little eyeliner back on?"

"No, thanks. I want to give my skin a rest."

"In that case, let me apply some moisturizer with sunscreen."

"Thank you. That I can really use."

Mey tanned easily, which was both unhealthy and not a good look on her.

Despite her protests, Derek dropped her off at the Starbucks nearest her home, which probably added at least half an hour to his drive.

"See you tomorrow bright and early." He waved before pulling into the street.

"Thank you for the ride." She waved back.

Inside the coffee shop, Mey did exactly what she'd planned, ordering a venti cappuccino made with whole milk and at the last moment adding a chocolate croissant.

She was going to pay for that, but right now she didn't care.

Choosing the corner seat next to the window, she sat with her back to the rest of the customers and pulled out her phone.

Her heart skipped a beat when she saw a message from

Shimon. It must have come in while she'd been placing the order because she'd checked her phone before Derek had dropped her off.

She called right back.

"Mey."

"Hi, Shimon. Thanks for getting back to me. Do you have anything about Jin?"

"Yes and no. She didn't book any flights, not under her name. And if she bought a train or bus ticket, she did it with cash. The last activity on her credit card was a charge from Bareburger, which she made the same day she left for her new job."

Mey slumped on the barstool. "So, you found nothing."

"Well, as I said, yes and no. I checked her phone records, and there were none. Everything was wiped clean, which is next to impossible to do. Everything ever said over a cellular connection, and every text message, it can all be retrieved. Whoever cleaned Jin's was a top-notch pro. Probably someone from your government. I can't think of anyone else who could have done it."

Mey shook her head. "It doesn't make sense. Jin is a twenty-four-year-old girl with nothing to hide."

Except for her special ability.

Mey tried to remember if they had ever talked about it over the phone or texted each other about it. If what Shimon was telling her about the phone records was true, and she had no reason to doubt him, then someone might have hacked into their communications and discovered their secrets.

"I wish there was more I could do for you," he said.

"You did plenty. Thank you for putting so much effort into this."

"For you, anytime. Are you coming home for a visit sometime soon?"

"I have no plans at the moment, and certainly not until I find out what's going on with Jin."

"When you do, give me a call."

"I will. And thank you again. You're the best."

He chuckled. "So I kept telling you. Bye, Mey."

Disconnecting the call, Mey smiled. Shimi was so full of himself, but at least it wasn't empty boasting. He had the right to be cocky.

It was a shame that things hadn't worked out between them.

Maybe he'd left because he'd thought she was too skinny, too.

Ugh, enough of that. She took a long sip from the cappuccino and grimaced. It was too heavy and didn't taste as wonderful as she thought it would.

After throwing the half-full cup into the trash, Mey took one last bite of her croissant and threw away the paper bag it came with.

She was still wearing the high heels from the photo shoot, but she had a pair of flip-flops in her bag, and she took them out before heading home. It was less than a ten-minute walk, but there was no reason to do it in four-inch heels and tower over everyone on the street.

Talk about stares.

So far, she had only two clues about Jin's new job. Her sister was most likely working on something top secret for the government, and it could be somewhere in West Virginia. Perhaps near that radio free zone, which would explain the communication problem.

Then there was the possibility that Shimon had made her aware of. If they'd mentioned their abilities over the phone, talking or messaging, then Jin might have been recruited for that top secret job because of her talent.

She could be the perfect spy. Heck, she could be the best spy anyone could dream of. All she had to do was to meet the suspect and touch him or her, and bam! She could spy on them wherever they were and report what she saw and heard.

But if they, whoever they were, knew about Jin's ability from tapping into their phone conversations and texts, then they also knew about Mey's special talent. It could also be used as a spying tool, maybe not as good as Jin's, but still useful. Mey didn't need to meet the person or touch them. All she had to do was be in a room that person had occupied recently.

That could explain Jin's cryptic comment about Mey's modeling career. Was it a hint not to accept job offers that seemed too good to be true?

As the clues started to form a possibly scary picture, Mey's senses went on high alert, and she looked over her shoulder.

Was the guy in the baseball cap following her?

Nah, it was probably paranoia. If the government was involved, they had no reason to send someone to follow her. They knew where she lived, and most likely also about her Mossad days. And if they hadn't known before, they might know after her phone call to Shimon. The word Mossad hadn't been mentioned, but she had a feeling that the American Secret Service could find out anything about anyone.

Just in case the guy was a creep, Mey didn't turn into her street and continued walking straight ahead. After a few minutes, she glanced over her shoulder again, but the baseball cap guy was gone.

That didn't mean he was gone for good. If he was following her, he might employ evasive maneuvers, staying out of sight for a little while and then popping up again. Or, he could have taken the cap off. Without it, she wouldn't recognize him.

Mey kept on walking, stopping here and there and pretending to look at storefronts while casting inconspicuous glances back.

He wasn't behind her, but then she caught his reflection

from the other side of the street, leaning against a lamppost and pretending to read on his phone.

Damn.

What was she going to do now?

Going home was a no-no. The guy might not be from the government, but he might be a would-be rapist stalking her.

She could go into another coffee shop and wait him out, or she could call Yamanu.

He'd told her to call him if she sensed something suspicious, right?

And besides, even if she got rid of the creep following her, she would be afraid to go home and sleep in the apartment alone.

Pulling out her phone, she found Yamanu's contact and called him, at the same time committing to memory everything about the guy across the street.

He answered right away. "Are you in danger?"

"Are you psychic? I'm on the street not far from my apartment and I have a feeling someone is following me. You told me to call you if I sensed something suspicious."

Damn, what if he thought that she was making it up just to see him?

"Are you near a busy coffee shop or a restaurant?"

"There is a steak house about two minutes' walk ahead."

"What's the name?"

"Barron's. I mean Barron's Steak House."

"Get in there. I'll join you in less than five minutes."

She felt the tension leave her shoulders. "I really hate inconveniencing you like that, and I might be panicking over nothing. But I'm scared."

"It's not an inconvenience. Now get moving. Don't stay in one place and hold your purse close to your body. How are your self-defense moves?"

She heard him opening a door and then closing it. "Decent."

"Do you have anything you can use as a weapon?"

"A high-heeled shoe?"

"Are you walking in them?'

"No, they are in my satchel. I was on my way from a photo shoot."

"Then put your hand inside and grab a hold of one. Be ready to use it."

"Yeah, good idea."

"Don't hang up. Keep the line open."

"Okay."

YAMANU

*Y*amanu ran all the way to the steak house, ignoring the startled looks of passersby, the few *watch it* shouts, and the many gaping mouths. He was running at an unnatural speed, but with his height and his long black hair flying behind him, people probably thought that he was an athlete turned actor shooting a commercial.

He didn't care. Mey had sounded frightened, and she didn't strike him as someone who panicked over nothing.

He still heard her over the earpiece, asking for a table for two, thanking the waiter, and then ordering a glass of water. So, he knew she was okay, but she'd sensed something, and that was enough to turn on his fight or flight instinct, or rather just the fight.

No one scared his woman and got away with it.

Wait, whoa. His woman?

Where did that come from?

His friend. Mey was his friend, not his woman.

And no one threatened Yamanu's friends without suffering his retribution. Yeah, that was better.

Crossing a distance that would've taken a human about twenty minutes at top speed in less than ten, Yamanu stopped at the door and took a deep breath. When he pushed it open, he saw Mey sitting at a table in the back but facing the entrance.

Smart girl.

To never turn your back on a potential threat was basic survival instinct, but not everyone had it. Humans, especially those living in big cities, had lost their sensitivity to danger triggers.

She smiled at him. "How did you get here so fast?"

"I ran."

"No way. Did you steal someone's bike?"

He pulled out a chair. "I wouldn't do that. I would offer to pay for it."

"What if you didn't have time to negotiate?"

"Then I would yell that it's an emergency, throw the money together with my business card at the biker, and take off."

She narrowed her eyes. "Good solution. I'll remember that next time I have to confiscate someone's bike."

"I'm glad you've relaxed enough to joke about it. You sounded frightened over the phone."

"I'm sorry about that. I don't know why I freaked out. After I called you, the guy didn't follow me. I was watching the street through the window the entire time."

"What did he look like?"

"Average height and build. He wore jeans, faded but not ripped, a brown T-shirt, a blue baseball cap that didn't have anything written on it, and aviator sunglasses. And he had white converse high tops on." She closed her eyes. "His hair was closely trimmed, and he was clean shaven."

"I'm impressed. You remembered a lot of details. Did he carry anything with him? Like a shopping bag or a backpack?"

Mey shook her head. "Just a phone. He was leaning against a lamppost and pretending to read on it, or really reading. He might have been just someone walking in the same direction as me, and I jumped to conclusions."

He reached across the table and took her hand. It was a little clammy, belying her dismissive statements.

"I'll tell you what. We will order dinner, and after we are done, we will go for a walk. If he is still following you, I will know."

Her brows rose. "How?"

He smiled and tapped his temple. "Sixth sense."

"Really? You believe in that?"

"Of course. Always trust your intuition. It's not some mystical mumbo jumbo. Your subconscious is constantly collecting information that your conscious self ignores. We can't process all the input that is coming our way, and most of it is stored as raw data. The gut feeling you get, or intuition, or sixth sense, that's your subconscious processing some of it and sending it to you as a nonverbal warning."

All of what he'd told her was true, but Yamanu had a few extra tricks up his proverbial sleeve that he couldn't reveal. He wasn't as strong an empath as Arwel, but he could sense nefarious intentions if the perpetrator was close enough.

"That's fascinating. Did you study psychology?"

He flashed her a grin. "I've studied many things, but none of them officially. I'm a self-taught kind of guy."

"That's awesome."

The waiter came over. "What can I get you folks?"

"I'll have the Caesar salad, please," Mey said.

Yamanu cast her a questioning glance. "That's all you're going to eat at a steakhouse?"

"I had a huge cappuccino and a chocolate croissant before I came here. I'm not hungry."

He waved a dismissive hand. "Bring me your largest steak with a side of mashed potatoes and a smaller one for the lady."

She narrowed her eyes at him. "I don't want a steak."

"If you are full after the salad you can take just a couple of bites of the steak, and I'll finish the rest. How about that?"

She shook her head. "I can't eat meat. If you insist, I can order fish." She looked at the waiter. "Can you bring me a side of grilled salmon with my salad?"

"Of course."

"Thank you."

When the waiter took the rest of their order and left, Yamanu leaned forward. "You ate beef yesterday. Are you following some special diet?"

Her eyes widened. "I was supposed to come over for dinner tonight. With the scare I had, I totally forgot. Arielle is going to be disappointed. I need to let her know."

"Don't worry about that. We can join her and the rest of the gang for dessert." He pulled out his phone. "I'd better let her know that you're okay."

He typed a quick message to Alena, telling her he was with Mey and that they were eating dinner and would come later.

Mey sighed. "I feel so bad for scaring everyone. If my room-mates were in, I would have just gone home. But I was afraid of being alone in the apartment."

He put the phone away and took her hand again. "You did the right thing. Now, tell me what's the deal with you and beef."

She shrugged. "There is no deal. I had a cappuccino before I came here, and I ordered a Caesar salad that is also dairy. My parents keep kosher, and so do I, or at least I try to when I can. I'm not very strict about it, but I don't eat pork or shellfish, and I don't mix beef with dairy. That's about it."

She sounded apologetic, and he didn't like that. "There is nothing wrong with that. In fact, it's probably a healthier way of eating. I read that many people are sensitive to dairy and shouldn't consume it at all."

"I know. It's not good for my skin, but I was in a rebellious mood today." She leaned forward and whispered. "It was a venti sized cup, and it was whole milk, not skim."

Yamanu gasped dramatically. "The horror. You wicked, wicked lady. Where are the model police? I have to report you."

MEY

*a*s Mey laughed, the tension left her body.

Yamanu was incredible. Not only was he as handsome as a god, he was also protective, and he was funny.

What else could a girl ask for?

That he would like her as much as she liked him, that's what.

He baffled her.

Usually, Mey had no problem deciphering people's intentions, especially a man's. But Yamanu was unlike any man she'd ever met.

He seemed to enjoy her company, and he was even holding her hand like a boyfriend would, but he wasn't flirting with her. He was acting like a friend, not a boyfriend.

Still, he'd come running when she'd needed him, and she was enjoying his company even though his lack of romantic interest was disappointing.

Pulling her hand out of his, she tucked a strand of hair behind her ear. "We all have to make some sort of sacrifice. Nothing can be gained without giving up something in exchange."

The humor left Yamanu's eyes. "Ain't that the truth."

As the waiter returned with their order, Mey eyed the mountain of mashed potatoes on Yamanu's plate. There was probably a whole stick of butter in that mound, and even though her mouth salivated imagining how good it would taste, she would never touch it.

He caught her looking. "Do you want a bite?" Using a fork, he moved the mound of potatoes away from the steak. "No cross contamination." He winked.

"I can't."

He scooped a little with his fork and brought it next to her mouth. "One bite will not make a difference."

She chuckled. "That's where you are wrong. One would never be enough. Once I get the taste in my mouth, I won't be able to resist taking another one, and then another, until there is nothing left, and I've consumed two thousand calories."

Yamanu just stared at her, his big pale eyes sad instead of smiling.

She hated seeing him like that and wondered why it was so important to him that she ate his potatoes. "But if it means so much to you that I try, I'll take a bite. I don't want you to be sad." She opened her mouth.

He retreated his hand. "I don't want to be responsible for your succumbing to temptation." He put the scoop in his mouth, chewed and swallowed. "I know how hard it is to keep yourself disciplined and stay away from things that can potentially ruin the one good thing going for you."

Was he talking about himself or about her? Because if he thought that her looks were the only thing that she had going for her, he'd just insulted her.

"Modeling is not my only option. There are plenty of things I can do, even if I gain some weight. Maybe not as well-paying, but still."

His eyes widened and he reached for her hand again. "I

didn't mean it like that." He clasped her fingers gently. "I'm sure you can do whatever you put your mind to. I was talking about myself."

"I'm sure you have more than one thing going for you as well."

"I do. But there are levels of importance." He motioned at her salad. "You're not eating."

Was that his way of avoiding the topic?

She forked a few lettuce pieces together with a chunk of salmon. "You're being vague." She put it in her mouth.

"I'll give you an example. Let's say that you are a lifeguard. If you don't train regularly, you might not be able to save the next drowning victim. So routine training is crucially important. You must sacrifice your free time and comfort or change occupations. You also must protect your skin with sunblock and wear a hat, but that's one level down in importance because neglecting to do so will not put anyone else's life in jeopardy. Only yours."

"I get it. So, what's that one thing for you? The one you have to sacrifice for?"

His eyes darted sideways, which meant that he was about to lie to her. "I'm like the lifeguard. I need to keep training in order to be able to protect the people I care for. That's number one in level of importance for me."

"But you are a business manager. How do you train for that? Do you negotiate with yourself in front of the mirror?"

Yamanu laughed. "That's an interesting method. I might try it." He cut another piece of steak and put it in his mouth.

Regrettably, her Mossad training hadn't included interrogation techniques. It would have come in handy for pulling information out of Yamanu. He was damn good at evading and redirecting.

It was time to drop the polite and demure act and let her inner Israeli out. "If you don't want to tell me about yourself, just say so. I won't be offended. I get secrets, and believe me, I have plenty of my own. But I don't like evasiveness. I appreciate bluntness."

He put his fork down. "That's refreshing. You are right. There are things I can't tell you."

"That's fine. I know there is a lot of secrecy involving Arielle. Just tell me what you can without revealing anything you are not supposed to."

"Fair enough." He hesitated for a moment. "I'm not really Arielle's business manager. I'm in charge of her security team."

That made so much more sense. His alertness, his insistence on her calling him the moment she felt unsafe, the speed with which he'd arrived when she called.

"I should have guessed. You don't look like the business type."

"I don't?" He looked down at his button-down shirt. "I thought I dressed for the part well."

Was he teasing?

She pointed with her fork. "With waist-length hair, muscles galore, and a face to die for? Not a chance. An actor, a model, yes. Not a number cruncher."

"Tsk, tsk, Mey. Are you judging a book by its cover?"

"I'm not. But most people do. If you want to play a part, you need to adhere to the expected stereotypes. When you really are who you claim to be, you can afford not to."

He nodded. "Very well stated, my lady Mey."

YAMANU

*A*s they left the restaurant, Yamanu wrapped his arm around Mey's shoulders. "Let's walk at an easy stroll. I want to make sure that you are not being followed."

She leaned against him. "Perhaps you should check with Ari if it's still okay for me to come over. We spent a long time in the restaurant. She might want to get into her pajamas and relax."

He laughed. "I don't think Arielle owns even one pair of pajamas. She wears fancy nightgowns."

Mey lifted her eyes to him and smiled. "You're doing it again. It's actually fascinating. You pick up the irrelevant part of the question and expand on it while ignoring the main one. Are you doing it on purpose?"

Was he? Sometimes. But not this time.

"It wasn't intentional. I just couldn't imagine Ari in pajamas. But to answer your question, I don't need to check with her. She'll be mad if you don't show up."

"I'm just making sure."

They walked in silence for a few moments, with Mey leaning against his shoulder and him trying to control his breathing from getting heavy while at the same time letting his senses flare out and check for a possible tail.

"Are you getting anything?" Mey whispered.

"No."

She relaxed her grip on his arm. "That's a relief."

"It doesn't mean that you weren't followed before."

She'd admitted to keeping secrets from him, which was fine. But if those secrets were behind what was happening to her sister and her, she should level with him.

"Maybe I imagined it. I was having a mini panic attack, and suddenly I was sure that I was being followed. It's likely that one was the result of the other. The question is in which order."

"Why did you have a panic attack?"

She hesitated for a moment. "I have a friend who has other friends who can hack into anywhere. I asked him to find out if Jin bought airfare and to where, or if she bought train or bus tickets. I called him from the coffee shop, and he said that there was no record of her buying anything at all using her credit or debit cards. Not only that, he tried to hack into her phone records to check who she's been talking to lately, but it was all erased. He thinks it was done by the government because it is very difficult to do."

"It is. But it's also very difficult to hack into those records, especially if encryption is involved."

"Jin used a regular cellular connection. But what worries me about it is that whoever did that could be privy to all our phone conversations and texts. And that's really creepy. I was trying to remember if we had said anything that sounded suspicious, and that was when I felt like I was being followed."

Mey wasn't telling him half-truths, she was telling him quarter-truths, and he was tempted to reach into her mind and get to the bottom of what was going on.

Except, he didn't have any justification for doing that.

Keeping the clan secret was not the issue, and to do it for any other reason would be a major violation of clan law.

But if he couldn't make her trust him enough to tell him the truth, he would not be able to help her.

"Have you ever felt like you were being followed before?"

She shook her head. "Except for guys who wanted to get my phone number or start something, I don't think so."

"You said that you know how to defend yourself."

She chuckled. "It was part of my basic training."

"Did you enjoy your service?"

"Yeah, I did. I made a lot of good friends. Fifty girls sleeping in one barrack for six intense weeks encourages bonding."

Again, she was telling him partial truths. "Not every Israeli girl knows self-defense."

"That's true. The basic training is exactly what it sounds like —basic. I later took another course that was more thorough. But that was a long time ago, and I probably need a refresher."

He stopped and turned to her. "Look, Mey. I know you can't tell me military secrets. But can you at least tell me if there is a connection between what you did during your service and what's happening now?"

She shook her head. "There is no connection."

That was the truth as far as she knew it. He didn't scent any guilt.

"Okay. Thank you for telling me." He took her hand and resumed walking.

"I'm sorry that I can't tell you more. The gist of it is that my part was not important, but I really can't talk about it." She squeezed his hand. "If you think that I'm some superhero warrior woman, don't. I know enough to be scared, and I'm grateful that you offered me your help and glad that you are a pro at this. You make me feel safe."

Yamanu felt his chest expand involuntarily. There was

something immensely satisfying about protecting Mey. Which was strange.

Yamanu had been a protector for most of his adult life. His sole purpose in life was to shield the clan from its enemies, and since he was the only one who could do that, his entire self-worth was derived from that.

But for some reason, protecting this one woman and making her feel safe made him feel more of a man than all his years of serving the clan.

It was absurd. It was wrong. But it was nevertheless true.

LOKAN

"So, what's the verdict?" Lokan asked after the waiter had cleared their table.

Carol pursed her lips. "Four and a quarter stars."

She'd come up with an idea to keep herself busy. A foodie's blog rating Washington's finest eateries on a scale of one to five.

The food was delicious, and the service exemplary. He wondered what she'd penalized the place for.

"What cost them three-quarters of a star?"

"I deducted half a star for the bread. A fancy place like this should be baking their own and serving a variety of different ones. Theirs tasted like a store-bought baguette."

"And the quarter?"

"That's for how long it took the waiter to clear the table. He should have done it the moment we put our forks down."

"Is that how it works?"

Carol shrugged. "I don't care how others go about their ratings. This is my blog, and I'm going to write about things that matter to me." She leaned closer. "It will cost them another half a star if the coffee is less than great. I got spoiled by Kian's wife. Syssi makes the best cappuccinos outside of Italy."

He smiled. "When was the last time you had coffee in Italy?"

"Never. But it's supposedly the best."

Reaching over the table, he took her hand. "As soon as my schedule clears, I'll take you to Milan. I know a place where they make the best cappuccinos. You'll have something to compare with."

She sighed. "First, I want to visit home. I miss Syssi and Ella and the rest of the gang. I can't wait to see everyone. Did Kian tell you how it's going to work?"

"Not yet. I still have to call Losham and set up an appointment with him. That will determine the exact dates of our visit."

"So, call him." She waved a hand. "What are you waiting for?"

"Now?"

"Why not? I can pretend to be one of the movers and shakers you wine and dine."

He lifted her hand to his lips and kissed her fingers. "No need to pretend. You move me and shake me every day and every night."

The bright smile she flashed him was the best reward he could get.

"You're such a smooth talker, my love. But I'm not complaining, mind you. Keep 'em coming."

"Oh, I will. Did I already tell you how ravishing you look tonight?"

Her hand went to the diamond necklace he'd bought her on a whim. "You did. But you can tell me as many times as you please." She leaned forward and winked. "But first, call Losham. Enough stalling."

"Fine."

Sometimes he had a feeling that Kian had agreed to let

Carol go with him to Washington just so she could spy on him. There was no doubt in his mind or his heart that she loved him, but that didn't mean she wasn't reporting what she saw and heard to Kian.

His call to Losham wasn't confidential, but he needed to be careful about what he said in front of Carol. He should assume that she repeated every word to Kian.

Lokan pulled out his phone and selected his brother's number.

He's not my brother.

They weren't related in any way, and he still had a score to settle with the guy over what his sadistic son had done to Carol.

Taking a deep breath, he schooled his features, which helped him even out his mood and push the rage below the surface.

The call was answered after several rings.

"Lokan, what a pleasure it is to hear from you. How have you been?"

"Busy. I'm still playing catch up. I need to come down to Los Angeles for a meeting, and I was wondering whether you are there already so we could meet for lunch or dinner."

"Splendid. When is your meeting?"

"I wanted to check with you before scheduling it. I doubt I will have time for another West Coast visit in the near future, and I wanted to make sure that we can meet."

"I see. My assistant and I are flying down on Saturday, and the rest of the gang is driving down on Sunday."

That was a great opportunity to sneak a question about how many men Losham had with him. "Did you rent a moving truck or a bus?"

Losham chuckled. "Neither. We are not taking any furniture with us. I'm renting out my house fully furnished."

"Are you planning on returning to San Francisco?"

"I don't know. But I like the place too much to sell it. The house I rented in Bel Air comes fully furnished as well."

"Bel Air, that's fancy. I'm sure you're not supplying Bel Air lodging for your men as well."

"Of course not. I bought a modest apartment building in Koreatown. It only has twelve apartments, but that's plenty. The men can sleep two and three to a room, which is better than what they get on the island, so they will be happy enough."

Assuming each apartment had two bedrooms, it meant that Losham had between forty-eight to seventy-two warriors at his disposal.

"Will you be available on Monday?"

"Let's make it Tuesday. I want to make sure that my men are settled first."

"Sounds good. I'll schedule my other meeting for Monday."

"Who are you seeing?"

"A senator."

"Which one?"

Right. That was bold of Losham to ask.

"I'm not at liberty to discuss it. It's a preliminary meeting, and I don't know if anything will come out of it."

"I see. Well, you'll know better by Tuesday."

"I hope so. Dinner or lunch?"

"Let's do dinner. Lunch will make the meeting rushed because we both have things we need to do in the afternoon. Dinner will allow us the freedom to talk for as long as we please."

"You are absolutely right. Dinner it is. Are you making the reservation or should I?"

"I'll make it. After all, Los Angeles is my turf now, so I'd better get acquainted with the best places to eat over there."

As Lokan disconnected the call, he debated whether he should call Kian right away, and how much of the information he should share with him. He could tell him about the apartment building in Koreatown and the estimated number of warriors, but not about Losham's rented property in Bel Air.

Except, Carol had been listening to the entire conversation, and she might mention it to Kian.

Not that Lokan was under any obligation to share everything with his cousin. The deal was that he would warn the clan if Navuh decided to resume his offense against them. And he was also going to help with regard to the abductions, which he disapproved of anyway.

Kian hadn't asked for more.

But he still might, and Lokan wasn't sure he was okay with betraying his so-called brothers. After centuries of thinking of them as blood relatives, it was difficult for him to regard them as strangers.

"Why are you frowning?" Carol asked. "You got him to tell you everything that you needed from him."

"I still think of him as a brother, and it annoys the hell out of me. We are not related in any way. On top of that, I still need to find out whether he knew about what his son was doing to you. If he did, I'm going to serve his head to Kian on a platter." He smiled evilly. "In the shape of a meatloaf."

29

MEY

*W*hen they arrived at Ari's suite, Mey expected the living room to be filled with the rest of the gang, as Arielle had called them, but they must have already left.

Ari got up from the couch and came over to give Mey a hug. "I heard that you had quite a scare earlier."

"I did. But now I'm not even sure that anyone was following me. Yamanu didn't see anything on our way here."

"Where is everyone?" Yamanu asked.

Arielle took Mey's hand and led her to the couch. "Ethan got fussy, so Eva and Bhathian had to leave. And then Uisdean and Ewan decided to leave too. Arwel is in his room."

They all had foreign names that Mey wasn't sure about the origins of. Perhaps Scandinavian? Or maybe Scottish. Yamanu had said that his mother was from Scotland.

Was there still a Scandinavian monarchy? Sweden had a king, right?

Mey wasn't sure. It had been years since she'd graduated high school, and her memory had never been great. Her mind tended to race, which meant that she often didn't pay as much attention as she should have in class, thinking about a thousand

and one other things. It was a miracle she'd graduated with decent grades.

One of the bedroom doors opened, and Arwel walked into the living room. "I was waiting for you. Arielle didn't let us touch the cake until you got here."

"There is cake?" Yamanu glanced around.

"It's in the fridge."

Ari smiled. "I sent my butler to get fresh coffee and hot water for tea. When he's back, we will have us some cake."

Mey shook her head. "I can't. I already overindulged today."

Ari patted her knee. "We can share a slice. I'm only going to have a couple of teaspoons."

Yamanu walked over to the fridge and pulled out three slices of cheesecake. "Oh, that's rich even for me."

As he took the plates to the dining table, the butler opened the door and rolled in a cart with the coffee and tea Ari had ordered.

"Come." Arielle pushed to her feet. "Let's taste that deliciousness."

Arwel and Yamanu both took a full slice of cheesecake, while Mey and Ari shared one.

"It's delicious," Mey said after the first spoonful. "But I shouldn't eat any more of it."

Regrettably, no one argued with her, so she had no excuse to take one more.

"I want you to stay here tonight," Arielle said. "I don't want you sleeping alone in an empty apartment."

Frankly, Mey was grateful for the invitation, and would have loved to accept, but it felt like too much of an imposition and she was still wearing the clothes from the shoot.

"Thank you, but I can't. I have an early shoot tomorrow, and I need to change into the outfit I'm supposed to wear for it."

For a moment, Arielle looked disappointed, but then she

smiled brightly. "Yamanu can go with you. He can sleep over and keep you safe."

Yamanu's eyes shot daggers at his charge. "I can't do that. I'm here to protect you, Arielle. But Mey is more than welcome to stay the night, and I'll escort her home early in the morning."

Ari tilted her head. "I see that you spilled the beans." She waved a hand. "Oh, well. No harm done." She smiled at Mey. "I can lend you one of my nightgowns, and Ovidu can launder your things, so you'll have fresh clothes for tomorrow morning."

She couldn't refuse. The thought of going home alone was too scary. "Thank you so much. I don't want to inconvenience you more than I have to. If you have a spare blanket, I can sleep on the couch."

Yamanu cleared his throat. "You are going to sleep in my bedroom, and I'll take the couch." When she opened her mouth to protest, he lifted his hand. "I'm the Guardian. It is my duty and privilege to guard you both, and the best way to do it is by watching the entry."

The entire floor was secure because no one could get up there without a key, so Yamanu was talking out of his ass. But if he wanted to be gallant, she wasn't going to be a bitch and refuse.

"Okay."

His chest deflated. "That was easy. I was expecting to have to arm wrestle you into the bedroom."

"Kinky," Arielle teased.

Yamanu shot some more daggers in her direction, and Mey felt her ears getting warm.

She didn't blush often, but the image that Yamanu's innocent comment had evoked had been very arousing.

Damn. She needed to get her libido under control. No sex for six weeks shouldn't be a big deal. She'd gone without for longer than that. But back then she hadn't been staring at temptation personified.

It was easy to abstain when there was nothing to entice her.

Arielle pushed away from the table. "Let me get the night-gown for you, so you can get out of those clothes and take a shower." She ducked into the suite's master bedroom.

"I can go snooping around your apartment," Arwel offered. "Check if anyone is lurking around. And I can also bring you a change of clothes, if you don't mind me going into your closet."

The thought of him going through her underwear drawer made her a little uncomfortable, but if that was the only prob-lem, she would have swallowed her pride. "Thank you for the offer, but I still didn't pick up shoes and other accessories to go with the outfit that I need to wear tomorrow. I have to do it myself."

"I have a better idea." Yamanu leaned and put his hand on Arwel's shoulder. "Do we have any spare bugs left over that you can leave in Mey's apartment? It would be interesting to see whether anyone tries to get in."

Arwel grinned. "I have plenty."

"Excellent." Yamanu turned to Mey. "Is it okay with you?"

"As long as you take them down before my roommates return, I'm all for it." She reached into her bag and pulled out her keys. "I will write you the code for the entry door and my phone number." She pulled out a pen and jotted down the numbers on one of the napkins. "If anyone asks, you are from the agency, and I sent you to pick up things for me."

30

YAMANU

*Y*amanu lay awake and stared at the ceiling. The couch was too short, so he propped his feet on the armrest. But that wasn't what was keeping him awake.

He could hear Mey tossing and turning in his bedroom, and he wondered whether she was awake and having trouble falling asleep.

He couldn't hear her heartbeat from behind the closed door or discern her breathing pattern, but he could sense her unrest.

Was it because of him?

Probably not. Mey had enough on her mind to keep her awake at night. Her sister had possibly gotten herself into some kind of trouble, working for some shady top secret organization that could be a government agency or not, and then she herself had someone follow her around.

One had probably nothing to do with the other, and the creep who'd followed her had likely been interested in her feminine assets and not intelligence secrets.

Which was worse.

If he caught the bastard, he was going to make a pancake

out of him. Arwel had planted a hidden security camera over her front door and another one in the living room. So, if anyone tried to get in, they would know. Tonight, though, Arwel hadn't spotted anyone watching her apartment building, and no one had tried to get in.

Tomorrow, Yamanu was going to get Uisdean and Ewan to guard Alena, while he went with Mey to her morning shoot. Kian would not be happy about it, but he could deal with him later.

He wasn't going to leave Mey exposed for even a moment.

The soft sound of her footsteps confirmed that she hadn't been sleeping, and a moment later the bedroom door opened.

"Are you awake?" she whispered.

"Yes. Do you need anything?"

She walked over to the couch and sat on the edge. "I can't sleep thinking about you on this couch. It must be torture. You are way too tall for it."

"I'm okay."

She reached for a strand of his hair and ran it through her fingers. "I wanted to do this from the first moment I saw you. Your hair is like silk."

He chuckled. "It's not much different from yours."

"Mine is not as soft." She leaned forward, letting her long hair brush against his bare chest. "Touch it."

Stifling a groan, he smoothed his hand over the crown of her head. "It's soft," he murmured.

"Come to the bedroom. We can share the bed. I don't mind."

Yeah, but he did.

When a fake cough sounded from Arwel's bedroom, Yamanu sighed. "We can't talk in here."

Mey lifted her eyes and glanced at the closed doors. "They can hear us?" she whispered.

"Yeah, the acoustics in this place suck." He threw the

comforter off. "We can sit on the balcony outside my bedroom. That's as private as it gets."

Mey's eyes were stuck on his bare chest and she didn't budge.

"I need to get up."

"Oh." She pushed up to her feet. "Sorry."

"Don't be. It's okay to look."

"Just not to touch, right?"

Damn. The girl was direct.

Arwel coughed again, and then Alena did the same.

Busybodies.

It was a shame Yamanu couldn't reprimand Annani's daughter, but Arwel was another story. Tomorrow, he was going to have a man-to-man talk with his buddy, and he wasn't sure words wouldn't be exchanged.

"Come on." He took her hand and led her back to the bedroom.

When he opened the slider to the balcony, cold air blew in and Mey shivered.

"Wait here. I'll get you a jacket." He ducked into the closet and grabbed the first one off the hanger.

"What about you?" she asked when he handed it to her. "Aren't you going to be cold?"

"I'll get a T-shirt." The cold didn't bother him, but Mey's eyes on his chest did.

They were way too covetous, and he couldn't give her what she wanted.

Except, the white T-shirt he'd pulled on wasn't enough to shield his body from her gaze, and the worst part was that he enjoyed it way too much.

It felt like a soft caress, and he hadn't felt a woman's touch in so long.

"It's nice out here," she said.

"Good view."

She looked straight at him. "I agree."

Yamanu swallowed. "It's because we are so high up." It was a lame answer, but he couldn't think of anything else to say.

Mey closed her eyes and breathed in. "You smell nice. What cologne are you wearing?"

"Tom Ford."

"Which one?" She opened her eyes.

"I don't remember. I have several of them."

"You have good taste. In clothes too. You're stylish without overdoing it."

"Thank you."

Fates, this was awkward.

Perhaps he could steer the conversation to a safer topic.

"Do you miss your parents?"

"I do. I go back home twice a year, and they come here quite frequently too. My Bubbe is not doing so great. Her knees are bad, and she refuses to have an operation." She smiled. "That's grandma in Yiddish."

"I know. Where does your grandma live?"

"In Brooklyn. With my grandpa. And my other grandparents live in Miami."

"It's nice to have a big family."

"Yeah, but ours isn't. My dad is an only child and my mother has just one sister. How about you? Are your grandparents still alive?"

The last thing Yamanu wanted to do was talk about his lineage, but the other option was to reach for Mey, put her on his lap, and kiss the living daylights out of her.

Except, that was the worst thing he could do. It would be the first step on the road leading to hell.

31

MEY

ay to go, Mey.

She had a hot guy out on a bedroom balcony, and they were talking about their grandparents.

"Only my grandmother on my mother's side is still alive," Yamanu said.

How was she going to get him from there to kissing?

He wasn't going to do it, that much was obvious. But should she?

Mey wasn't shy, but she wasn't used to taking the initiative either. Hell, she didn't want to.

With her height, people assumed that she was assertive, and they weren't necessarily wrong. She was, but not sexually.

Her first had been the typical alpha male, who had taken charge and led in the bedroom, and he'd gotten her spoiled. She wasn't willing to settle for anything less than that. Being the aggressor didn't suit her.

She could be the seductress, though. That was feminine.

The nightgown Arielle had given her was beautiful, all satin and lace in soft creamy colors, and she was naked under it because she'd given the butler her undergarments to launder.

As if guessing her intentions and trying to stave them off, Yamanu lifted a hand and rubbed it over his jaw, which she noticed he'd shaved before going to bed.

"Your friend, the one who checked about Jin for you, how good is he at what he does?"

"He and the people he works with are the best. Why?"

"I know some people too. I can ask them to give it a try. Maybe they'll be able to find something that your friend missed."

"That would be awesome. I doubt that they will find something that he didn't, but I wouldn't say no to another go at it. Right now, I have basically nothing to work with."

"I'll make some phone calls tomorrow."

"Thanks."

It was hopeless. If she didn't do something, they would keep the polite conversation going until Yamanu excused himself and went to bed.

To sleep.

Being alone with him in the middle of the night, with a bed just a few feet away, was an opportunity that would not present itself again.

What was the worst that could happen?

Yamanu saying no?

The rejection would hurt, but then guys faced that all the time and still kept pursuing women. Those who gave up were doomed to spending their lives alone, holed up in their rooms, playing video games and masturbating. She didn't want to become the female equivalent of that.

Winners took action and didn't back down from challenges.

Here goes nothing.

Mey put on a seductive smile, rose up as sexually as she could, and lowered herself onto Yamanu's thighs.

"I don't want to talk anymore." She wrapped her arms around his thick neck and looked into his pale blue eyes.

They were glowing, but that must be a trick of the light.

She touched a finger to his lips. "I've been staring at those lips of yours for hours now, and all I could think about was kissing them."

He was so tall that even though she was sitting on his lap their faces were at the same level. Leaning, she started closing the distance between their lips, very slowly, giving Yamanu every opportunity to back away.

Consent was important, and she wasn't going to force him into doing anything that he didn't want to do. She was only providing encouragement.

With a pained groan, he lifted his huge hand and closed it around the back of her neck, practically encircling it, and then he smashed his lips over hers.

Talk about taking the initiative.

She was at his mercy. If he decided to close those powerful fingers, he could crush her windpipe, but Mey felt no fear.

Even though he was kissing her like a man who'd gone without for decades, his hold on her was gentle, and as his tongue swiped inside her mouth, it was only after she'd parted her lips for him.

He wasn't taking anything she wasn't offering.

Perfection.

That's what Yamanu was.

With his other hand on her back, he pulled her closer to him and kept kissing her like a man possessed, swallowing her moans, nipping at her lips, rubbing his thumbs over the wildly racing pulse at the base of her neck.

It was raw hunger.

Except, his thin pajama pants couldn't hide the fact that he was only semi-erect under her.

It dawned on her then that he might have a medical problem. The thought that this gorgeous hunk of a man couldn't have an erection brought tears to her eyes. Not because she was disappointed, but because she hurt for him.

What had she done?

Poor guy. Now he would have to explain himself, and that would be devastating for someone as proud as Yamanu.

How was she going to fix it so he would have an honorable way out of the situation?

God, what a mess.

32

YAMANU

*I*f not for the potion Yamanu had drunk before going to sleep, he would have been inside Mey by now.

She was his kryptonite, his Achilles heel, his doom.

It had been nearly impossible not to act on the attraction when she'd been keeping her distance, but when she'd gotten tired of waiting for him to act and had made her move, he was a goner.

He could kiss her, though.

As long as he didn't get a release, there was no harm in it. Except for the torture of not taking it any further than that.

Mey was slim, but what little curves she had molded into his body as if she was made for him. And her lips, oh Fates, those lips. Was there anything sweeter than that in the universe?

He kept kissing her, dreading the moment the kiss would be over and she would expect him to do more. What was he going to tell her?

Mey pulled away first and touched a trembling finger to her lips. "I'm so sorry. I don't know what came over me. I guess it was all the stress of the past couple of weeks. Can you forgive me?"

He hadn't expected that.

An apology?

She tried to push away from him, but he held on to her. "Don't go. I want you here."

"No, you don't. You were only humoring me, and that was very sweet of you, but I shouldn't have attacked you like that."

Yamanu could smell real guilt coming off her, but he couldn't understand why. Was she embarrassed about taking the lead?

"It's okay, Mey. I enjoyed the attack. I find assertive ladies super sexy."

"But I'm not. I mean, I am, but not in this. It's not feminine."

"Says who?"

She waved a hand in a circle. "Everyone. Please let me get up, so I can go to the living room and pull the blanket over my head in shame."

Now, that wasn't true. He could smell guilt, but not shame. She was putting on an act.

"Why are you doing this?"

"I told you. I don't know what came over me. I'm usually not like that."

The best thing to do was to let her go and end the episode there. But he just couldn't let go. Not of her, not of this night, not of this situation.

He couldn't have sex with her, but he could have a connection. Hell, it was already there, and he wasn't willing to give it up.

Yamanu shook his head. "Who is being evasive now? Be straight with me, Mey. What's wrong? Does my breath stink? I promise that I won't be offended if it does."

Her eyes softened, and she cupped his cheek. "You are such an amazing man, Yamanu. I was the one in the wrong, and you're giving me a way out. But no, your breath doesn't stink. In fact, everything about you is perfect, except that you don't really want me."

So that was the problem.

She didn't feel what she'd expected to feel and thought that he wasn't attracted to her.

"It's not that I don't want you. I do with every fiber of my body and every thought in my head. But I can't."

She nodded. "I get it. I totally do. Can I go now?"

"No."

"Why?"

That was a good question. He'd just told her that he couldn't have her, so why was he not letting go of her?

Because he couldn't do that either. And he couldn't let her believe that it was in any way her fault.

"I want to explain."

"You don't have to." She pushed against his chest, but he wasn't having it.

"Yes, I do. I took a vow of celibacy. That's why I can't be with you the way you want me to."

"I understand." The pain in her voice cut him like a knife.

"The vow I took prevents me from getting a release, but I can give you one if you'll let me."

She shook her head. "I want you. I won't deny it, but that would be torture for you."

"Not being with you is torture as well. I'd rather take what I can than have nothing at all."

33

MEY

*W*as Yamanu telling her the truth?

Not likely.

But if he was too embarrassed to admit that he had a physical problem, the supposed vow he'd taken was a good way to explain it without losing face.

And that was what she'd wanted, right? For him not to feel bad about his inability to achieve erection.

Could she enjoy a one-sided experience, though?

But if that was all Yamanu could have, then she shouldn't deny him the little pleasure he could derive from sex.

Not everything was about the release.

In fact, Mey valued the intimacy and the buildup more than the act itself, and there had been plenty of times she hadn't climaxed during sex but had still had a good time.

She could easily picture herself in Yamanu's situation.

If she couldn't achieve release, she wouldn't abstain from sex because she still craved the intimacy. And if a partner rejected her because of her inability to climax, it would be just plain cruel and selfish of him.

She would appreciate a man who was willing to work with

her limitations.

"Okay," she whispered. "But only if you want to. I don't want you to do it out of pity, or because you don't want to hurt my feelings, or anything like that. I need to know that you derive some sort of pleasure from it, or I won't be able to enjoy myself."

He looked at her with appraising eyes, the eerie reflective glow dimming a bit as he lowered his dark lashes. "Same goes for you, Mey. Are you agreeing because you feel sorry for me?"

"Not at all. I value the intimacy more than I value orgasms. If I had to make a similar vow to yours, for whatever reason, I would choose to sacrifice my climaxes but, if possible, retain my right to intimacy. And if a man was willing to take what I could offer and be satisfied with that, I would appreciate it."

"For how long?"

"What do you mean?"

He shook his head. "Never mind. I shouldn't have asked that."

She understood what he'd been trying to say. Cupping his cheeks in both hands, she kissed him softly. "Forever if there was love."

"What if he couldn't give you children?"

She smiled. "Did you forget that I was adopted? There are so many children who need parents, and I feel like I owe it to the world to pay forward the kindness that was bestowed on me."

His palm cupped the back of her head. "You are a very special lady, one of a kind. Do you know that?"

She shrugged. "Not at all. A lot of women would have given you the same answer. You are incredible, Yamanu, and you are so worth it."

He tilted his head. "How do you know that? We've only just met, and we barely know each other."

She put her hand on his chest. "There is a big heart beating under this ribcage, and I don't mean its size. You are brave, dedicated, honorable, and an all-round mensch. The only thing that I thought was missing was you liking me back. But now that I know that you do, everything is perfect."

"In that case." He rose to his feet with her in his arms. "Let me show you how incredible I really am."

Laughing, Mey wrapped her arms around his neck. "Give a guy a compliment and he immediately thinks that he is Casanova."

"Oh, but I am. Only my goal is to please just one lady, not an entire city of them."

"How marvelous for me."

As he laid her on the bed, his eyes roamed over the contours of her body. "You are so beautiful."

He sounded sincere, but Mey was painfully aware of her hipbones sticking out like twin upside-down boomerangs through the soft satin of her borrowed nightgown. And her small breasts didn't begin to fill the lacy top, her erect nipples doing the heavy lifting.

That was the price she paid for her modeling career. Until she switched professions, the gaunt look had to stay.

But this was not the time to think about all the things she knew were less than perfect about her body.

Yamanu's eyes were in agreement with his words, telling her that she was beautiful, and tonight she was going to believe him.

He seemed lost, though, as if he didn't know what to do next.

How long had it been for him?

Should she take off the nightgown and show him what to do?

No, that would be a terrible mistake.

Even if he fumbled, she was going to try to make him feel like the manliest of men.

34

YAMANU

*G*orgeous.

Yamanu's eyes travelled the length of Mey's long body, taking in the slender ankles peeking from under the long nightgown, her elegant curves, her tightly budded dark nipples, clearly outlined by the cream-colored satin, and all the way up to her lush, parted lips that were letting out short, panting breaths.

Fates, he wanted her. All of her, and not just what he could give her now.

Fortunately, the potion was preventing him from doing what his willpower was too weak to resist.

Leaning over her, he kissed those parted lips, his tongue delving in and exploring while his palms smoothed over her silky shoulders, sliding down her arms the thin straps holding the nightgown up.

Even though he couldn't wait to see Mey without a stitch of clothing on, Yamanu went slow, relishing the reveal and prolonging her anticipation.

The scent of her arousal was so strong that he had no doubt

Arwel and Alena could scent it all the way from their rooms, but at this point he didn't care.

In fact, he cared about little else than the woman sprawled out on his bed.

Thank the merciful Fates for the potion keeping him from getting fully erect.

When the fabric caught on her nipples, he lifted the neckline and slid it under her breasts, sucking in a breath as she moaned and arched up in invitation.

He dove for one sweet berry, taking it between his lips and twirling his tongue around it. The groan that started deep in his throat sounded tortured and ravenous at the same time.

How long had it been since he'd touched a female intimately?

Centuries.

Guilt over his sins and duty to the clan had carried him through the long years, the potion and hours of meditation helping to keep his resolve. But all of that was coming to a screeching halt as he faced a life-altering crash between his past and his present, between duty and realization.

Hadn't he paid for his sins already?

Hadn't he earned the right to be selfish?

"Oh God, yes…" Mey murmured as he moved his mouth to the other sweet berry.

And when he thumbed the one that he'd been sucking on before, she uttered a throaty moan that caused his semi-erect member to twitch despite the potion that was supposed to keep it flaccid.

But there was no going back for him. Whatever happened, he was going to pleasure Mey until she climaxed like a firecracker, and if the potion failed him, so be it.

As his tongue swirled around one nipple, his fingers pinched and tweaked the other, eliciting moans and whimpers from Mey's lips and wild gyrating from her hips.

Sliding the gown down her ribcage, he kissed the undersides of her small breasts, kept kissing down her concave belly, and then when he reached her hips, she lifted up for him to take the gown all the way down.

The sight of her smooth and hairless feminine center made his mouth salivate. He'd heard that human females were lasering unwanted hair these days, but he hadn't expected how arousing he would find it.

As he slipped his palms under her small bottom, Mey moaned and parted her thighs for him, and the aroma of her arousal hit him so hard he got momentarily dizzy.

"Intoxicating," he murmured before kissing the very top of her puffy lips.

She jerked up, her hands fisting the sheet under her as she struggled for control.

"It's okay, my beauty. Let go."

He tilted her hips further up and licked around her opening, marveling at the satiny feel of her skin and the softness of her engorged petals.

Fates, it had been so long.

As Mey's bottom twitched in his palms, he squeezed it and speared his tongue into her core, keeping her in place for his ministrations.

"Yamanu," she breathed. "Don't stop."

He had no intention of stopping before he brought her so many orgasms that she passed out from the pleasure.

Alternating between penetrating her and flicking his tongue over her most sensitive feminine spot, he moved one hand to cup both buttocks and freed the other one.

He couldn't penetrate her with his shaft, but he was blessed with a long tongue and even longer fingers. Putting two in his mouth, he slicked them before pushing them inside her.

"Oh, oh, yes…" Mey's sheath convulsed around his penetrating fingers, and as he took her clit between his lips, it closed around them tightly.

As Mey's orgasm erupted, she uttered the most unusual sound, coating his fingers with copious nectar. It was a cross between a whistle and a groan, and it was the sexiest thing he'd ever heard.

He kept licking, not letting any of that delicious elixir go to waste.

The satisfaction he felt was almost as good as if he had climaxed with her, but the potion worked, keeping him subdued enough to prevent his balls from pumping semen into his shaft and his glands from producing venom.

Yamanu didn't know whether he should feel happy or devastatingly sad about that. On the one hand, he hadn't broken his vow, so that was good, but on the other hand, he was reminded of what he was missing.

That feeling of power, of dominance, of conquering this amazing female and making her his, that was absent. He couldn't help imagining what it would have felt like to sink his hard shaft into her welcoming core and his fangs into her long neck as she offered him her submission.

MEY

ey sighed and curled against Yamanu's big body, her head resting on his magnificent chest and her arm draped over his tight abdomen.

She was boneless, exhausted in the most wonderful way, and thoroughly satisfied.

After the series of explosive orgasms Yamanu had pleasured her into, the only way he'd allowed her to repay him was with kisses, only on his face, and caresses only above the waistline.

He hadn't even allowed her to kiss his flat nipples or nip at his neck.

The message was clear. He was open to intimacy, and he was fine with pleasuring her, but he refused reciprocation.

Which was a damn shame.

Even though he couldn't get fully erect, he could probably feel pleasure if he let her lick and suck on his shaft.

But it was likely a matter of pride for him.

He had to maintain the illusion that it was his choice to abstain from sex and not a disability.

Perhaps in time, when he felt more comfortable with her,

he would confess the truth and allow her to pleasure him back. It might not bring him to a climax, but it would be pleasurable.

In either case, his problem was definitely not a deal-breaker for her. She could spend her life with this man regardless of his erectile dysfunction. He had so much to offer that his inability to penetrate and impregnate her was insignificant in comparison.

Well, not insignificant, that wasn't true, but it wasn't of utmost importance either.

She would have loved to have kids of her own one day, but this relationship would probably not last until she was ready to have them anyway. Something would come up that would either end it or it would fizzle and die on its own.

For some reason, men hadn't stuck with her. Was it because she was too independent?

Nah, that wasn't it, and she knew it. The real reason was that she hadn't really loved any of her other boyfriends. She liked them, enjoyed their company, but her feelings had never run deep. Not even with Shimon, who she'd thought she'd been in love with. If she had really loved him, she would have been heartbroken over the death of their relationship. Instead, she had been a little sad for about a week.

"You should get some sleep," he murmured. "It's after two in the morning."

"I don't feel sleepy. I need to use the bathroom, but I'm too boneless to move."

He chuckled, sounding very satisfied with himself. "I can carry you."

"I think you've worked hard enough for one night." She sat up in bed and glanced at the mess they'd made.

The sheet was rumpled, leaving part of the mattress exposed, and the blanket was on the floor.

Yamanu's eyes trained on her breasts and he licked his lips.

"I would love another taste, but I think you've had enough of my attentions."

Her nipples were a little sore from all the pinching and nipping, but in a good way.

She leaned and kissed his lips. "I loved every moment, but I really need to use the bathroom."

As she slipped off the bed and turned toward the door, he slapped her bottom playfully. "You have a great ass."

She cast him a smile over her shoulder. Her butt was the only place on her body that had a little padding. No wonder he found it appealing.

"I'll be right back."

In the bathroom, she used the commode and then got into the shower for a quick wash. Wrapped in a thick towel, she stood in front of the vanity mirror and wiped the condensation with her hand. Her hair was all tangled and messy, her cheeks were rosy, and her eyes sparkled despite the lack of sleep.

This had been by far the best sexual experience of her life, and not because her other lovers had been subpar.

It had been different with Yamanu, and not only on the physical level. She felt a connection with him like she hadn't felt with men she'd dated for months. Not with Shimon who she'd believed she'd been in love with, and not with Oliver with whom she'd lived for over a year.

Was it because Yamanu was so unique? Or was it because she was at a vulnerable stage in her life and needed a protector?

Probably both.

In either case, she wasn't going to analyze it to death. The bottom line was that she wanted a relationship with Yamanu, and she was going to do her best to make it work.

After brushing her teeth and her hair, Mey opened the bathroom door, half expecting Yamanu to be asleep. Instead, she found him standing next to the dresser with a small brown vial tilted over his mouth.

It was smaller than a shot glass, so it wasn't alcohol, and liquid medications usually came in larger containers as well.

Emptying the contents down his throat, he grimaced and threw the bottle into the trashcan.

"What was it?" she asked. "Vitamins?"

He shook his head. "I need this to control my sex drive." He smiled sadly. "Without that, it would have been impossible for me to keep my vow. In fact, since I met you, I've had to double the daily dose. I tripled it today."

He'd been telling her the truth?

Stunned, Mey sat on the bed. "What made you make such an extreme vow?"

Sitting on the bed beside her, he wrapped his arm around her shoulders. "That's one of the things I cannot tell you, but I can give you a hint. If you knew that your sister was in mortal danger, and that the only way to save her and keep her safe required you to make a great sacrifice, what would you be willing to give up?"

"Anything."

"Same here."

36

YAMANU

"Can I make you coffee?" Mey asked as they entered her apartment. "It will take me about half an hour to get ready."

Yamanu glanced at the kitchen through the open door. "I'll make the coffee. Is there a particular way you like it?"

"A little bit of cream and no sugar, thanks." She cast him an apologetic smile. "I'll be as quick as I can."

Once he was done loading the coffeemaker, Yamanu decided to sweep the apartment for bugs. Arwel had planted two, one over the front door and the other one on top of the bookcase, but he hadn't thought to check if there were other bugs in there already.

If the government was involved, he was not likely to find anything without the proper equipment. Those with access to unlimited resources and the newest technology could plant bugs the size of a fly or even smaller.

On top of that, the place was a bug heaven.

Dozens of framed photographs were hanging on the walls, and each frame could hide a tiny bug. Other than that, there were plants and figurines and books and DVDs, not to mention the assortment of throw pillows. Each item could be hiding a miniscule camera, and that was in the living room alone.

It would take hours to perform a thorough sweep. The smart thing would be to come back with the proper equipment that would pick up the signal. William could probably order one for him online and have it delivered to the hotel.

In the meantime, Yamanu could do it the old-fashioned way, patting items one by one.

By the time Mey emerged from the bedroom, he was partially done with the bookcase.

He put his hand over his heart and whistled. "Stunning, my lady Mey. Absolutely stunning."

And he wasn't saying it to make her feel good. Wearing spiky black heels and a red wrap dress that flared from her hips and reached just below her knees, Mey looked like the cover model she was. Elegant, sophisticated, confident.

"Thank you." She put her large bag down and twirled around. "I like this dress, and I get to keep it, which is a nice bonus."

He rubbed his hand over his jaw. "The coffee is ready."

"Thanks. I'll grab a paper cup. Derek is going to pick us up in five minutes."

"What did you tell him about me?" He followed her into the kitchen.

"That you are Arielle's business manager and that you want to check out a live shoot." She poured the coffee into a paper cup and closed it with a lid. "Do you want coffee to go as well?"

"No, thanks. I already drank mine. Did he buy it?"

Mey shrugged. "It doesn't matter if he did or not. He and Julie are going to guess that we hooked up. But there is no reason for me to spell it out for them."

He didn't like her thinking of them in terms of hookups. This was much more than that. Then again, she might have been hesitant to use the term boyfriend. It wasn't as if they'd made any long-term promises to each other.

Should he tell her that he wanted more than that?

Right, like that was a good idea. Mey was incredible, and forgetting her would be impossible, but she was a human and he couldn't keep her. Once this assignment was over, and he went back home, it would be the end of it.

His heart squeezed hard at the prospect of losing her, but his mind slapped the silly organ into compliance.

He would have to double his meditation time to get over her.

Mey took the cup and walked back into the living room. When she bent to lift the bag, he reached for the strap.

"Let me." He took it from her.

"Are you sure? It's not unisex."

The thing had hearts and the word love printed all over it.

"You don't say." He slung it over his shoulder. "What do you have in there?"

"A pair of flip-flops, yoga pants, a T-shirt, and a change of underwear. I'm probably going to sleep over at your place again." She looked at him, the high heels making her so tall they were almost at eye level. "If you don't mind, that is."

"I wouldn't have it any other way."

Her shoulders relaxed. "Thanks. I'm scared of sleeping alone in here. During the day it's okay. I'll go back tomorrow morning." Then her lips lifted in a mischievous smile. "Besides, I'm looking forward to a repeat performance. I need to make sure that it was as good as I remember it." She winked.

Laughing, he wrapped his arm around her shoulders. "It would be my pleasure to prove that to you, my lady Mey."

As they entered the elevator, she leaned against him and whispered in his ear, "Had you been checking the bookcase for bugs?"

"That's very perceptive of you," he whispered back. "And

yes, I was. Thank you for not saying anything out loud in there."

She smirked. "The moment I saw what you were doing, I figured that I shouldn't mention anything about you suspecting bugs in the place." She frowned. "But if they are monitoring my phone conversations, they know about you."

She was right, and he should have thought about that. His phone was safe, but hers wasn't, and he couldn't suggest her switching to a burner phone because her sister might call or text her. Still, it was a good idea to stash the thing inside the safe once they were back in the hotel. It was possible to use the device to listen in on people even when it was off. Which meant that they should watch what they were saying while it was in her purse.

He leaned to whisper in her ear again. "We shouldn't talk freely while your phone is near."

Her eyes widened. "Oh, crap."

He put a finger on her lips. "All they know is that you called a guy when you were scared that some creep was following you and that you slept over at my place. Nothing unusual about it. But just to be safe, call one of your girlfriends and tell her about how you were scared for no good reason and called your new boyfriend for help."

She smiled. "Are you my boyfriend, Yamanu?"

The elevator reached the lobby level and he took her elbow as they stepped out. "I'm an old-fashioned kind of guy. In my book, what we did last night makes us a couple." He stopped in front of the lobby's door. "If that's okay with you."

Mey turned to him and wrapped her arms around his neck. "It's more than okay." She kissed his lips. "It's what I want."

"Good." He pushed the door open. "Because I want that too."

37

MEY

"So, you are the famous Yamanu," Derek said as they entered the van.

To make room, Julie moved to the third seat while mouthing "hot" and fanning herself. As if Yamanu couldn't see what she was doing.

When Mey rolled her eyes at her, Julie fanned herself some more, and then she added a few more mouthed words that Mey couldn't decipher.

Was the last one stud muffin?

Who used that anymore?

Stifling a laugh, Mey mouthed, "Stop it."

"Depends on what you've heard," Yamanu said. "If it's bad, then I'm not that guy."

"It's all good. Mey said that you are managing the new girl's career. Arielle, right? She is going to do that Korean beauty line."

"That's the one. Are you going to be the photographer?"

Derek looked at Yamanu in the rearview mirror. "I'm not a studio photographer, and makeup is always done in a studio."

"Not in Europe." Mey rushed to save the situation. "They do outdoor shoots for everything."

Yamanu nodded, but smartly didn't say anything. Oftentimes keeping quiet was the best strategy. Especially when not knowing much about the subject.

"We are going back to Central Park today," Derek said.

"Why? The client didn't like what we shot there. That's why we are redoing everything."

"He changed his mind. His only instructions were to find a less shitty corner where everything was green and not wilting. His problem was that the background wasn't manicured."

"You could've Photoshopped it."

"Dalia tried that angle. It was a no go." Derek shrugged. "He is the client, and he gets what he pays for."

Mey crossed her arms over her chest. "I hope he pays a bundle."

"What do you care?" Julie asked. "We get paid by the day."

"Yeah, but I don't want some prima donna client screwing Dalia over."

"Don't worry about the dragon lady." Derek glanced at her through the rearview mirror. "Dalia can take care of herself."

Mey wasn't so sure. "You know her motto. The client is always right. She will take a loss on a project rather than have the agency's reputation suffer. The schmuck might be taking advantage of that."

"Not our problem," Derek said as he turned into the paid parking lot.

As they unloaded the equipment, Yamanu took Julie's chair and makeup case, and he also insisted on carrying Mey's bag.

"He is a keeper," Julie whispered.

"I know."

The question was for how long. Mey was still giddy over him declaring them a couple, but it was too early to celebrate.

Besides, things always seemed perfect in the courtship stage, with the nasty little things hiding until much later.

One thing she could be sure of, though. He wasn't going to cheat on her while she was away on a shoot.

Except, if a vow of fidelity could be broken, so could a vow of celibacy. Yamanu didn't strike her as the type, but she didn't know him well enough to be sure.

At the park, Derek led them to the spot he'd scouted yesterday afternoon.

It was early morning, so the only passersby were joggers, and they tended to mind their own business. They had jobs they needed to get to, and they didn't have time to stop and gawk.

"Over here is good?" Yamanu unfolded Julie's chair.

"Perfect. Thank you."

He put her makeup case down by the chair. "How long will the makeup part take?"

She waved a dismissive hand. "Ten minutes tops. Mey has beautiful skin. I can go light."

"I think I'll take a walk. Is that okay?" He looked at Mey.

He probably wanted to scope the area.

"Sure. Take your time. Derek is going to spend the first half hour testing."

He saluted her with two fingers and walked away.

"Girl, you are so lucky," Julie said as Mey sat in the chair. "I've never seen a man as gorgeous as that. He should be a model."

"Hey, what about me?" Derek asked. "I'm gorgeous too." He flicked imaginary hair back.

"Yes, you are, just in a different way." Julie winked. "For a teddy bear," she whispered as she applied primer to Mey's face.

"How come this Arielle didn't grab him?"

"She has a boyfriend, and he's also very handsome."

"Oh, yeah? I'm sure he is not of Yamanu's caliber. No one is. Where do they make guys like him?"

"Nowhere." Mey chuckled. "Yamanu is one of a kind. Arwel's charm is different. He rocks that tortured soul look. I bet women fall for that left and right. It's the motherly instinct to fix whatever is wrong and provide comfort."

"I don't have it," Julie said. "I cured myself of it. God knows that I've dated enough broken ones. This time I want a guy who doesn't need any fixing. Like that hunk of yours."

If Julie had only known.

Not that Yamanu needed fixing, but perhaps he needed a change in perspective. He'd taken that vow years ago, and whatever situation had prompted it was probably long over.

Besides, it was nothing more than wishful thinking. God, or whatever power that Yamanu believed in, didn't listen to vows and fulfill the wishes of those who made them.

Yamanu was denying himself for no good reason. But it was too early in their relationship for her to suggest that it was time for him to move on.

Hell, she'd been willing to accept him the way he was when she'd thought he had a medical disability. Except, now that she knew that the possibility existed, she was less willing to settle for what he was willing to give her.

Was she a bad person for thinking like that?

Yamanu was entitled to his beliefs, and it wasn't her place to question them. If he insisted that she forget about kosher rules, she would be upset that he demanded it of her.

Then again, she might be willing to do that if it meant being a couple in every sense of the word. Every gain required a sacrifice—it was a universal law.

Keeping kosher wasn't the same as a celibacy vow, though. Besides, she had a feeling that Yamanu would never ask her to give that up or anything else that was important to her.

YAMANU

*W*ith his distinctive appearance, Yamanu wasn't the best man for a recon job, but then he had tricks up his sleeve that humans could only dream about.

Not the good kind of dreams, though. Nightmares about the invisible boogeyman were more likely.

The thing was, he couldn't vanish from sight while someone was watching him, and everyone in his vicinity was doing that.

It took him a while to find an isolated spot with no joggers in sight, and the moment he did, Yamanu cloaked himself in a shroud, sound and smell included.

As far as humans were concerned, it was as if he entered a bubble of nothingness. The only exception to that was if someone bumped into him. But that wasn't a problem either. First of all because he was careful to skirt any passersby, and second because he could thrall the bumper to forget that he or she had hit an invisible man.

Shrouded, he went back to where Mey was getting ready for her shoot and sat on a bench across from the spot.

It was fun watching her unawares.

She was a little tense, probably because of the possibility of someone following her, but other than that she was friendly and easygoing with her crew of two, and they seemed fond of her.

Not that it was a big surprise.

Mey was awesome. She didn't have an ounce of prima donna in her, which for a beautiful woman like her was uncommon. Especially one who was a bona fide beauty queen and worked as a model. Not only that, Mey was the most understanding and accepting person he'd met.

Most women would have been weirded out by his celibacy vow, or would have asked a ton of questions, but she'd asked only one, accepted his answer at face value, and hadn't walked away.

As the sense of someone focusing on Mey filtered through Yamanu's awareness, he had to stop his pleasant musings and concentrate on the job he'd come to do.

There was no malicious intent in that focus, so it could have been just someone stopping to look at a beautiful woman getting her pictures taken, but just in case that was about to change, Yamanu went on high alert.

Scanning the area, he couldn't see the watcher and wondered whether the guy was using a scope. It was a man, that much was obvious, and his focus on Mey was tinged with a dose of attraction, but it was mild and not something to cause Yamanu's hackles to rise.

Still, when several moments passed and that focus hadn't wavered, Yamanu pushed to his feet and went to investigate.

Circling the shoot area, he checked the bushes and trees, but there was no one hiding nearby. Walking in ever increasing circles, Yamanu added his nose to the search, but there were so many different smells around that it proved to be of little use.

Regrettably, the sense of someone watching Mey wasn't the

kind that increased with proximity, so the only way to catch the watcher was to spot him.

Yamanu got lucky when the cloud cover cleared, letting the sun through. For a moment, the angle was just right to bounce off a lens someone was using about five hundred feet away.

Breaking into a jog, Yamanu closed the distance in two minutes. The guy was sitting up in a tree and watching Mey through a scope that had a mic attached to it.

What he hoped to hear through that was questionable. Yamanu's super hearing could pick up some of the conversation, but other noises interrupted.

Perhaps the guy wasn't trailing Mey but was there for another reason, and he just happened to spot her and couldn't take his eyes away?

Easy to find out.

Yamanu didn't even have to climb the tree and touch the guy to do that. He could reach into his mind from where he stood. Which was good because he wasn't sure the branch the dude was sitting on was strong enough to hold both of them.

Besides, if the guy was there to do some bird watching and had stumbled upon Mey by chance, there was no reason to wrestle him down and scare the shit out of him.

It was a free country and watching a woman in a park wasn't a criminal offense.

Except, when he reached into the guy's mind and tuned into his thought stream, it quickly became obvious that he was there specifically to watch Mey.

He was enjoying the view, but he was sure that he was wasting his time because he thought that there was nothing special about the model except for her killer legs. She hadn't done anything weird or unusual yet, and he didn't expect her to. But he was getting paid to watch a hot woman, so what did he care.

Yamanu frowned. What exactly was the guy hoping to see Mey do?

And who'd sent him?

Those were questions Yamanu couldn't get answers for without getting closer. The guy was a hardheaded fellow, and he was resistant to thralling, but he wasn't immune. A closer, more intense thrall might unlock the hidden memories that would give Yamanu some answers.

Or he could just beat them out of the dude.

Sometimes the more mundane methods of interrogation worked better for loosening tongues.

Instead of climbing the tree and jumping down with the guy, Yamanu sent a suggestion into his mind—an urgent need to take a piss.

"Damn it," the guy grumbled. "I just went." He used the strap attached to the scope to hang it on a branch and then climbed down.

Yamanu was waiting for him at the foot of the tree, and the moment the guy was within reach, he wrapped his arm around his middle and dragged him down to the ground.

The dude struggled without making a sound, which marked him as a pro, but he was no match for Yamanu's superior strength.

In seconds, Yamanu had him face down on the ground, arms pinned behind his back and legs pinned under Yamanu's knees.

When it became obvious to the watcher that he wasn't getting out from Yamanu's grip, he stopped struggling. "You can take the money. My wallet is in my back pocket. Take it and leave the wallet. I need my driver's license."

The guy was scared, but he wasn't terrified.

That was going to change soon.

"I don't want your money. I want to know why you were watching the model."

"She is hot."

"You were waiting for her to do something weird. In what way? And don't lie to me because I'll know, the same way I knew what you were thinking."

The guy resumed his struggles.

"It's not going to work, buddy. The only way you are getting away is if you talk. So, I'll ask again. Weird in what way?"

"I don't know. I was told to watch for anything unusual, but they didn't tell me what exactly to look for."

"Who are they?"

"I don't know. The assignment was emailed to me and money was deposited into my account. I don't ask questions. That's why I get the jobs."

He was telling the truth.

Damn.

"Were you following her?"

"On and off. All I need is to catch her doing something unusual. I don't need to watch her all the time."

That was only partially true.

"Did you plant surveillance cameras in her apartment? And don't you dare lie to me or I'm going to pull this arm out of its socket and it's going to hurt like hell." Yamanu demonstrated with a yank but let go before the joint did.

The guy hissed in pain. "Yes."

"Where. Tell me the exact locations of each one."

"There is one in the living room attached to the curtain rod and one in her bedroom."

Pervert.

Yamanu gave another yank.

"I swear it wasn't because I was going peeping Tom on her. But if she were to do something weird, like chant curses and stab voodoo dolls, I figured she would do it in private."

He was telling the truth.

"How about her phone?"

"It's tapped, but not by me. I was told to leave it alone because they got it."

Again, he was telling the truth.

Holding the guy down with one arm, Yamanu reached into his pocket and pulled out the wallet. Going through the slots, he found a business card and pulled it out. Placing it and the driver's license on the guy's back, Yamanu got his phone out and snapped a picture of both.

When he was done, he returned the things to the wallet, the wallet into the guy's pocket, and then flipped the dude around.

Reaching into his mind, he erased the memory of what had just happened. "You needed to take a piss and you slipped and fell down. You are going to wake up in two minutes and feel sore all over because of the bad fall."

With the suggestion planted in the watcher's mind, Yamanu let go of him and resumed his shroud.

He was definitely missing an important part of the puzzle. Whatever Mey and her sister were into had courted the interest of the government or some other powerful organization with lots of money.

The question was what?

The other question was whether Mey was going to tell him, and if not, did he have justification enough to reach into her mind and get it that way?

And the third question was what was he going to tell her about the watcher?

He needed to warn her because the guy would keep reporting to whoever had hired him, and she needed to be aware of that. Getting rid of the guy was not an option either. Whoever had hired him would just send someone else.

At least with this one, he had a name and a driver's license. Perhaps William could hack into the detective's email and try to trace it to the client.

39

MEY

"Can we take a break?" Mey asked.

Yamanu had been gone for a long time, and when he returned his expression was troubled. Had he found the guy following her?

Derek sighed. "Fine. But no more than five minutes. The sun is out, and I want to take advantage of it for a few more bright shots."

"Maybe ten? I want to take a short walk." Hopefully that would do.

He shook his head. "You know that I can't say no to you." He waved her away. "Go. I know you want to hang out with your guy."

"Thanks. You're awesome." She kissed his cheek and hurried to her satchel to pull out her flip-flops.

After more than an hour in the high heels, her feet were killing her.

"Let's go." She threaded her arm through Yamanu's and waited until they were about ten steps away before asking, "Did you find him?"

He leaned to whisper in her ear. "Wait. I want some background noise."

When they reached one of the fountains, Yamanu sat on the lip and pulled her down beside him. "Now we can talk."

"Who was he? Was he just a creep? I hope you didn't beat him up too badly."

Yamanu laughed. "I didn't beat him up. And whether he's a creep or not depends on your definition of one. He is a private investigator hired to spy on you. He's watching you through a scope with a mic attached to it. That's why I wanted us to talk here. The fountain's noise will cover our voices."

"Why is he watching me?"

Yamanu shrugged. "I hoped you could tell me. Once I figured out that he is a private investigator, I didn't want to alert him to the fact that we are onto him, so I couldn't ask him."

"Then how do you know he is a private investigator? A creep can have a scope too."

"I overheard him talking on the phone, but what he said didn't make any sense. He told whoever was on the other line that you didn't do anything unusual so far. He said that if you weren't such a looker, it would have been a total waste of his time. Do you have any idea what he was talking about?"

As Yamanu's eyes bored into hers, reaching down into her soul, Mey cringed. Should she tell him about her and Jin's special abilities?

But what if the comment the detective had made wasn't about that?

Suddenly, it occurred to her that Yamanu had showed up in her life shortly after Jin had left. What if there was a connection?

What if he'd been sent to befriend Mey and get her to talk about her ability?

If Jin had been recruited because of her supernatural spying talent, whoever hired her would logically assume that her sister had some talent too. But if Jin kept it a secret and claimed that Mey was just an ordinary person, they might not have believed her and sent people to investigate.

This whole setup might have been a trick to get her to talk to Yamanu. Maybe the other guy had been sent to scare her, and then Yamanu, the knight in shining armor, had come to her rescue, seduced her, and made her trust him.

Except, he hadn't seduced her and had resisted her flirting attempts pretty damn hard. If that had been all an act, then Yamanu was wasting his time working for the government. He could be an Oscar-winning actor.

"Well?" Yamanu prompted. "Anything come to mind?"

"I'm still thinking."

He might not have intended to seduce her, only to befriend her. And the reason that he'd made up the story about the vow was because he wasn't rotten to the core and had thought that it was the decent thing to do.

Except, that made her feel even worse. Not only would it mean that her perfect guy was a potential spy, but also that he didn't find her desirable. Because if the vow of celibacy and the arousal suppressing medication had been a charade, then she'd failed to stir his desire.

The thing was, she could find that out quite easily by listening to the walls in Arielle's hotel suite. She could say that she needed to meditate in the living room because the bedroom was too cramped for that. She would also have to ask them to leave for a short while because she needed to concentrate.

They would think her an ungrateful prima donna, but that was a small price to pay for knowledge. In the meantime, she needed to stall.

"Perhaps he is working for the government. They might

think that I know something because I served in Israeli intelligence."

That wasn't a total lie. Mossad was a separate entity and worked on different things than regular army intelligence, but it was close enough without spilling secrets she wasn't supposed to.

He shook his head. "The guy was a hired private investigator. He wasn't CIA."

"How do you know?"

"Because he talked about the money deposited into his account for the job of following you around."

"The government might have hired him. They could be outsourcing."

"That's possible. But then what could they learn by having him observe you? I understand tapping your phone and putting surveillance cameras in your home. That way they can listen to your phone conversations and catch you talking about secrets from your time in the intelligence services. But something weird or unusual doesn't sound like military secrets."

Mey shrugged. "He might have meant suspicious." Then the rest of what Yamanu had said registered. "Wait, so they have my phone tapped and cameras in my apartment? Did you hear him say that?"

Yamanu nodded.

"Crap. I talked with my friend Shimon and asked him to help me find where Jin was. He's from my intelligence days, and he's still on active duty. Maybe that triggered the tail?" She stopped and calculated the timeline. "I called him on Tuesday, and then we talked again on Thursday. That was when I felt someone following me." She looked into Yamanu's eyes. "I think that the first call triggered it. My phone was already tapped, and when I started investigating where Jin was, they sent someone after me."

Yamanu shook his head. "Did Jin serve in the intelligence service as well?"

"No."

"So, she is not connected to this and your call shouldn't have triggered anything."

"But I called an active duty intelligence officer and asked for his help. They might think I'm some big shot with important connections."

His brows drew together. "Are you?"

Mey chuckled. "Shimon was my boyfriend, and we parted as friends. That's why I could call him, not because I have such great connections."

Yamanu lifted a finger. "Aha! It could be the ex-boyfriend connection. Maybe they want you to make him tell you his secrets."

"Right. He didn't tell me anything when we were together. He isn't going to tell me anything now."

"But they don't know that."

"Yeah, maybe you are right."

40

YAMANU

*M*ey was hiding something.

Yamanu was sure of that now more than ever. It was possible that she'd been involved in something big during her time in the military, and the part she'd played wasn't as insignificant as she was trying to make it sound.

No wonder she wasn't admitting it. She probably couldn't.

The problem was that without knowing what those people were after, he couldn't help her. All he could do was try to protect her, but once Alena started shooting, he wouldn't have time to follow Mey wherever she went. And then he would go back home, and she would be left without a protector.

That bugged the hell out of him.

Perhaps she would be safer back in Israel where she had people who could provide her with protection.

"Is there any way you can take a vacation and go back home?"

She lifted a pair of questioning eyes at him. "Are you trying to get rid of me?"

He enveloped her in his arms and set her in his lap. "If it were up to me, I would never let you go. But I can't be with you every moment of the day to protect you. Not once Arielle starts working on Monday. I have to be with her. I was thinking that you'd be safer in Israel where you can get protection from your old buddies in the military."

"You'd be willing to give me up so easily?"

"Not easily. But your safety comes before my wishes. Obviously, you can't tell me what you've been involved in, so I don't know how serious this is and what kind of danger you are in. I'm trying to find a solution without knowing what the problem is."

She rested her forehead against his, sighed, and then pushed back to look at him. "I asked Dalia for time off because I want to go looking for Jin. The problem is that I don't know where to start. Besides, I need to finish this job for this very picky client before I can take time off, and then I can't go anywhere until I know what's going on with my sister."

And that was another thing. How did Jin fit into the theory he'd come up with?

On the face of things, she didn't.

Perhaps Mey wasn't telling him the whole story about her sister either?

What if Jin had been taken to put pressure on Mey?

Nah, that wasn't it either. When he'd asked her what she was willing to sacrifice to save her sister, Mey had said anything and had meant it.

The question was whether she was willing to betray her adopted country as well. That wasn't a personal sacrifice. She could be potentially putting a lot of people in danger by revealing military secrets.

It seemed that to help Mey, he would have to find Jin. Perhaps William and Roni could do more than her old boyfriend could. After all, Roni still had a backdoor to government data, and the facial recognition software William had improved on was the best in the world.

Or so he claimed.

"Do you have a picture of Jin on your phone?"

"Yes. I have many."

"Great. Could you share some of them with me? I know a guy who can hack into anywhere. He might be able to find out where she went by hacking into airport security surveillance footage."

Mey's eyes widened. "That would be awesome." She pushed up to her feet. "But in my rush to hear what you have found out, I stupidly left my phone in my purse." She started walking briskly, her flip-flops flapping noisily against her soles. "What if Jin tried to call? Or sent me a message? How could I have just left it there?"

He shook his head. Whatever Mey had done during her service, she hadn't been a spy.

"Did you forget what I told you about your phone? The conversation we had shouldn't have been made anywhere near it. I thought that you left it behind on purpose."

She slapped her forehead. "Talk about being stupid. I totally forgot about that. The thing is, I'm glued to that phone because I'm waiting for Jin to contact me. I should have cut this short."

"Relax. She told you that she would try to make contact once a week. It hasn't been that long since her last text."

"I know. But I can't help thinking what if?" She cast him an apologetic glance. "It's not logical. But I have to check."

"Of course."

Mey practically ran the rest of the way and snatched her purse off the ground as soon as they got there.

"Oh, thank God." She put a hand over her chest. "There have been no calls."

"Are you ready to get back to work?" Derek glared at her. "That was much longer than ten minutes and the clouds are back."

"I'm sorry. Just give me one more moment." She brought up

her photo application and started scrolling quickly. "I think that should do it. I'm texting them to you. I have more if your friend isn't happy with these. Jin really has the perfect look for what he has in mind."

That was no doubt for the benefit of whoever might have been listening in.

Yamanu looked at the images she sent. "Looks good. I'm going to call him while you finish the shoot." He turned to Derek. "How much longer is it going to take?"

Derek lifted his eyes to the sky. "I need to fiddle with the lighting now, so it will take longer than it should've. Maybe an hour." He looked at his watch. "No longer than that because I'm getting hungry. It's time for lunch."

"I'm going to walk around a little more." Yamanu winked at Mey.

He wanted to check on the guy in the tree and whether he was still there, and then he was going to text William and ask the dude for a favor.

After that, he was going to take Mey out to lunch.

The good thing about starting a workday early in the morning was finishing it early in the day, and he was looking forward to spending it with Mey.

When he found a secluded spot, Yamanu shrouded himself and headed back to the tree.

While talking with Mey, he hadn't been paying attention to people's intents, but now that he was alone and let his senses flare, he no longer felt the guy's intense focus on her.

Just in case, he checked the tree as well as a wide area around it. The guy wasn't there, and Yamanu wondered if the watcher had left because of the roughing up he'd given him.

He hadn't used much force, but it had been enough to cause the human some nasty aches and pains for at least several hours.

MEY

"It's nice having a big strong guy like you around," Julie said as Yamanu once more collected her things. "I feel like I'm on a mini vacation."

Mey cast her a glare.

Flirting with Yamanu was not allowed. He belonged to her.

"Do you have plans for the weekend?" Yamanu asked, probably just to be polite, but Julie smiled from ear to ear as if he was asking her out.

"I was planning on relaxing at home, but I'm open to suggestions."

Yamanu glanced at Mey over Julie's head. "Mey and I are going to spend the weekend with Arielle and Arwel. How about you?" He turned to Derek before Julie had a chance to respond and invite herself over. "Any exciting plans?"

"I'm driving down to my parents' house. My brother and his brood are going to be there, and my mom practically begged me to come help out. Those boys are a handful."

Mey felt a pang of sorrow. She would have loved a house full of kids, and chasing around three rambunctious boys sounded like fun, not a chore. But then she was young and in good shape, while Derek's mother had bad knees and couldn't keep up with her grandchildren.

It reminded her of a saying that poignantly described the situation.

God gives nuts to those without teeth.

Mey was healthy and capable, but her adoptive family was tiny, and no one had young children.

She cast a sidelong glance at Yamanu. He had the most pleasant personality. Just being around him calmed her nerves. He would have made such a wonderful father. Did he intend to keep his vow forever, or was there a time limit? She hadn't thought to ask, but that was a very important question. There was a big difference between not right now and never.

As Yamanu loaded Julie's chair and case into the van, his phone pinged with an incoming message, and Mey instinctively tensed. Even though there was no way his hacker friend had already found something, she couldn't help the surge of hope.

He pulled out his phone and read the message. "Arielle wants to take a walk down Wall Street and eat lunch over there. Are you in the mood for it?"

Mey looked down at her red dress and the four-inch heels that went with it. She should have taken them off right after the shoot, but she'd wanted to look nice for Yamanu. It wasn't often that she could walk in heels next to a guy and not tower over him.

Except, she hadn't expected to do much walking. They were supposed to go somewhere nice to have lunch, and the elegant dress would look funny with flip-flops.

Frankly, she wouldn't have minded skipping lunch. Right now, sitting down on the couch and relaxing with a cup of tea in front of the dumb box was much more appealing.

She looked at Yamanu, who didn't look overjoyed at the prospect either. "Do you have to join them?"

He nodded. "The entire bunch is coming, including Eva, the baby, and her husband."

That was his way of telling her that Arielle needed her entire security detail when going out.

Had he said baby, though?

Suddenly, the prospect of a walk didn't seem so daunting. "Well, why didn't you say so? I want to see Eva's baby. Heck, I want to hold him. Do you think she will let me? Or is she one of those overprotective mothers?"

He helped her into the back seat of the van. "She's protective, but she has no problem with people holding him. Back home, that little guy is in high demand. All the single ladies want their baby fix."

Back home. Did it mean that Yamanu worked for Arielle and her family on a regular basis? And why were there so many single ladies there, and just one baby?

Questions and more questions. Both Yamanu and Arielle were enigmas.

"Where do you want me to drop you off?" Derek asked.

"Would you mind driving to Wall Street? We can take a cab if the traffic is bad."

Derek shrugged. "Traffic is always bad. I'll get you there."

Yamanu looked at his phone. "Do you know where Delmonico's is?"

Derek whistled. "That's a fancy place. Who's paying for lunch?"

"Arielle."

"Yeah, Mey told me that she comes from money." He glanced at them through the rearview mirror. "European aristocracy."

Yamanu slanted a reproachful look at Mey.

She lifted her hands. "That's all I said, I swear. Derek asked how Ari could afford to stay at a pricey hotel with her entire retinue, so I said she came from money. Models don't get paid much, and she hasn't even started working yet."

"I would appreciate it if you kept it to yourselves. Arielle's safety depends on it."

Julie turned back. "Is it her real name?"

Mey had wondered that as well and had decided that it couldn't be. If Ari was trying to work incognito, she must be using an alias.

Yamanu lifted a brow. "What do you think?"

"I think that it's not. But it's a good choice. I like it."

By the time Derek dropped them off next to the restaurant, Ari and her gang had already been seated, which was good because Mey had decided to keep her heels on until after lunch.

If she was going to eat at a fancy place like that, she wasn't going to do it in flip-flops.

"Mey!" Arielle jumped up. "I'm so glad that you are joining us." She pulled her into her arms and hugged her like one would a sister. "Come, I'll introduce you to everyone."

Taking Mey by the hand, she brought her around the table to where Eva was sitting with her baby in her arms.

"This is Eva, and this is Ethan."

Mey crouched next to the sleeping baby. "He is adorable," she whispered.

"No need to keep quiet," Eva said. "He is used to people talking around him. In fact, conversations put him to sleep even if they are loud."

"He must be a friendly baby." Mey smoothed one finger over his soft hair.

"He is." Eva leaned and kissed his cheek. "My sweet little angel. He's such an easy boy."

"Hi, I'm Bhathian." Eva's husband offered her his hand.

"Nice to meet you."

The guy was a hunk, and he looked a bit younger than his

wife. Good for Eva. She was a beautiful woman and could have any guy, regardless of age.

The other two bodyguards, Ewan and Uisdean, were very handsome too. Their entire group looked like they'd just stepped off a movie set.

It probably wasn't a coincidence. Arielle, or whatever her real name was, probably liked to surround herself with good-looking people, and since she was paying their salaries, she could pick and choose.

The thing was, she didn't seem like the type. Maybe it had been her mother or father who'd chosen her crew?

Ari seemed so nice and friendly, and she wasn't stuck up at all. She had the mannerisms of a princess, but it was more about the grace with which she carried herself and the fluidity of her movements. She must have taken ballet for years to achieve such poise.

"Come sit next to me." Ari motioned for Arwel to move one seat over. "You look gorgeous in this dress. Red is your color and so is the wrap style. Not everyone can pull it off. My younger sister likes Diane von Furstenberg's dresses. Amanda has a similar build to yours and she is almost as tall. Maybe an inch shorter."

"Do you have any other siblings?"

Ari nodded. "I have two sisters and a brother, but we are scattered all over the world. I don't get to see them much."

42

YAMANU

*A*s they waited for the second course to be served, Yamanu held Mey's hand under the table, giving it a little squeeze every time she shifted nervously on her chair.

The conversation was stilted, with everyone trying to sound like regular humans with everyday human concerns, and not doing a great job of it.

If Mey wasn't as sharp as she was, she might have missed the blunders, but even a less observant person would have wondered about the long moments of silence amongst a group of people who knew each other well.

"I need to visit the ladies' room." Mey pulled her hand out of his grip and got up.

"Do you want me to come with you?"

"Don't be silly." She bent and kissed his cheek. "It's right over there." She pointed toward the back. "And you can see anyone who goes in and out of there."

"Not necessarily. There might be a back door."

"There isn't," Arwel said. "I checked."

As Mey took her satchel, slung the strap over her shoulder, and walked toward the bathroom, Yamanu watched her hips sway enticingly, the fluid fabric of her red dress alternating between flaring and clinging.

She was a fine, fine woman.

"You are falling for her," Arwel stated. "In fact, I think you are already in love with Mey."

Alena nodded in agreement but said nothing, waiting for him to respond.

Bhathian and the other Guardians pretended to be busy with whatever they could get their hands on. Bhathian rearranged the blanket around his son, Ewan grabbed another piece of bread, and Uisdean checked his phone.

Yamanu shook his head. "Mey is beautiful, but this is just a fling. It's going to end as soon as we are done here and go back to Los Angeles."

The words tasted like a lie to him, but he couldn't allow himself to think otherwise. Not only because of his vow, but because she was a human and there could be nothing permanent between them.

Arwel sighed. "I've known you for a long time, and you've never shown interest in a woman beyond a casual glance."

He shrugged even though that was mostly true. The potion that he'd gotten the recipe for nearly seven hundred years ago was still working well. In the past he'd brewed it himself, but he'd found an herbalist in Chinatown to do it for him. Gertrude could have done it as well, but then his secret might have been revealed.

He preferred for everyone to keep guessing rather than providing a solid clue that he was actively medicating himself. He'd almost spilled the beans when Andrew had needed help with his rampant sex drive after his transition. Nathalie had been still human and pregnant, and at the time Bridget hadn't figured out yet that using condoms would have been enough to prevent her from transitioning.

Although Nathalie might not have wanted to take the

chance anyway. Protecting her unborn baby had been top priority, and condoms were known to malfunction on occasion.

"No response?" Arwel cocked a brow.

"What do you want me to say? I like Mey. I like her a lot. But falling for her would be stupid of me. She's a human."

"She might be a Dormant," Eva said. She then glanced around the restaurant to make sure that no one was listening and then lowered her voice to a near whisper. "Does she have any special abilities?"

"Not that I know of."

"Did she do anything unusual since you met her?" Eva continued.

"Like what?"

"Like zone out or stare into the distance. Vivian and Ella do that when they communicate telepathically. But even if she's not telepathic, all paranormal talents require concentration, which can result in her appearing scatterbrained." Eva glanced at Arwel. "Even in your case, I'm sure that when you were young, you were easily distracted by the human emotions flowing at you." She turned back to Yamanu. "Does she ask you or the people on her crew to repeat things they've said?"

"No. I would say the opposite is true. She's very alert and doesn't miss much."

Except, Eva's line of questioning resonated with what the detective he'd caught earlier had said. Whoever had sent him was also interested in catching Mey doing something unusual.

As a surge of hope rushed through Yamanu, Mey walked back to the table and sat down.

Unable to help himself, he wrapped his arm around her shoulders and pulled her in for a quick kiss on the mouth.

Arwel cleared his throat, and Alena tried to stifle a chuckle.

Mey smiled. "Did you miss me while I was gone?"

"Yes. Terribly."

43

MEY

"I'm going to take a shower." Mey put her satchel on the dresser and pulled out a change of clothes and the few toiletries she'd brought with her.

Yamanu sat on the bed and kicked his shoes off. "Did you have fun today?"

"Oh yeah. Arielle and Eva are really fun to hang out with, and the guys are nice too."

They were all a little odd, though, and not only because the men had hardly spoken two words to her, and the ladies kept talking about trivial things like the best places to go shopping and dining in New York.

They were all young looking, and yet very old-fashioned in their mannerisms and even in their patterns of speech.

Maybe it was because they were foreigners, or at least some of them were. Eva was clearly a New Yorker, but even she sometimes used phrases more suited to someone triple her age. Arwel, Bhathian, and Yamanu spoke American English with no accents, but Ewan and Uisdean had a bit of Scottish in theirs.

The most logical explanation was that they had all lived in

Europe for a while, probably in the country where Arielle was from, and that's why they sounded a little off.

Still, Mey couldn't shake the feeling that there was more to it.

The first moment she got a chance, she was going to listen to the walls and find out what they were hiding.

"What did you enjoy the most?" Yamanu asked.

"Being with you." She smiled. "And the restaurant was amazing. I don't usually dine in places like that." She chuckled. "None of my dates have taken me to such fancy places."

His brows rose. "A beautiful woman like you didn't date any millionaires?"

She pretended to think about that and then shook her head. "Nope. But just so you know, today's fantasy boyfriend is a billionaire. Millionaires are so seventies."

"Interesting. Is that because of inflation?"

"Not likely. Jin told me that prices double every fifteen years or so. A million in the seventies would be worth eight million today, not a billion. The inflation happens in the imaginations of today's Cinderellas."

He rose to his feet and pulled her into his arms. "And what would be this Cinderella's dream?"

She sighed. "I don't wish for anything fancy. My best fantasy is owning my own business and running it with my sister."

"What about your dream boyfriend?"

Mey smiled. "I've found him." She lifted on her toes and kissed him.

"Children?"

"At least ten. We can adopt them from China, so they will look like me."

She hoped he knew that she was teasing. They had met only four days ago.

Yamanu frowned, but she could see amusement in his eyes.

"How are you going to run a business and take care of ten children?"

"You are going to be a stay-at-home dad."

"I wouldn't mind. But what's the point of having ten kids when you are working long days instead of enjoying them?"

"Yeah, you're right. I haven't thought it through. I have to admit that the highlight of my day was getting to hold Ethan. He is so adorable and friendly. Usually babies don't like it when strangers hold them."

"He's used to that."

"Yeah, you told me."

She wanted to ask him about the single ladies back home, and why there was a shortage of babies to go around for everyone to get their baby fix, but nature was calling and she couldn't wait to get out of the clothes she'd been wearing since five in the morning.

"Do you need to use the bathroom before I get in there?" She shifted from foot to foot.

He chuckled. "I can use one of the others. Go ahead."

"Thanks."

Tucking the bundle of clothes under her arm, she took the pouch with toiletries and ducked into the bathroom.

As she stood under the spray, Mey closed her eyes and tried to imagine herself with a house full of kids. Ten was a bit much, especially if she wanted to fulfill her and Jin's dream. But it had been fun indulging in a fantasy for a couple of minutes and imagining having a life with Yamanu.

Except, she wasn't Cinderella and he wasn't a prince. He only looked like one.

The truth was that she knew next to nothing about him, and before she allowed herself to dream about a future with a guy, she needed to find out who he was and what was his deal.

The problem was coming up with a good excuse to be left alone in the suite's living room. Her previous idea of saying that she needed to meditate and that she couldn't do it with other people around wasn't a good one. Someone would no doubt suggest that she could do it in Yamanu's bedroom, and she couldn't claim that it was too cramped because it wasn't.

Maybe something about beds?

How about intruding thoughts of sex because of the proximity to the bed she and Yamanu had had it in?

Not likely.

She might have been comfortable to say something like that to her friends. But not to Arielle and her crew.

They were all so formal and remote with her.

Except for Ari, who was the opposite and treated Mey like a sister. But that didn't mean that Mey would have been comfortable talking with her about sex either.

Ari was like a princess, and everyone in her crew was treating her as one. Not because she was a spoiled prima donna or anything like that, but because they respected her and deferred to her.

Why someone like Arielle would pursue a modeling career was another mystery.

She was gorgeous, but she had so much more than looks going for her, and she obviously didn't need to work for money. She was loaded.

Mey chuckled. She should apply the same logic to herself.

As Jin had often pointed out, Mey could do so much more than pose for the camera. Except, she needed to work to earn a living and to save for the business she and Jin were going to open one day, and modeling paid better than any other job she could get without a college education.

44

YAMANU

*M*ey had been teasing, but Yamanu had sensed the deep yearning she'd tried to cover with humor. She really wanted a house full of kids, and he wanted her to have that. But the thought of her marrying some random human and having babies with him was enough to make his venom glands pulsate and his fangs elongate.

Luckily, her pressing need to use the facilities had distracted her from noticing what was going on with him. He had to get himself under control before she was done with the bathroom.

What a mess.

He shouldn't have allowed himself to get attached to her. Hell, he couldn't believe that it had happened so quickly. When she'd reminded him that they had met only four days ago, he'd had to count back the days to make sure. It felt like so much longer than that.

Which brought back to mind Eva's suspicion that Mey might be a Dormant. Supposedly, there was a special kind of affinity that immortals felt for Dormants, and if that was coupled with physical attraction, the pull became incredibly strong.

Except, unlike his fellow clansmen, Yamanu hadn't wished for a mate because he couldn't have one even if she fell into his lap.

He snorted. Like Mey had.

But Mey hadn't done anything unusual or strange since he'd met her, and they had been spending a lot of time together.

The only thing that could indicate otherwise was what the detective had said.

Then again, not all Dormants had special abilities. Mey could be one of those. The problem was that the only way to test it was to have unprotected sex with her and bite her, which he couldn't do.

Rubbing his hand over his jaw, Yamanu wondered how the others had done it.

It was a catch-22 kind of thing. It was wrong to induce a Dormant's transition without her consent but telling her about immortals and what it took to transition was forbidden unless she was a Dormant, but determining that required inducing unless she exhibited very strong indicators like Syssi had.

The only way around it was to tell her, and if she agreed to try, lock her up until she transitioned, provided that everything turned out well. If she didn't transition, her memory would have to be erased. End of story.

Talk about a convoluted situation. Lucky for him, he wouldn't have to go through that with Mey.

Or rather unlucky.

Depending on how he looked at it.

But what if she was a potential Dormant?

What if she wanted to transition?

Would he break his vow to induce her?

He would have no choice because he wouldn't be able to stand aside and have another immortal male do it.

Someone kill him now.

There was no way out of this mess.

If Mey was a human, he would have to let her go, and that would be bad. If she was a Dormant, he would have to break his vow to induce her and rob the clan of its best defense. And that was even worse.

He couldn't bring himself to hope for either eventuality.

"Yamanu?" Alena said from the other side of the door. "I ordered coffee, tea, and desserts. Are you and Mey going to join us?"

He walked over to the door and opened it. "Mey is in the shower, but I'll ask her when she's done."

"Ovidu went down to get it. He should be back any moment now."

"Are the others coming too?"

"It's just the four of us."

As he closed the door behind Alena, Mey stepped out from the bathroom. Clean faced and dressed in a pair of stretchy pants and a long T-shirt, she looked young and fresh and good enough to eat.

Which he was planning on doing later. It wasn't the smartest decision, but for as long as his sojourn in New York lasted, he was going to enjoy as much of her as he could.

When it ended, he was going to be more miserable than he'd ever been, but at least he would have memories of her to sustain him.

Reaching for Mey's hand, he pulled her against his chest. "Arielle invited us to coffee and desserts."

"I heard." She wrapped her arms around his neck. "But after all I ate today, I shouldn't eat anything more. I probably gained at least two pounds."

Yamanu chuckled. "And people think that a model's life is all about glamour. They don't realize that it's mostly about going to bed hungry."

"And no partying because we need to be in bed early. Beauty sleep is important. Also, little or no alcohol, no dairy products, and the list goes on. I feel like a criminal when I order a milk-based cappuccino instead of soy."

"You can have some tea." He led her to the door. "With no sugar." He winked.

"That would be nice. But let's not stay for long." She smiled suggestively. "I want to get to bed early." Her tone of voice didn't leave room for misinterpretation.

Which caused a twitch where there should have been none.

"Yeah, me too." He opened the door. "Go ahead. I'll be out in a minute. I need to use the bathroom."

"Okay."

That was a lie.

What he needed was another dose of potion.

It was good that he was an immortal and couldn't cause himself permanent damage by overdosing on the stuff, or so he hoped. The herbalist had warned him not to take it more than twice a week or he would risk irreversible impotence.

But that was good advice for humans. As an immortal, he could safely take one dose a day and sometimes two if he knew he was going to face strong temptation.

Except, since meeting Mey, he'd increased the dosage to three a day. Perhaps he needed to consult with Merlin. Doctors were sworn to secrecy, right?

Merlin wouldn't let his secret get out.

45

MEY

*a*s Ari's butler cleared the dishes and loaded them on the cart, Ari lifted the remote and flicked the television on. "Let's see the movie offerings for today."

Mey cast a sidelong glance at Yamanu, trying to figure out whether he wanted to stay and watch a movie with his boss or retire to the bedroom for some private production time.

He hadn't said much in the past hour, but then Arielle had monopolized the conversation, asking Mey a ton of questions about every topic under the sun.

It had started with the usual about moving from the States to Israel, then coming back, and how her parents were taking it that both their girls had left the nest. Then Ari had moved on to the topic of feminine intuition and if that was what had alerted Mey to the guy following her.

They'd had a long discussion on whether intuition was real or not, and Mey had expected Yamanu to repeat what he'd told her about the subconscious collecting information and spewing it out when needed, but he'd seemed to be a million miles away.

He still did. His pale blue eyes were trained on a random spot on the wall, and his expression was somber.

She wondered what was going on with him. Had he had second thoughts about spending the night with her?

Pushing to her feet, Mey stretched. "I'll have to take a rain check on the movie. I'm exhausted."

Ari clicked the screen off and waved with the remote. "Yeah, it was a long day. Do you have to work tomorrow?"

"I don't. I have the weekend off. I'll finally get to sleep in."

"Wonderful. We can go shopping tomorrow. If you are up to it that is."

"Sure. Just not too early."

"No problem. Anyway, it takes Eva an hour to do my face. I'll ask her if she wants to join us. She can leave Ethan with his daddy, and we can have us a girls' fun day." Arielle yawned. "I'm going to bed too. I might watch something to help me fall asleep, though. It's so noisy in here. I'm not used to that."

Noisy?

They were on the top floor of the hotel, and with the windows closed almost no streets noises could be heard. Had Ari been referring to the sounds of last night's activity in Yamanu's bedroom?

Mey felt a blush spreading over her cheeks. Fortunately, with her skin tone it wasn't noticeable.

Or so she thought.

As soon as they were alone in Yamanu's bedroom, he pulled her into his arms and asked, "What were you thinking that brought about that enticing blush?"

She answered with a whispered question. "What did Arielle mean by noises disturbing her sleep? Could she hear me moaning all the way from her bedroom?"

Yamanu shrugged. "And what if she did?"

Mey pushed on his chest. "It's damn embarrassing, that's

215

what. But you wouldn't understand because making a woman climax is a badge of honor for you."

"I promise you that the thought has never even crossed my mind. And there is no shame in orgasms, received or delivered."

"True, but that doesn't mean that they should be advertised either."

Frowning, he stroked her hair for a long moment. "If it bothers you that much, we can put on loud music."

"That's a great idea. Thank you."

She pushed out of his arms and reached for the remote. The hotel offered a good selection of music channels, and after flicking through them she settled on jazz.

"Is that okay?"

"Perfect." Yamanu took her hand and led her to the bed.

He didn't seem in a hurry to get her undressed, though. Lying on his side, he wrapped his arm around her waist and leaned in to kiss her.

It wasn't a ravenous kiss, but a gentle, loving one that speared through her heart. Kisses like that could make her fall in love with him.

Or maybe she already had?

No, that was stupid. She still didn't know much about him, and one tender kiss didn't mean that he was in love with her either.

"What's wrong?"

Damn, the guy was perceptive. "I might be falling for you, and I was berating myself for being stupid."

A sadness settling over his eyes, Yamanu nodded. "I understand. I can't give you what you want. I can't fully satisfy you, and I can't give you a house full of kids."

Feeling like a jerk, she cupped his cheek. "That wasn't it at all. You satisfied me and then some." She chuckled. "I don't think I've ever climaxed so hard and so many times as I did with you last night. The only thing missing was me responding in kind. I feel selfish."

The gleam back in his eyes, Yamanu smiled. "It brings me immense pleasure to witness your rapture. Hell, just holding you like that is priceless to me, and not because I've been lonely. I was doing fine until you showed up in my life and made me crave things that I shouldn't."

Damn. He was making it really difficult not to fall for him.

Mey closed her eyes and decided to take the plunge, asking the question that had been paramount on her mind but was probably too soon to ask. "Is there a time limit on your vow? Or is it in effect until the day you die?"

46

YAMANU

*M*ey's question had taken Yamanu by surprise even though it shouldn't have.

It made perfect sense for her to wonder about that, but the truth was that he'd never thought about the length of his commitment.

When he'd made his vow, Yamanu had believed that he was only giving up meaningless hookups, and if he could get over the physical cravings, it would take most of the sting out of his sacrifice.

After all, meaningful relationships with women had not been possible, and with the physical part subdued, it had felt like not much of a loss.

But now that more and more Dormants were being discovered, perhaps he could be blessed with one as well. If the Fates indeed rewarded those who had sacrificed a great deal with truelove mates, then he'd certainly earned the right.

Hell, he should have been first in line.

And as to his vow, hadn't he done enough?

Perhaps finding his truelove mate would be the sign that it was time to re-evaluate his priorities?

Was Mey a Dormant?

Was she his truelove mate?

How would he know if she was either without having intercourse with her?

Mey sighed. "I'm sorry. I shouldn't have asked."

"No, that's okay. I've just never considered putting an expiration date on my vow."

Her eyes flared with hope. "And now you do?"

"It's not something I can decide on without giving it serious thought."

"Of course not." She was still smiling, and her fingers were combing through his hair, making him want to purr. "Take as long as you need. Just knowing that this is not permanent is good enough for me."

It was just as he'd thought. Mey wanted a full partner, not just a partial one, and all her talk about adopting had been a joke. No big surprise there. He'd figured as much.

"So, my celibacy is a deal-breaker for you. You just didn't want to admit it because you didn't want to hurt my feelings."

"No way. I was angry with myself for believing that I was falling for you after four days of knowing you, not because of your vow and the limitations it imposed on our lovemaking. I meant it when I said that you had me orgasming harder and longer than I ever had before."

She was telling him the truth.

Yamanu let out a stifled relieved breath. "Careful. You are inflating my ego. Soon I won't be able to squeeze into my clothes."

"You'll be fine." She lifted a strand of his hair and wound it around her finger. "I know that it's too early to talk about the future, but I was dead serious when I said that I was fine with adopting children and not having them myself." She looked into his eyes. "The way I feel now, I wouldn't give you up even if you kept your vow of celibacy for the rest of your life."

Dear merciful Fates. That had sounded more like a proclamation of love than if she'd spoken the words themselves. And not only love, but also commitment.

Mey could very well be his truelove mate.

Provided that she was a Dormant.

But to prove it, he would have to break his vow sooner rather than later.

It was one hell of a dilemma. Lokan had thought that giving up the island's location was a difficult decision, but that had been easy compared to what Yamanu was facing.

He leaned in and kissed her gently. "You are a remarkable woman, my lady Mey." He smiled. "But after all that ego boosting you've given me, I feel that I have to prove myself."

He kissed down her neck, but the T-shirt was in the way.

"This has to go."

As he gripped the hem, Mey lifted her arms so he could slide it off them easily. The bra was gone a moment later, and then he was staring at Mey's perfectly shaped breasts.

As her dark nipples stiffened in front of his eyes, he smacked his lips. "I think those twin berries are sending me subliminal messages." He pinched both lightly and then took one into his mouth.

Confident in the background music masking the sounds she was making, Mey let out a throaty moan.

"Yes," he murmured around the nipple he was suckling. "I want to hear the sounds of your pleasure. All of them."

Her hands went to his head, holding him to her breast. "They are yours."

Alternating between the two, he licked, nipped, thumbed, and pinched, getting her to make many more of the sounds he craved.

Yamanu could listen to Mey's moans all day long and not tire of it. It was a much better music than the jazz playing in the background.

"Thank you," he said as he kissed down her ribcage.

Mey giggled as he swirled his tongue around her bellybutton. "I'm ticklish there."

He did it again just to hear the sound of her laughter, then kept going and pushed her stretchy pants down her hips to expose her feminine treasures.

She kicked them off the rest of the way. Her panties remained stuck on her hips, and he helped her get rid of those with one strong yank.

Sitting on his haunches, he stared at the beauty sprawled on the bed before him, offering herself to him like a feast on a platter.

Kneeling between her parted legs, he murmured, "Just look at you. Gorgeous."

She smiled coyly. "I'm glad that you approve."

"Oh, I more than approve. I worship." He dipped his head and nuzzled her puffy folds. "I can't get enough of your scent." He licked the length of her slit. "Or your taste."

Mey's hips surged up, and he was rewarded with a soft moan.

He delved deeper, spearing his tongue into her opening and then licking upward to pay homage to her throbbing clitoris.

That elicited a different kind of moan, more high-pitched.

Was it too much stimulation for her?

Pulling his tongue back, he pressed a soft kiss to the engorged nub and slipped a finger inside her. As her undulating hips and deep throaty moan signaled that he was doing it right, he wedged in a second finger, pumping both in and out of her while alternating between licking around her clit and pressing soft kisses to it.

As tender muscles tightened around his penetrating fingers, he knew that she was getting close. Evidently, the centuries of abstinence hadn't made him forget how to properly pleasure a woman.

He'd been quite the Don Juan in his previous life—the one he'd forced out of his mind until Mey had entered the picture and turned everything upside down.

Ladies had sought him out, and he'd been happy to oblige, naively believing that he was spreading the joy and teaching women how wonderful sex could be with the right partner.

He'd been so cocky, so overconfident, not realizing that the sex hadn't been as inconsequential for them as it was for him.

But this was not the time to dwell on past sins.

Flattening his tongue over that most erogenous spot on Mey's body, he curved his fingers and rubbed the tips over that other highly responsive spot inside her sheath.

When she cried out and the delicate muscles inside her fluttered against his fingers, Yamanu felt a corresponding tightening in his balls.

After four doses of potion, that should not have happened. He had a feeling that soon the concoction was not going to be enough, and that he would be forced much sooner than he'd hoped to choose between keeping Mey and keeping his vow.

MEY

*a*s Mey drifted down from dreamland, Yamanu's absence in bed was the first thing she became aware of. To make sure, she reached with her hand, but instead of his muscular chest, she found only pillows.

That was disappointing.

Since the breakup with Oliver, she'd gotten used to waking up alone, but that didn't mean that she liked it. It was much nicer to wake up nestled against Yamanu's chest.

Where was he?

Last night he'd pleasured her into several wonderful climaxes, proving that the night before hadn't been a fluke or that she'd orgasmed so hard because she hadn't had sex in a long time.

It was all Yamanu.

He was such a selfless man, and it was such a rarity in today's world, and especially her generation of me, me and more me.

Yawning, she stretched her arms over her head and glanced at the window. By the position of the sun, it was late morning, and she wondered whether Arielle had gone shopping without her.

The truth was that Mey would have gladly skipped that in favor of spending the day with Yamanu, but she couldn't say no to Ari. After all, she was sleeping in the hotel suite Ari was paying for and taking up her bodyguard's time.

The door opened and Yamanu walked in, looking showered and dressed. She must have slept like the dead not to feel him get out of bed or hear the water running in the bathroom.

"Good morning, beauty." He sat on the bed and planted a closed-mouth kiss on her lips. "Do you want me to heat up breakfast for you?"

"Sure. How long have you been awake?"

"A couple of hours." He ran his palm over her arm.

"You should have woken me up."

"Nah." He smirked. "You needed the rest. But now you need to eat. So up you get."

"What, no breakfast in bed?" she teased.

He shook his head. "Not this time. Arielle is waiting to take you shopping."

"Right. I kind of hoped she'd left without me. I'd rather spend the day with you."

"You're going to. I can't let her go out alone with Eva and you as she's planned. My job is to protect her." He leaned and kissed her cheek. "And you. Eva can take care of herself."

"Are you saying that because she isn't your boss or your girlfriend, or because she is a kickass lady?"

He grinned. "I like hearing you say that you're my girlfriend. And as for Eva, she's a tough cookie. Besides, she has her husband to protect her."

Mey yawned again. "Is Bhathian coming along with the baby?"

"I don't know. But if you get out of bed, you can ask Eva yourself."

Flinging the comforter away, Mey enjoyed the glow in Yamanu's eyes as they roamed over her nude body.

"Gorgeous." He smoothed his hand over her hip. "I could spend days just looking at you."

"Same here." She lifted up and kissed his cheek. "But I'd rather do it after I brush my teeth and get dressed."

"Should I put your plate in the microwave now, or is it going to take you longer than a minute?"

"Make it two." She swung her legs over the side of the bed.

"That's all?"

"I showered last night, and I'm not going to put makeup on. So yeah."

It ended up taking five minutes instead of two, but her plate was still hot to the touch.

"Scrambled eggs and hash browns. I must have died and gone to heaven. Do you know how long it has been since I last indulged like that?"

"Modeling is a bitch of a job." Arielle joined them at the table. "You are as thin as a twig, and you still have to worry about your weight. It's good that I'm not a fashion model." She patted her nonexistent belly. "I'm only showing my face to the camera. So, are you coming shopping with Eva and me?"

"Yes."

"Good." Ari pushed to her feet. "I'm going to her suite to get my makeup done." She winked. "Can't go out without my public face on. We might encounter paparazzi."

"Are Bhathian and Ethan coming with us?"

"I don't think so. Motherhood is the most fulfilling thing in the world, but every mother needs a break from time to time to keep from going insane."

"You sound like you're talking from experience."

"Oh, well." Arielle waved a dismissive hand. "I should go if I want to be ready by noon. It takes her an hour to put my face on."

When Arielle left, Mey looked at Arwel's opened door. "Where is Arwel? Is he going to come with us as well?"

"He's doing some shopping of his own, but he'll be back in time to join us. The protocol is to have at least two guards with Arielle at all times." He pointed at her plate. "After all that excitement over the eggs and potatoes, I don't see you eating. Your food is getting cold."

"True." She scooped some hash browns on her fork and put it in her mouth.

Her eyes rolled back from pleasure. This was such an unhealthy and fattening breakfast, but it tasted so good.

As Yamanu's phone pinged with a message, he pulled it out and looked at the screen. "The big boss wants to talk to me. I'm going to call him from the lounge."

She chuckled and pointed with her fork. "Ha! You just revealed that Arielle's super important parent is her father."

He arched a brow. "Who said that my boss is Ari's parent? It could be her brother, or it could be the head of the security firm I work for."

"Damn it." She let her shoulders slump. "I thought I had it figured out."

He cupped her cheek and kissed the tip of her nose. "I won't be long."

Her heart doing flips, she nodded and watched him walk to the door. This was the opportunity she'd been waiting for. She finally had the place to herself and could do some snooping.

Waiting for the door to close behind Yamanu, Mey abandoned her breakfast and sat on the floor in the middle of the room. Assuming her meditative pose, she closed her eyes and concentrated.

Arielle wasn't coming back anytime soon, and hopefully Yamanu's boss was going to keep him on the phone for a while.

Worst case scenario they would catch her meditating. No one would know what she was actually doing.

YAMANU

*Y*amanu entered the executive lounge and locked the door behind him. Even though Ragnar had promised to keep it for the team's exclusive use, and only their keys could open the door, it was better to err on the side of caution. Mey had seemed very curious about the man he'd called boss, and he wouldn't put it past her to try and listen in on the conversation.

After all, she'd served in intelligence, and even though she claimed that her role had been insignificant, there must have been a good reason for her to get chosen for the department. An inquisitive mind was probably a prerequisite for that kind of work.

Choosing the armchair furthest from the door, he pulled out his phone and selected Kian's contact.

His call got answered after the second ring. "Yamanu. How are things in New York?"

"Nothing is happening yet. Alena starts shooting on Monday, and after that it will take time before the advertising campaign begins. It's a long-term project. And frankly, I don't think Kalugal will take the bait. He might miss his mother, but he isn't looking for a replacement lookalike. Not as a mother and not as a lover."

"I know it's a long shot. But that's the only thing we've got. Besides, Annani wants it done, and I don't see a reason to refuse her. Not that I could even if I wanted to. Arguing with the Clan Mother is futile. Besides, the operation doesn't cost us much, and it's an opportunity for Alena to have a breather away from our mother, which I'm sure she needs."

Yamanu wasn't sure about that. Alena wasn't the wallflower everyone thought her to be. She was just as assertive and commanding as her other siblings, and she could handle Annani just fine.

"How long do you want to keep it going?"

"Once the campaign goes live, Alena will do some press conferences, and we will post tons of social media updates for her. I think a month or two should be enough. If Kalugal doesn't surface by then, we can claim to have done our best."

Which meant more time with Mey. The question was whether it was bad or good.

Kian continued, "But that's a problem because I need you back here."

That wasn't good. "Why?"

"Lokan got us information about the building his brother bought to house his men. We found it, and we plan on taking the Doomers out before they manage to snatch any girls. The thing is, the building is smack in the middle of Korea town, and we need you here to shroud the area during the raid."

It was a chilling reminder of why he couldn't break his vow.

As much as things had gotten peaceful in the last seventy years, Yamanu's services were always needed for something.

"I can't be in two places at the same time, and you put me in charge of Alena's security."

"I know, and I have a solution. We need you for three days tops and then you go back. I'm sending Kri and Michael as reinforcements. The kid has strong telepathic ability, and Kri can pretend to be another model."

Yamanu chuckled. "Kri a model? Maybe for motorcycle gear. She's built like a lumberjack."

"Don't ever let her hear you say that. Kri is a badass with killer fighting instincts, but she hates it when people think of her as masculine."

Yamanu was well aware of that, and he would have never said it in her presence, even though he thought it was silly of her, but it surprised him that Kian was aware of that as well. The guy had the emotional intelligence of a brick.

"Since when are you so attuned to people's feelings?"

"Since I have Syssi to point things out for me. You think I would have realized that on my own?"

"Nope. That's why I was surprised. How is your wife by the way? The pregnancy going okay?"

"Thank the merciful Fates, everything seems fine and Syssi is glowing with happiness. Merlin is flooded with requests for his potions."

Yamanu switched the phone to his other ear. "Can I ask you a personal question?"

There was a moment of silence. "That depends on the question. Ask and I'll decide if I want to answer."

Fair enough.

"How did you know that Syssi was the one for you? Your truelove mate?"

Kian chuckled. "I didn't. Not consciously, anyway. I'm a stubborn bastard, and I couldn't accept that one look into her eyes and one touch of her hand were enough to ensnare me. But the connection was so powerful that the realization eventually penetrated my thick head. Amanda helped too."

"How?"

"She showed me the error of my ways, basically telling me that I was full of shit, and that I was lying to myself and hurting

Syssi's feelings in the process. Sooner or later, I might have reached the same conclusion, but Amanda saved me from making an even bigger ass of myself."

That was helpful, but only to a certain extent. Kian's situation with Syssi had been different than Yamanu's with Mey. Because of Syssi's powerful precognition talent, Amanda had had good reasons to suspect that she was a Dormant.

"Why the sudden interest? Did you meet someone?"

Yamanu sighed and let his head drop against the chair's back. "Yeah. I did. Her name is Mey and she is a model in the same agency that signed Alena up. I feel the connection, but she doesn't have any paranormal abilities. I know that some of the other Dormants didn't have them either, so it is not a prerequisite, but then how would I know if she is a Dormant or not? It's a bloody catch-22. Without paranormal abilities as an indicator, the only way to find out is to attempt her transition, but that's a no go without her consent. But for her to agree, she needs to be told the truth about us, and that's a no go as well. The only option is to have her locked up somewhere while trying to induce her transition, and if it doesn't work to thrall her memories away. Except, then I'll be forced to erase myself from her memory and never see her again. I can't stand the thought of that." He clutched his chest. "Every time I think about it, I feel as if a vise is squeezing my heart and it's going to burst."

And to complicate things even further, he had his vow to think of.

What a bloody mess.

"Don't quote me on this, but if it's meant to be, it's going to somehow work itself out. The Fates will find a way, like they did with Callie and Brundar and Tessa and Jackson and all the others. Give it time."

That was the second surprise of the day. Since when had Kian become a believer? He was a staunch skeptic.

"I guess that's the only thing I can do." Yamanu sighed. "When do you need me back?"

"Unless there is a change in plans, Wednesday. We are planning the raid for Thursday night."

"Is Turner involved?"

"Not this time. The guy has volunteered enough lately. With you providing the shroud, we can handle this one ourselves."

MEY

*I*t was so damn frustrating.

The thing about hotels was that rooms changed occupants frequently, so there were a lot of echoes to sift through, and fast-forward was not available.

Mey had to watch and listen to heated arguments between spouses, witness strangers having sex on the couch, and worst of all waste the precious time she had.

Yamanu would be back anytime now, and she hadn't gotten any of his team's interactions yet.

Probably because none of them had been emotionally charged. Regrettably, mundane chitchat didn't leave imprints on the walls, but it could have revealed what she was looking for.

A clue to the small oddities she'd been noticing about Arielle, Yamanu, and the rest of the team.

Except for Ethan.

He was just a cute little baby and perfectly normal.

Then finally she got something.

Arwel stood in front of Arielle's door and knocked. "Alena, may I have a word with you?"

So that was her real name. It suited her better than Arielle, which evoked images of Little Mermaid in Mey's mind, complete with the red hair and pixie face. Alena sounded like someone stately and more dignified, which this particular bearer of the name personified.

Alena opened the door and glared at Arwel. "I don't need an escort of five Guardians for a walk down Wall Street. What do you think might happen to me there? Doomers jumping out from coffee shops? Don't tell Kian, but Annani and I go out by ourselves all the time."

Doomers?

Who or what were Doomers? It sounded like a synonym for boogiemen.

Arwel shook his head. "That's not true. You always have a couple of Odus with you. They can protect you."

Ari, aka Alena, waved a dismissive hand. "The most Ovidu can do is frown indignantly at an attacker. The Odus might have been designed with fighting capabilities, but I'm pretty sure that they got erased with the rest of their memories. In the thousands of years that Annani's had them, they haven't fought even once."

Thousands of years must have been a figure of speech, but the rest of what Alena said about her butler didn't make any sense either.

Perhaps her meaning had been lost in translation? Perhaps she'd meant trained instead of designed? And by erased she'd meant lost?

Except, Alena had been faking her foreign accent, and what little there actually was sounded English, not Eastern European. She shouldn't have any trouble with the language.

"Perhaps you are right about their fighting skills, but they can still shield you and your mother with their indestructible bodies, and they have done that when it was needed."

Okay, that was totally inexplicable. Indestructible bodies? What in hell was he talking about?

Perhaps they were rehearsing a movie script?

"Fine," Alena sighed in exasperation. "I'll take Ovidu with me and Eva and the rest of you can stay here."

"Why? Are we such bothersome company?" Arwel put a hand over his heart. "I thought that you liked me."

She laughed. "You sly, sly, Guardian. Fine. You can come as well."

"Bhathian would feel offended if you left him behind with the baby. After all, he is a Guardian."

Alena rolled her eyes. "Okay, he can come too. But what about Ewan and Uisdean? You can't convince me that they are going to feel left out. I'm sure that the last thing they want to do is go sightseeing with me."

"They've never been to Wall Street."

Throwing her hands up in the air, Alena went back into her bedroom but didn't close her door. "I give up. You win. Everyone can come. Do you want to invite Ragnar as well?"

Arwel rubbed his hand over his jaw. "That's not a bad idea. I'll check with him."

"Don't!" Alena turned around. "I was joking."

"I know. I was joking too."

And that was when the echo fizzled and dissipated.

As soon as Alena and Arwel had reached an agreement, their emotional state had gone back to normal, which meant no echo.

Mey was about to get up, when another scene started playing. This time it was from the very same morning.

A cup of tea in hand, Alena turned to Yamanu. "Is Mey going to get up anytime soon? It's after ten in the morning."

The smirk on her face was a sure sign that she'd heard what they'd done last night despite the background music. Either that or she was guessing.

Yamanu ignored the hint. "She had a long week and needs her rest."

"I'm sure," Alena said. "But if she wants to join me on my shopping expedition, she should…"

The sound of the suite's front door opening threw Mey out of the scene, the voices and images blinking out of existence instead of slowly fading away.

"What are you doing?" Yamanu asked.

Her heart pounding against her ribcage, Mey forced a smile. "What did it look like I was doing? I was meditating. Then you walked in and broke my concentration."

"I'm sorry. If I had known, I would have waited. But you didn't tell me that you were going to meditate while I was gone."

She waved a hand. "It was a spur of the moment kind of thing."

It was difficult to keep her breathing even and her facial muscles relaxed. What she'd heard was so bizarre, and she hadn't had time to process it yet.

Crouching next to her on the floor, Yamanu stroked her hair. "You don't have to stop on my account. I promise to be quiet as a mouse."

"I can't meditate when there is someone with me in the room. I get too easily distracted."

"Then I'll go to the bedroom."

She put a hand on his knee and used it to push herself up. "It's not going to work. Besides, Ari is probably about done with her makeup, and I should get ready." She glanced down at her yoga pants. "I wish I had something nicer to wear. But I thought that I'd be going home in the morning."

Yamanu smiled, his eyes roaming over her body. "You look mighty fine to me, my lady Mey. I like seeing you like that, casual and comfortable."

That was nice to know. Some guys wanted the model look

twenty-four seven, and she was glad Yamanu wasn't one of them.

Still, if Alena was putting on her Arielle makeup, she was going to dress appropriately too. Mey would feel uncomfortable in her homey attire while going out with her.

"Perhaps Ari can lend you something of hers?" Yamanu suggested.

Mey shook her head. "Is there any way we can stop by my place on the way so I can change? It will only take me a minute. I'll just pull on a nice dress and grab some decent shoes and that's it. I'm not one of those women who try a hundred outfits before deciding on what she wants to wear. I'm quick."

She was babbling, which wasn't like her at all. It was a dead giveaway that she'd been up to something, and Yamanu was no fool. But perhaps he would attribute her nervousness to worry about looking schlumpy next to the decked-out Arielle.

"I can ask Ari if she doesn't mind waiting. But you need to remember that your place is being watched, and that you have to be mindful of that. No talking about Arielle or about going shopping with her."

Mey grimaced. "It's so creepy that I don't feel like going back there. I'll just wear what I have on and buy something to change into."

"That's a better option."

50

YAMANU

"This is my definition of hell," Arwel murmured.

Yamanu agreed. They'd been all over the shopping mall, waiting outside clothing stores while the ladies tried on outfits, outside shoe stores while they tried on countless pairs, then bathrooms, jewelry stores, and more of the same.

If he could help it, Yamanu was never going to do that again, but he had a feeling that more shopping was awaiting him over the next six weeks. Alena was bored, and apparently that was her way of entertaining herself. It wasn't about the act of purchasing things, it was a fun way to pass the time for her.

Women, for some reason, enjoyed shopping in packs. For him, it was more of a solitary activity that was usually completed as fast and as efficiently as possible, and most of it was done online. Mall stores didn't carry his size, not in clothing and not in shoes.

For some inexplicable reason, though, he'd thought that it would be fun to hang around the mall with Mey, just enjoying each other's company. But he'd forgotten about the stares his looks attracted, and Mey was keeping Alena company while he was stuck with the guys.

He had a nagging suspicion that she was doing it on purpose.

She'd been so nervous when he'd caught her meditating, as if what she'd been doing was a crime.

Did that count as strange and unusual behavior?

Maybe, but not in the way that mattered to him. Neither meditation nor nervousness belonged in the paranormal realm.

Eva patted Arwel's arm. "I understand. It must be difficult for you with all these people around."

"That too. But I'm talking about being dragged from store to store and waiting for you ladies to be done. It's mind-numbingly boring."

Eva nodded. "I'll try to get Ari to stop for ice cream. How about that?"

"Awesome idea."

"I'll go check on her and Mey."

"Thanks."

She motioned for Bhathian to follow her into the store with the stroller. "There is a place for you to sit outside the changing room."

He grimaced. "The suffering husbands' corner."

"Indeed." Eva laughed and threaded her arm through her husband's.

Watching them together, so comfortable, so familiar with each other, suddenly wasn't just an observation. Yamanu wanted that, and he wanted it with Mey.

Was he an idiot for believing she was his fated mate after knowing her for only five days?

If he were human, yes, it would have been idiotic. But he was an immortal, and for some reason the Fates had been kind to his clan lately, arranging fated matings left, right and center.

Was Mey really his? Delivered to him by the merciful Fates? Or did he want her to be and therefore believed that she was?

"What is tormenting you?" Arwel asked. "The shopping is bad, but it can't be responsible for the anguish you are feeling."

Having an empath as a best friend and roomie had its disadvantages.

"Stop focusing on me and spread your awareness wider. We are here to search for a certain someone and to guard Alena."

"As if there is a chance in hell he's going to be here." Arwel shifted to his other foot and then leaned against the railing. "Don't worry, I'm alert. But all I get is a lot of human crap, and it's driving me nuts. I need to get out of here."

"Perhaps you can play on Alena's sympathy and save us all? Tell her that you can't handle the onslaught and that you need to go back to the hotel."

Arwel snorted. "Right. After the fabulous job I did of convincing her to take us along wherever she goes? I don't think so. She wanted to go alone with Eva and Mey."

"Is she nuts?"

"No, she is fearless. There is a slight difference. She's used to accompanying Annani on her excursions, and you know how Annani is. She thinks she is invincible. Alena seems to think herself equally strong, which is, of course, absurd."

"Who knows? Alena might be powerful. It's not like we know much about her and what she can do. I thought she was a recluse, a gentle soul, and a wallflower. I was wrong about all three. And as for Annani, she has a good reason to be fearless." Yamanu glanced around to make sure no one was listening. "She's the most powerful being on earth."

Arwel shook his head. "That might be true, but she is still vulnerable. I agree that there is very little chance of anyone getting the upper hand with her, but freak accidents happen. Take Lilen for example. A rotten human cut his head off by striking him from behind. On the battlefield, the stenches of fear and aggression are so strong that it is difficult to feel someone coming at you, especially when you are busy fighting off several opponents. Not only that, that human could have been an anomaly like Turner who didn't emit any emotional scents."

Yamanu nodded. "I wonder if there are humans out there who are immune not only to our mind manipulation, but also to Annani's."

"I have no doubt. And that's why she shouldn't go places without bodyguards galore to protect her. There is no substitute for trained warriors watching her back."

"Yeah, but if we are talking extremes, there are things even a bunch of bodyguards cannot prevent. A sniper with special ammunition aiming at her heart or brain, a nuclear bomb or a plane crash. Following your logic, she should never leave the sanctuary."

Arwel smiled. "Precisely. She shouldn't. And that's why Kian is so stressed out whenever she visits."

"You can't expect her to be holed up there forever. It's a nice place, but come on, would you have liked to live there and never venture outside?"

Arwel arched his brows. "You are jesting, right? I would have loved to. With no humans around, it would have been a real paradise for me."

"So why don't you ask for a transfer? Not that I want to get rid of you, but that's a viable solution."

Looking down at his shoes, Arwel shook his head. "I can't. And you of all people should get it. The clan needs me and what I can do."

It seemed like Arwel had figured out why Yamanu had been abstaining, but thankfully his friend had kept his mouth shut about it.

Except for that one time when he was drunk and asked questions he shouldn't have.

They were both sacrificing for the clan.

"Alaska is like a retirement colony," Arwel continued.

"Think of the Guardians who serve there. Anandur says that they are a bunch of out-of-shape guys who are happy with doing basically nothing."

"And that is who we entrust our Clan Mother's protection to? Kian should assign proper Guardians to her."

"Kian has no say in it. Annani decides who lives in the sanctuary."

"That's regrettably true."

51

MEY

"That was fun," Arielle, aka Alena said as they waited for Arwel to open the door.

Mey smiled. "Yeah, I got several nice outfits, and the best part was having the guys carry the bags. Now I understand why you brought them along."

Yamanu was holding her two shopping bags, and Arwel and the two other Guardians were carrying Alena's. Eva's were stashed on the bottom of Ethan's stroller. Thank God for the little guy getting fussy. If not for him, the shopping expedition would have lasted until the mall closed.

It hadn't been all shopping, though. They'd eaten lunch and dinner at the place and had stopped for ice cream between the meals. Enviably, Alena didn't seem concerned with calories at all, eating whatever her heart desired. She must have one hell of a metabolism going for her.

Arielle, not Alena.

Mey needed to keep thinking of her as Arielle or she might let slip the name she wasn't supposed to know.

"I'm going to change into something more comfortable,"

Arielle said as she waited for the guys to drop her many shopping bags in the bedroom. "Join me for a movie?"

That wasn't a request. It was a command.

"Sure. I'll just change back into my yoga pants and T-shirt."

The new dress Mey had put on in the mall was comfortable enough, but she wanted to take her bra off, and the fabric was too clingy and would show her nipples.

Yamanu followed her into the bedroom. "Do you want to go to your place tomorrow and pack a bag? Or did you buy enough things to hold you over?"

Kicking her shoes off, Mey pulled the dress over her head. "It can wait for Monday. But are you sure that it's okay for me to stay here for so long? I can rent a room of my own."

Naturally, that wasn't what she wanted, but she felt like she had to ask.

For a long moment, Yamanu didn't answer, his eerie eyes roaming over her nearly nude body. "You're not going anywhere."

She struck a pose. "Is it because of this?"

"That too. I like having you in my bed and knowing that you are safe."

She walked up to him and sat on his lap. "That's so sweet of you to say, and I know that you want me here. But what about the others?"

"Everyone likes you."

"Arielle does, and I think Eva likes me too, but I'm not sure about the guys. They seem uncomfortable around me."

"That's because you are a gorgeous, sexy lady. You make men nervous."

"But they know that I'm with you." She chuckled. "It's not a secret that I'm sleeping in your bed and that you are not sleeping on the couch."

Thinking of secrets, she was reminded of the weird conversation she'd summoned from the walls earlier. "By the way, I was wondering where Arielle's butler sleeps. Does he stay with Uisdean and Ewan?"

"He sleeps on the couch in her bedroom."

"Isn't that odd?"

Yamanu shrugged. "She's had him since she was a little girl. He's taking care of her and keeping her safe."

Strange didn't begin to describe it. Even if Ovidu was Alena's father, he shouldn't have slept in the same room with her. It wasn't the Middle Ages when families slept in one room.

Mey shook her head.

If this were a science fiction movie, or an Asimov book, she would have thought that Ovidu was a human-looking robot, and that Alena turned him off and put him in the closet for the night.

52

MEY

*A*s the movie dragged on, Mey's eyelids became heavy. The others had retired at various stages, and now it was only her, Ari, and Yamanu.

Perhaps if she pretended to fall asleep on the couch, they would leave her there, and she could listen to what the walls had to tell. Perhaps the conversation she'd overheard between Alena and Yamanu had continued into something interesting.

Except, that required her staying awake while they fell asleep, and she was losing the battle with her eyelids.

They just refused to stay open.

A strange dream started as soon as she drifted off, starring Arielle's butler and a thousand copies of him marching in formation like an army of robot soldiers. For some reason, it terrified her. Perhaps because they didn't look quite human, but the discrepancies were so minute that most people wouldn't have noticed them. It took careful observation to get that uncomfortable feeling that something wasn't right about them.

Except, Mey was aware that she was dreaming, and figured

that her mind had been affected by what she'd heard before. The real Ovidu didn't look like that. Or did he?

She woke up when Yamanu lifted her into his arms. "Whoa, what's going on?"

"The movie is over. I'm taking you to bed."

"Oh."

Crap, it seemed like there would be no snooping around tonight.

As Yamanu laid her on the bed and covered her with the comforter, Mey turned on her side and tucked her hands under the pillow.

The nightmare about Ovidu and his thousand replicas marching in formation was still fresh in her mind, and falling asleep could mean a return to that disturbing dream. Besides, the nap she'd taken had given her a second wind, and she was wide awake.

Which presented her with two options. She could let Yamanu know that she was up for some playtime, or she could pretend to sleep, wait until he was out, and then go back to the living room and do some more snooping.

Actually, it was straight-out spying, but calling it snooping sounded better in her head, and made her feel less guilty.

The choice wasn't difficult. Her pleasure could wait, but finding out more about Yamanu couldn't. As it was, she was falling in love with a man she knew next to nothing about who was surrounded by mystery and intrigue.

Safety always came first.

Done in the bathroom, Yamanu climbed into bed behind her and wrapped his long arm around her middle, pulling her closer to him.

She let out a contented sigh. "That's nice."

"Uhm." He nuzzled her neck.

It didn't take much more than that to awaken her libido, but

Mey forced it to stand down. She had a mission to fulfill, and getting frisky was not part of it.

Thankfully, Yamanu's breathing evened out in two minutes or so, and then he started snoring lightly.

Damn, even his snoring sounded melodic and soothing, and Mey fought hard to stay awake.

As she waited to make sure he was deeply asleep, she thought about what the walls in the living room could reveal and realized that it wasn't much. The exchange between Arwel and Alena she'd heard was from the day before, and the one between Yamanu and Alena was from this morning. Nothing from before had come up, and there couldn't be much that happened after. What were the chances that they had another heated discussion this morning before she'd woken up?

Probably slim to none.

How about Yamanu's conversation with the boss, though?

He had seemed somewhat perturbed when he'd returned from the executive lounge, but she'd attributed it to him catching her red-handed. Except, he'd had no reason to be upset about her meditating because he didn't know that she had been spying.

So, it must have been something about that phone conversation, and if he'd gotten upset or excited, then the walls of the executive lounge might hold the echoes of that.

She had to get in there.

The problem was that the lounge was one floor down, and she didn't have a key to activate the elevator on the way back. The emergency stairs could solve that part. But she also needed the key to enter the lounge and then get back to the room.

She would have to steal Yamanu's. Hopefully, he wasn't a light sleeper. But if he woke up when she tried to sneak out of bed, she'd pretend that she was going to the bathroom.

Sliding as gently and as slowly as she could from under his arm, she made it out of bed without waking him, and then crouched on the floor for a long moment listening to his breathing.

When there was no change, she pushed up and tiptoed to the dresser where he'd left his wallet and the room card. Thankfully, the card was not in the wallet because she would have felt doubly bad about taking it out.

Snatching the card, she pushed it inside the waistline of her yoga pants. With her loose T-shirt covering the contraband, she tiptoed to the door and opened it quietly.

Thank God the hinges didn't squeak, and she made it out nearly soundlessly. When the front door opened and closed just as smoothly, Mey let out a relieved breath.

Using the emergency staircase, she padded to the lower floor and used Yamanu's room key to get into the lounge.

She nearly had a heart attack when the lights came on, but then she realized they were motion activated and she rushed to turn the switch off.

With its large windows, the lounge had plenty of illumination from the moon, and Mey had no trouble moving around. An armchair at the far end seemed like the perfect place to meditate. It even had a footstool.

Now the only problem was getting her anxiety under control so she could relax enough to get into a meditative state.

It took a while, but eventually she did it, and the scene with Yamanu holding his phone and talking with someone started playing.

Thank God.

Mey had been afraid that she would have to listen to countless conversations before getting to the right one. Apparently the lounge hadn't been used often, and when it had, nothing overly exciting had taken place in there.

Unfortunately, the echo provided just Yamanu's side of the conversation, and she had to guess what his boss was saying.

It started with Yamanu holding the phone to his ear, his frown deepening the longer he listened to the other guy.

"I can't be in two places at the same time, and you put me in charge of Alena's security."

Okay, nothing new there.

Yamanu chuckled. "Maybe for motorcycle gear. She's built like a lumberjack."

Surely he wasn't talking about Alena. She was delicately built and very feminine.

"Since when did you become so attuned to people's feelings?"

The other guy said something to which Yamanu replied, "Nope. That's why I was surprised. How is your wife by the way? The pregnancy going okay?"

Yamanu smiled as he listened to the response, so the boss's wife must have been doing well.

He switched the phone to his other ear. "Can I ask you a personal question?"

The boss must have said okay because Yamanu asked, "How did you know that Syssi was the one for you?"

Syssi was probably the boss's wife, and the answer was lengthy.

"How?" Yamanu asked.

There was a pause, and then Yamanu sighed. "Yeah. I did. Her name is Mey and she is a model in the same agency that signed Alena up."

Mey's heart skipped a couple of beats, almost throwing her out of her meditative state. She forced herself to calm down and keep on listening.

"I feel the connection, but she doesn't have any paranormal abilities. I know that some of the other Dormants didn't have them either, so it is not a prerequisite, but then how would I know if she is a Dormant or not?"

Startled, Mey lost her concentration and her eyes popped open.

Paranormal abilities? Dormants?

Her heart pounding a thousand beats per minute, she found it difficult to breathe as she tried to decipher the cryptic remark.

Yamanu felt the connection, which was good because she felt it too, but he needed her to have a paranormal ability, which was apparently a prerequisite for being a Dormant, whatever that meant.

53

YAMANU

"Your girlfriend was busy last night," Arwel said as Yamanu entered the living room.

"I know. I heard her going out."

"Any idea where she went?"

Yamanu shrugged. "Wherever it was, she couldn't get far. She was barefoot. I figured she couldn't sleep and went outside to call her parents without disturbing us. It was daytime on their side of the world. Besides, she isn't a prisoner here. If she wants to go somewhere, she can."

The truth was that he'd been suspicious when she'd slinked out of bed, but after seeing her go out without her shoes, he'd come up with the phone call explanation, which seemed logical enough to him. The safe he'd put her phone in was in the living room, and Mey had the code.

What other reason could she have for wandering the hotel's corridors in the middle of the night?

"Mey must feel lonely now that her sister is gone and her roommates are away," Alena said. "I'm glad that we can be here for her. She's such a nice person. You should wake her up and have her come get something to eat."

Lifting the thermos, Yamanu poured coffee into two cups, put them on one plate and added two pastries. "Yesterday, Mey said that she wanted to have breakfast in bed. I thought to oblige her today."

Alena looked at what he was holding and grimaced. "You call this breakfast?"

"It will do for now." He took the plate and went back to his room.

Not surprisingly, Mey was still sleeping. She'd come back to bed after three in the morning. If he weren't so selfish, he would have let her sleep longer, but he'd gotten so used to her company that he missed her even though she was right there.

Wednesday, he would have to leave her behind, and the thought of three days without her made him cringe. How was he going to survive it?

Worse, how was he going to survive letting her go if it turned out that she wasn't a Dormant?

And how the hell was he going to find out whether she was or wasn't?

Lifting his eyes to the ceiling, he uttered a silent prayer for the Fates to give him a sign.

Except, nothing happened, no thunder boomed, and no lightning struck. Perhaps he was expecting it too soon.

Putting his makeshift tray on the night table, he leaned and kissed her cheek. "Time to wake up, my lady Mey. I'm lonely without you."

Her lips lifted in a smile before her eyelids fluttered open, revealing her gorgeous brown eyes. "Good morning." She sniffed the air. "I smell coffee."

"You wanted breakfast in bed." He motioned toward the plate on the nightstand.

The smile turned into a grin. "You remembered." She lifted up and wrapped her arms around his neck. "Thank you. I'll hop into the bathroom for a moment and when I come back, we can both have breakfast in bed."

He kissed the tip of her small, upturned nose. "I like the way you think."

While she ducked into the bathroom, Yamanu fluffed up a bunch of pillows and stacked them against the headboard. Then he kicked his shoes off and got in bed.

As she'd promised, Mey got out in a matter of minutes and joined him on the bed. Except, something must have spoiled her mood while in the bathroom because she suddenly looked troubled.

"Anything wrong?" he asked as he handed her a cup.

She shook her head. "I can't believe how perceptive you are. You notice the slightest changes in my mood."

"You are easy to read."

She cast him a sidelong glance. "Really? You are the first person to say that about me."

He wrapped his arm around her shoulders. "For me, you are easy to read because I pay attention."

"Why?"

"What do you mean, why?"

"Do you pay attention because you feel a special connection to me, or because you are trained to notice things?"

"Both. What is this about? Did I do something to upset you?"

Mey didn't answer, but instead she lifted the cup to her lips and sipped on the coffee until the cup was empty.

He had a feeling she needed a little time to decide whether she wanted to share with him whatever was bothering her or not.

Perhaps it was somehow connected to calling her parents last night. She'd probably told them about her new boyfriend, and when they'd asked questions, she hadn't had answers for them because she didn't know much about him.

He could imagine calling his own mother and telling her that he'd met a girl. She would grill him for hours. The truth was that he knew only general facts about Mey, but he didn't need to know how she'd spent every moment of her life until meeting him. He knew the kind of person she was, and he liked everything about her.

Hell, he loved it.

She was his perfect lady. Not too timid, and not too assertive, gorgeous, but not stuck-up about it. Smart, caring, kind, and passionate. There was nothing he would have changed about her, except her genetics.

"What's a Dormant?"

It was good that he'd already swallowed his coffee, or he would have spat it all over the white duvet.

"It's a synonym for latent. A talent or an ability that hasn't manifested yet."

She turned to look at him, her brown eyes turning nearly black as she stared him down. "I didn't ask for the dictionary definition. What is a Dormant to you?"

Desperately, he tried to remember if anyone on his team had mentioned the term with Mey around, but they all had been careful not to talk about anything that might seem suspicious to her.

"Why? Did you hear anyone saying that?"

54

MEY

*M*ey debated her next move. If she told Yamanu where she'd heard the term Dormant, her secret would be out, but then he wanted her to have a paranormal ability for some reason. It sounded as if being a Dormant was a prerequisite for them having a long-term relationship, but paranormal ability wasn't a sure indicator of someone being a Dormant.

She had to find out what a Dormant was, and her curiosity wouldn't let her rest until she had.

It should be a good thing, right? Something desirable.

"I heard you talking with your boss."

He frowned. "How? Were you just pretending to meditate when I came back? Had you been eavesdropping outside the door and ran upstairs as soon as I was done?"

He was angry, and she didn't like it. Not when his anger was directed at her.

It would have been easy to say that yes, she'd been eavesdropping outside the door. After all, her culpability was the same whether she'd listened to the conversation while it was taking place or later to its echo.

The thing was, if she'd went with the mundane explanation, Yamanu would find a way to explain away the use of the term Dormant and wouldn't tell her the truth. Just as she kept secrets from him, he kept secrets from her. Perhaps if she revealed hers first, he would respond in kind.

"I didn't listen outside the door."

"So how did you hear me?" He got even angrier. "Did you somehow plant a bug on me?"

Damn, he was jumping from one wrong conclusion to an even worse one and escalating the stakes. It was time to put an end to it.

She took in a long breath and then let it out slowly through her nose. "You told your boss that I didn't have any paranormal ability. That wasn't true because I actually have the most bizarre talent, one that you've probably never heard of." She snorted. "I certainly have never heard about anyone who can hear echoes of past conversations that are trapped within the walls they've been held in."

By the confused look in Yamanu's eyes, he hadn't understood what she'd been trying to say.

"If I meditate in a room, I can hear and see things that happened there before. Not everyday stuff, but things that were emotionally charged. It's like watching a film. I've noticed oddities about you and your team, and since I was falling for you, I figured I should learn who you really were before it was too late for me. So, while everyone was gone, I meditated in the living room, and I heard Alena talking with Arwel about her butler. It was such a strange conversation, but it didn't tell me anything about you. The only thing I learned was that Arielle's real name is Alena. Not a big scoop there. I knew she was using a fake name along with her fake accent."

He nodded. "So last night you snuck into the executive lounge and listened to me talking with my boss."

"Yeah. I couldn't hear his side, just yours. I almost lost my concentration when you told him that you felt a special connection with me. Somehow, I managed to hold on to the meditative state and heard you talking about paranormal abilities and Dormants. That was when I lost the echo. I got so excited that I couldn't concentrate anymore." She looked into his eyes. "I know that I heard things out of order, and I might have misunderstood, but it sounded to me as if you needed me to have a paranormal ability to prove that I was a Dormant, whatever that is, and that the dormancy was a prerequisite to us having our happy ending. Did I get it right?"

Yamanu nodded, but he still looked as if a bomb had exploded at his feet, and he wasn't sure whether he was still alive or not.

Mey put her hand on his thigh. "Are you okay? You look a little gray."

55

YAMANU

*M*ey was a Dormant.

Yamanu had no more doubts.

That explained the irresistible temptation she was. He'd been celibate for centuries, and thanks to the potion and his daily meditative routine he'd become so adept at resisting temptation that he hardly even felt it.

Until he laid eyes on Mey, and his resistance had become paper-thin.

What was he going to tell her? What was he allowed to?

Before he explained about immortals and dormant genes and how a female Dormant's transition was induced, he had to talk to Kian again and explain the situation.

Or did he?

No one had the right to dictate to him how he led his life, but he owed the boss at least a forewarning before eliminating one of the most powerful weapons in the clan's arsenal.

"Yamanu?" Mey prompted. "Are you going to talk to me or keep staring into the distance? I just told you my most guarded secret and that's what I get?"

"What do you want me to say?"

"How about you share a secret of your own with me and tell me what is a damn Dormant, and am I one?"

Looking into her smart eyes, it suddenly occurred to him that Mey might have made her talent up just to get him to talk. She could have eavesdropped on his conversation with Kian the conventional way and come up with a scheme.

After all, Mey was so much more than a beautiful woman. She'd been trained by one of the best military intelligence agencies in the world.

She'd said that she'd learned Alena's name by meditating in the suite's living room, but she could have learned that from his conversation with Kian as well.

So that wasn't a proof of her so-called talent. Unless she could come up with something that she couldn't have overheard by normal means, he couldn't trust her admission.

Especially since he wanted it to be true more than anything. He was vulnerable and susceptible, which meant that he had to be doubly diligent in checking the facts.

"What did you hear Alena talk about with Arwel?"

The hurt look in her eyes cut through his heart. "You don't believe me, do you?"

"I have to be sure before I let you in on my secret. I'm in charge of Alena's security, and I don't take my duties lightly. You've been trained to collect information by Israeli intelligence. I have to be careful."

She nodded. "Fine. But just so you know, my feelings are hurt. I feel the connection too, and your doubt cuts deep. It wasn't easy for me to tell you about my ability. Other than Jin, no one knows about it. Not even our parents, and certainly not anyone in the intelligence community. Do you know what they would have done with me if they had known? I would have been forced to work for them whether I wanted to or not. My life would not have been my own anymore."

As Yamanu took Mey's hand and was about to apologize, something occurred to him. "Is Jin your biological sister?"

Mey shook her head. "I'm not going to answer that before you tell me what a Dormant is. But I can tell you what I heard Alena and Arwel talk about."

"I understand, and I'm sorry for hurting your feelings. But I have to be sure. When did that conversation between Arwel and Alena happen?"

"It was the day we joined them for a walk down Wall Street. Alena didn't want to go with all her bodyguards in tow. She wanted to go just with Eva. Arwel pretended that he was offended by her not wanting him around, so she agreed for him to come. Then he said that Bhathian would feel bad about being left behind with the baby. So, she said that he could come as well, but not Ewan and Uisdean because they would rather stay in the hotel and do their own thing. But Arwel said that they'd never been to Wall Street and that they were looking forward to it. Alena gave up and said that everyone could come."

That sounded real enough, and he knew that Mey couldn't have overheard it because she'd been with him while that was happening. Unless Alena told her the story at some point, but then he would have heard her telling it and he hadn't.

Except, he still wasn't convinced.

"You said that something about their conversation had sounded odd, and that it prompted you to investigate further. What was it?"

"The butler. Alena said that she and her mother go out alone all the time, and that they can take care of themselves. Arwel pointed out that they take the Odus with them, and that the Odus protect them because they were designed with fighting capabilities. I didn't know who the Odus were, but then Alena said something about Ovidu, and I figured out that Odus might be the word used for butlers in her country. Then she said that their fighting capabilities were most likely erased together with the rest of their memories. What I found strange about that was her choice of words. Designed instead of trained and erased instead of lost. She might have confused the terms if English was really a second language to her, but I know it isn't."

He could no longer doubt that she'd heard that conversation. Could it be that she'd planted a bug in the living room?

He hadn't checked her bags. She could have brought one with her.

Mey cast him a glance from under her lowered lashes. "When I'm not around, she speaks perfect English with just a hint of Scottish accent."

"What else? Until now everything could be explained away."

"Right. But then Arwel said that even if the Odus forgot how to fight, they could shield Alena and Annani with their indestructible bodies. Can you explain that away?"

"Kevlar vests."

She narrowed her eyes at him. "Try again. What are they? Robots? Cyborgs? Are you guys aliens from another planet?"

He chuckled, but she wasn't that far off.

"Can you do me a favor?" he asked.

"What?"

"Can you wait here while I call my boss? I can't tell you anything without his approval."

Crossing her arms over her chest, she jutted her chin out. "Do you believe me now? Or do you need more proof?"

Before he answered that, Yamanu was going to do one more thing.

The device he'd asked William to order for him had arrived the day before. He'd intended to use it in Mey's apartment, but after catching the detective, he had decided against that, wanting the people following her to think she wasn't aware of the surveillance.

It wasn't going to waste, though, because he was going to check the suite for transmissions. And then he was going to check the executive lounge as well.

"Give me twenty minutes. Can you do that?"

Grabbing the remote from the nightstand, she flicked the television on. "Go."

As he opened the door, the scent of tears hit his nose and he looked over his shoulder. "I'm sorry."

She waved with the remote. "Just go."

56

KIAN

"I'm sorry to bother you so early on a Sunday, but I need to talk to you." Yamanu didn't sound like himself.

Usually he was laidback, his tone smooth and relaxing, but now there was an edge to it that raised Kian's hackles.

"Give me a moment." Kian took the phone and stepped out into the backyard.

It was seven in the morning, and he'd been awake for a while, but he'd been taking it easy, browsing on his phone while sipping coffee in bed. Hopefully, Yamanu wasn't about to deliver news that would ruin his weekend. It had been relatively peaceful lately, and he hadn't expected any trouble from New York, but there was always something.

Sitting on his favorite lounger, he pulled out a cigarillo from the pack he'd left there last night and lit it. "Okay, talk to me. What's going on?"

"Alena is fine and so is everyone else on the team. It's about Mey. She's been hiding a paranormal talent all along."

Kian smiled. Now, that was news he was willing to hear any day and twice on Sunday, as the saying went. "Congratulations.

I told you the Fates would find a solution. How did you get her to admit it?"

"I'm afraid that there is a long backstory I need to fill you in on first."

Lying down, Kian took another puff from his 'stinky stick' as Amanda called his cigarillos. "I'm not in a hurry. Go ahead."

"Mey has a younger sister who's recently graduated from NYU and was immediately offered a very well-paying job. The thing is, that job sounds fishy."

By the time Yamanu was done, Kian had finished his cigarillo and lit another one. "I see where you're going with this. If Jin is Mey's biological sister, she might possess a similar paranormal talent, which would make her incredibly valuable to any spy organization."

"Precisely. I think that Jin wasn't as secretive about it as Mey, and somehow someone learned about her ability. The job offer might have been a way to lure her in, or she might have been told the truth and tempted by the large bonus she was promised at the end of the five-year contract with her new employer. Naturally, whoever hired her suspected her sister might be a valuable asset as well and sent people to find out."

The gears in Kian's head were spinning. "It makes me think of what Lokan told us. He believes that the government is collecting paranormal talents. They might be behind it."

"My thoughts exactly. It reminds me of the unit Mark worked for. Not all the brains they recruited had come voluntarily. Bribes and extortion were used in equal measure. Playing on people's patriotic feelings and sense of importance was the cherry on top. The bottom line is that if the government wants someone, they get him or her one way or another. And I think they got Jin."

"Maybe. The one thing that doesn't add up is the private detective. That's not how the government operates. They send their own people."

"Budget cuts?" Yamanu suggested.

"I'll have to talk with Turner and get his thoughts on this. He knows much more than we do about how the government operates."

"What do I do in the meantime? Mey is waiting for me to explain about Dormants, and I'm not sure what I can tell her while I don't have her in a contained environment. Not only that, she's being followed, and she's stayed with us for the last couple of days. If the government is behind it, I think that our team risks exposure if we stay. We should fold and come home."

"What about Mey?"

"We bring her home with us."

Kian took another drag from his cigarillo. "You said that you checked the suite for bugs and it was clean."

"That's right."

"Can the device detect surveillance from outside?"

"We are on the top floor, and the hotel is the tallest building on the block. I haven't seen any drones flying around either. So, no visual surveillance. And the device would have picked up any transmissions from the inside. They could be watching the entrance, though, or have people inside the lobby or posing as guests of the hotel."

"And what could they learn from that? Not much. I say we continue our mission as planned. As far as they are concerned, Mey befriended another model and hooked up with her business manager. But you probably should get Mey out before they decide to snatch her without proof of her paranormal abilities. They might get impatient."

"Yeah, that's what I thought. Besides, she already knows too much about us, and if anyone snatches her, that's dangerous to us as well."

"You should wipe her memories."

"Before I tell her about Dormants or after?"

"Is she your one?"

"I believe so."

Kian was glad that Yamanu hadn't had to ponder long before giving his answer. "Then tell her. But before you do that, check whether she's immune. If she is, you should get her out of there as soon as possible and bring her here. We can have her contained in the keep's underground until she transitions. We can't have her falling into the government's hands."

There was a long moment of silence. "Are we going to keep her locked up?"

Kian chuckled. "Not for long. Only until she transitions."

"What if she's not a Dormant? Not all humans with paranormal abilities are."

"The Fates have not messed up yet. When they pair people, they don't do it unless it can work out."

"Since when are you a believer?"

"Since I've seen enough proof to convince me that there is something to this mystical mumbo jumbo."

There was another long moment of silence. "Can I bring Mey to the village? There is no safer place for her."

"I'd rather not risk it. But let me think about it, and I'll get back to you. In the meantime, don't let Mey out of your sight even for a moment. Kri and Michael are arriving tomorrow, so you'll have reinforcements to keep Alena safe. From now on, Mey is your top priority."

Yamanu let out a relieved breath. "Thank you."

"Don't thank me yet. You don't know how she'll react to what you are about to tell her. In any case, good luck."

57

MEY

*a*fter Yamanu had left, Mey spent long moments crying her eyes out.

He didn't believe her, and he didn't trust her.

All those tender moments and loving looks had been a lie. Love couldn't exist in the absence of trust. It was possessiveness cloaking itself in the illusion of love.

Then again, hadn't she been guilty of the same?

If she had trusted Yamanu implicitly, she wouldn't have gone snooping around to find out more about him.

Wiping her tears with a corner of the duvet, Mey took in a shuddering breath and tried to get her head working on what really mattered right at the moment.

Yamanu had gone to talk to his boss, and he was going to tell him that Mey had uncovered some truths about them. The question was how important the things she'd overheard were. If Dormants having paranormal abilities was a huge secret, the boss might consider Mey a threat and tell Yamanu to eliminate her.

As kind and as considerate as Yamanu appeared, he was a soldier at heart and his loyalty to his people was absolute. If he had to choose between her and them, Mey had no doubt that he would choose them.

His vow of celibacy was proof of that.

He still hadn't told her how his abstinence helped protect his people, but he obviously wasn't willing to break his vow for her, which proved where his priorities lay.

Not that she could fault him for that.

He'd only known her for a few days.

As strong as the attraction between them was, and as powerful as the connection felt, it would have been selfish and irresponsible for him to abandon a lifelong commitment to his people for her.

The bottom line was that she could be in danger and should probably run.

Except, Alena and Arwel were in the living room, and Yamanu knew where she lived. She could probably overpower Alena but getting past Arwel was doubtful. Mey's training was old, while Arwel was an active bodyguard and seemed in top shape.

He would swat her like a fly.

She chuckled. A big-ass fly, but still, she had no doubt he could overpower her with ease.

Maybe she could make a rope out of the bed sheets and rappel down the side of the building?

That was an even sillier idea. They were on the twentieth floor and she didn't have enough sheets.

What about calling the police? Or the fire department?

She could fake an emergency, and when they got there, she could say that Yamanu and Arwel were about to rape her and that's why she called with the fake fire or whatever else she came up with.

Yeah, that could work.

She had to act fast, though. Yamanu had been gone for more

than ten minutes, and he was going to be back any moment now.

Jumping out of bed, she lifted her satchel and rummaged for her phone, forgetting that it was in the safe in the living room.

Damn.

Perhaps she could use the hotel's landline to make the call?

She paused with her hand on the receiver.

What was she doing?

If she pulled a stunt like that, she could kiss goodbye any chance she had with Yamanu. He would never forgive her. And for what?

A surge of panic over something that might not happen?

There was a chance that it would, though, and the question was whether she was willing to risk her life because she didn't want to lose a guy.

The logical thing to do was to err on the side of caution and call the police. But everything inside her was rebelling against it. In her gut, she knew Yamanu would not harm her or let anyone else do that no matter what.

He wouldn't betray his people for her, but he wouldn't obey a command to eliminate her either.

YAMANU

"*W*hat's going on?" Arwel asked as Yamanu returned to the suite.

He'd run out without giving an explanation, but then he'd assumed Arwel and Alena had overheard his conversation with Mey.

"Didn't you hear what Mey told me?"

"I had my earphones on, and Alena is in her room on the phone with her mother. They've been talking for the past hour."

Evidently, he'd been too distraught to notice. "Long story short, Mey has a very interesting paranormal ability."

Arwel grinned. "Congratulations, my friend. The Fates have smiled upon you."

It was the same response he'd gotten from Kian, and as before, he thought that the congratulations were premature. There were more variables that needed to fall into place.

"I didn't tell her anything yet. First, I wanted to get Kian's approval."

"Good call. He always gives it, but with conditions."

"Everything he said made sense." Yamanu rubbed his hand over his jaw. "I would appreciate some privacy for this. Is there any chance that you and Alena could go down to the hotel's restaurant or to Eva's suite? I'm not suggesting the guys' place. It's probably a disaster area."

Arwel pushed to his feet, walked over to Yamanu, and pulled him into a bro hug. "I got you covered."

"What's going on?" Alena walked out of her bedroom.

Arwel let go of Yamanu and took her elbow. "I'll tell you on the way."

"Where are we going?" She cast a perplexed glance at Yamanu over her shoulder.

"Down to the hotel's restaurant." Arwel opened the door.

"We just had breakfast," Alena still protested, standing at the door and refusing to budge.

"Yamanu and Mey need some privacy. If you can contain your curiosity for one more minute, I'll fill you in on the way down."

"Just tell me if it's good or bad."

"It's good."

"Then let's go." She turned, winked at Yamanu, and then let Arwel lead her out.

Taking a fortifying breath, Yamanu pulled two bottles of water out of the fridge and headed to his bedroom.

As he entered, he found Mey sitting cross-legged on the bed, a worried look on her face. In fact, the entire room had a strong scent of fear. And of tears.

She'd been crying.

Mey eyed the water bottles. "I don't think those will be enough for water torture."

She was joking, but she was still scared, and he had to reassure her.

"You have nothing to fear from me."

"How about your boss and the rest of your team?"

"No one is going to harm you. You are under our protection."

He walked over, sat on the bed, and handed her one of the water bottles.

As he debated where to start his story, Yamanu suddenly remembered that he needed to test her susceptibility to thralling first.

The memory he decided to erase was of what she'd heard about the Odus. Eliminating that memory would be a good enough proof.

Taking Mey's hand, he looked into her eyes, freezing her in place as he sifted through her recent memories. He cringed when he encountered what had caused her anxiety.

How could she have thought that he would kill her? Even if Annani herself ordered him to do that, he wouldn't. Not only that, he would defend Mey until he drew his last breath.

It gladdened him that she'd decided to go with her gut and not call the police. Subconsciously, Mey had known that she could trust him.

Good girl.

When he was done suppressing the memory about the Odus and released her mind, Mey shook her head. "What was that? Did you just hypnotize me?"

He smiled. "It's the mesmerizing effect of my eyes."

Mey looked doubtful.

"I'll tell you everything in a moment. But first, tell me what you think of Ovidu?"

Her eyebrows lifted. "Arielle's butler? What about him?"

"Do you think that he's odd?"

"A little. He has that fake smile plastered on his face, and the fact that he sleeps on the couch in her bedroom is just creepy. I don't know how she allows it."

"It's so he can protect her in case an intruder gets past Arwel and me."

"Pfft." Mey waved her hand. "What can he do? Block the intruder by bowing to him?"

"Maybe he's had military training."

Mey narrowed her eyes. "Why are we talking about Ari's butler? You promised me answers."

"This was a little test I had to run. What I'm about to tell you is my people's most guarded secret, and it puts all of us in danger. I had to ensure that I could erase your memories of it if necessary. Not everyone is susceptible to thralling."

She tilted her head. "Thralling? Erasing memories? What are you talking about?"

"That's what we named the ability to manipulate human minds."

Her eyes widened. "You are aliens? For real? Like from a different planet?"

He chuckled. "We are a divergent species. But we are not sure about our origins. Our ancestors are the mythological gods, who obviously weren't deities but a species of superior beings. No one knows where they came from. They might have been refugees from a different planet or the last survivors of their kind who got lost in one of earth's life-obliterating natural disasters."

Mey's lips lifted in a mocking smile. "So, you are a god? That would explain your looks."

"I'm not a god, but I'm a descendant of gods. Actually of one particular goddess, but that's a later part of the story. The gods had an extremely low birth rate and a limited gene pool. So, they decided to take human lovers. The children born from those unions were immortal, but their powers paled in comparison to the gods'. They were nearly indestructible, their senses were more acute, they were stronger and faster, and most importantly, they had the ability to manipulate human minds. That's what helped us stay hidden for thousands of years."

"You are serious, aren't you? This is not a joke, right?"

"No joke." He squeezed her hand gently. "Are you doing okay so far?"

MEY

*W*as she doing okay? Mey wasn't sure.

She was an open-minded person and believed that there must be many intelligent species out in the mind-bogglingly enormous universe. So, discovering that one had been secretly coexisting along with humans shouldn't be shocking news.

"Are the gods still around?"

Yamanu shook his head. "Just one, the mother of our clan." He chuckled. "Actually, there are two, but we've only discovered the second one recently, and she lives in complete seclusion. She isn't very powerful either."

"What happened to the others? Did they go home?" Mey asked half hopefully and half jokingly.

She had a feeling that their end hadn't been as pleasant as returning to their home world.

"A rogue god dropped a nuclear bomb on their assembly and killed them all. He was probably caught in the nuclear wind because he perished too. Our Clan Mother escaped to the far north and that was how she survived. Her sister also went north, but until recently we didn't know that she survived as well."

"Why did he do it? I mean the god who killed the others?"

Yamanu shrugged. "He was insane and hungry for power. Our Clan Mother was what you would call the crown princess, and she was promised to him in marriage. He thought he would rule over the gods once her father stepped down. But our Clan Mother chose to marry the god she loved instead. Mortdh, the rogue god, murdered her husband, was found out, and was sentenced to entombment. He must have decided that the only way he was going to escape that end was to eliminate all the other gods. But instead of becoming the ruler he'd hoped he would be, he died along with all those he'd murdered. The entire population of that region was wiped out. Humans, immortals, and gods."

"That's such a tragic story."

"I'm surprised that you aren't asking about how immortals and gods could die?"

"You said they weren't deities, and everything that is flesh and blood eventually dies. Or gets killed."

"That is true. Our bodies can repair most injuries quite rapidly, and we are hard to kill, but it can be done."

It hit her then. Yamanu was immortal.

Up until now the story had been just a story. Fantastic, interesting, but remote. Now it got personal.

"You are immortal," she stated, more to hear herself say it than to get confirmation.

Yamanu nodded. "And so is everyone else on my team. But that's not all. You might be a dormant carrier of those godly genes, and if you are, they can be activated, and you can become immortal. And so can Jin provided that she's your biological sister."

The mention of her sister raised Mey's defensive shields. Could this be an elaborate ploy to get her to reveal Jin's talent?

Yamanu hadn't provided proof of his story, and all she had were snippets of overheard conversations that could have been made on purpose.

"Are you basing your assumption that I'm a carrier of immortal genes on my paranormal ability?"

"Yes, but not exclusively. The powerful connection we feel for each other is another indicator. Not all Dormants possess paranormal talents."

"So, if Jin doesn't have any, she could still be a dormant carrier?"

"If you were both born from the same mother, and you are proven to be a Dormant, then she must be as well."

"How can it be proven?"

"If you are induced and enter transition then you are obviously a carrier. If the induction doesn't work, then you are just a human with a paranormal talent."

"How does the induction work?"

The pained expression on Yamanu's face didn't bode well. "To explain that, I need to backtrack a little. Other than the rapid repair abilities and enhanced senses, there are a few other oddities about our physiology. The males of our kind have fangs and venom glands. The venom serves two purposes and its composition changes according to what it's needed for. In battle, the venom can incapacitate an opponent or kill him. That's one of the few ways to kill an immortal. During sex, the venom induces a euphoric state and powerful orgasms."

Yeah, he'd just skirted around an important detail. The fangs were used to deliver the venom, which meant that biting was involved. Yamanu's people were like a cross between vampires and snakes.

It should have grossed her out, or maybe even scared her a little, but for some stupid reason the idea aroused her.

Very odd for a woman who didn't have even one masochistic bone in her body.

"What about the bite delivering the venom? That must be painful. And probably dangerous for a human female. Unlike immortal women who can rapidly heal from the injury, the humans cannot. I can just imagine the bruises the biting leaves."

"No bruises. Our saliva contains healing properties. In minutes, no sign is left of the bite. That's how immortal males can have sex with human females. Once the euphoria subsides, the marks are already gone, and sometimes no thralling is needed because the woman thinks it was a hallucination."

Mey crossed her arms over her chest. "Does it also contain analgesic? Because I'm sure it hurts."

"It does, but the bite is painful only for a couple of seconds until the venom takes effect." He smiled. "Then the fun begins."

Mey would be lying if she claimed she wasn't curious to find out how it felt.

Then a suspicion entered her mind. "You didn't bite me and make me forget, did you?"

Looking uncomfortable, Yamanu shook his head. "The concoction that suppresses my sex drive also eliminates the need to bite."

Bummer. She'd been kind of looking forward to experiencing that. The prospect of euphoria and powerful orgasms was very tempting despite the initial pain involved.

"What about when you need to fight another immortal? If the venom is one of the only effective weapons against an immortal opponent, then you are exposing yourself to mortal danger by drinking that stuff."

"The trigger is either arousal or aggression. My venom glands still respond to aggression."

"That's a relief. I was afraid for you."

He shook his head. "I have to say that you are taking all this with remarkable calm. And the questions you ask are so different from what I expected."

"What did you think I'd ask?

60

YAMANU

*Y*amanu swallowed.

Mey had actually asked the question that he'd dreaded, but he'd bought himself some time by explaining about the fangs and venom. She also hadn't asked him to prove his claims.

Perhaps he could buy himself a little more time by going in that direction first. Leave the worst for last.

"I expected you to ask for proof. All that I've told you so far could have been a fantastic story I've made up."

She tilted her head. "Is there a way you can prove it? Can you jump off the balcony and keep on running?"

He laughed. "You're funny. If I do that, I wouldn't die, but I would break a lot of bones in my body, which would hurt like hell and take a long time to heal. Those are not the kind of injuries that our bodies mend in minutes. Not only that, they would probably heal all wrong and our doctor would have to break them again to reset them."

"Ouch. So, no jumping off the balcony. What else?" Her eyes brightened and she lifted a finger. "Where are your fangs? I didn't see them. Do they come out on command?"

"Now, that's a question I was expecting." He opened his mouth wide and pointed at his canines. "That's their resting size, which allows us to pass for human. But if I get very aroused or aggressive, they would elongate."

Mey got closer, then lifted a finger and touched one fang.

The pulse of erotic energy that coursed from her finger straight to his loins caused an erection that shouldn't have been possible with the amount of potion he'd been drinking lately.

"Oh my God, it actually elongated." She moved her finger to the other fang.

He caught her hand. "Don't."

"Why? Does it hurt?"

"In the best way, but it's dangerous for me. I shouldn't have gotten aroused from that, but I did. You are overpowering a potion that has worked for me for centuries."

She lifted her eyes to his. "Centuries? How old are you?"

He forced a smile. "That's another question I was expecting. I'm seven hundred and fifty-three years old."

Mey's back slumped. "That's really old."

"Does it gross you out?"

She snorted. "Not really. You talk and behave like the age you look. Most of the time, anyway. I've noticed a few oddities about you and the other guys."

He arched a brow. "Like what?"

"You treat me like a lady. You even call me your lady Mey, which I really like."

He rubbed his jaw. "How would a human my age, or rather the age I appear, act toward you? Should I be rude to blend in better?"

"Not rude, it's not about that. Just less formal."

"I don't think I'm overly formal."

"You are not treating me like you treat your buddies, that's for sure. You censor your words around me. You don't cuss, you don't tell me inappropriate jokes, and you hold the door open for me." She giggled. "And you don't fart. Do immortals fart?"

He laughed. "You see? That's a question I'm sure no other Dormant has ever asked."

"Why not? It's a legitimate one, and you didn't answer me."

"We have the same bodily functions as humans, but flatulence in mixed company is not acceptable."

"Ha! That's what I meant. Who uses words like flatulence or mixed company? In today's world it's considered sexist to say that."

"Flatulence?"

"No, silly. Mixed company. You should just say company."

"I'll try to remember. So many things are considered offensive these days. It's hard to keep track."

There was nothing like a fart joke to defuse tension, but now that the joking was over, Yamanu found himself lost for words.

"So, what's next?" Mey asked. "How am I going to transition if you can't bite me?"

"Do you want to transition?"

She looked at him as if he was missing a screw. "Who doesn't want to become an invincible immortal? Did anyone ever decline the offer?"

"Not that I know of, but there are a few disadvantages that you should consider before deciding. We spend most of our lives in hiding, and we have to be very diligent about keeping our existence secret."

She waved a dismissive hand. "Not a problem. I'm very good at keeping secrets."

"Your parents. It's going to be difficult to explain why you are not aging. And if your sister transitions as well, then both of you would need to keep lying to them and use elaborate makeup to hide the fact that you remain untouched by the passage of time." He rubbed his jaw. "Although we might have a solution for that."

"What is it?"

"A young boy who recently turned immortal has developed a very rare ability. He can compel humans. Which means that he can compel your parents to never talk about what they know with anyone outside the four of you. The problem is that he is just a twelve-year-old, and his powers are not yet fully developed. But in a few years, he might be able to do that."

"So, he is the only one who can do it? Out of all the immortals? And how many immortals are there?"

"Our clan is small. We are less than one thousand people. But our enemies the Doomers have thousands of warriors. We don't know exactly how many, but we know that it's better for us to hide than engage them in battle."

"Whoa, hold on. You didn't mention enemies before. How dangerous are they? And why the animosity? Is it over territory?"

He chuckled. "Yeah, the whole territory of Earth. They want to rule it, and we don't want them to. That kind of sums it up."

"Tell me more."

"Gladly." As long as he could keep talking about things that had nothing to do with Mey's transition and his problem with inducing it, he was happy to postpone the inevitable.

61

MEY

*F*or over an hour, Mey listened to Yamanu retell the history of their people, trying to interrupt as little as possible, and only asking questions when she absolutely had to. He was a great storyteller, and to listen to him was like watching the events unfolding before her very eyes.

He'd started at the very beginning, with the young goddess falling in love and choosing to follow her heart instead of duty and obligation. And he'd finished with the present day and the miracle of finding Dormants. Finally, after thousands of years of lonely existence, a few lucky clan members had mates to form lifelong relationships with.

It was utterly fascinating, captivating, and Mey wanted to become part of that wonderful community of people almost as much as she wanted Yamanu to be her truelove mate.

What a concept. A bond so strong that it could last forever and feed energy into a relationship, never letting it go stale.

"Wait until Jin hears about this. She's going to flip."

"What about you? Are you flipping?"

"Am I ever?" She rolled her eyes. "I want that. All of it. I want you to be my truelove mate, and I want to live in your village, hang out with Wonder and hear details about the ancient world. And I want to talk with Annani and bask in her godly presence, and I want all these wonderful people to be my family."

Yamanu smiled, but it looked forced. "I'm so glad that you feel this way. But there is a slight problem."

"What?"

"My vow of celibacy. In order to induce you, I'll have to either break my vow or have another male do the induction. But I can't break my vow without potentially harming my people, and I can't conceive of another male touching you."

That was a problem. "What about artificial insemination?"

"I don't think it can work. Besides, I don't want any other male's venom in you either. I want you addicted to me and not anyone else."

Her shoulders slumped. "Yeah, I forgot about that. And you can't produce venom without getting aroused."

"Right."

"I know that you don't want to talk about it, but since we are laying it all out, how is your vow of celibacy protecting your people?"

He shook his head. "I haven't told anyone about it. My friends suspect that I'm celibate, but they don't know for sure. I want to keep it this way. At least for a little while longer until I decide what to do."

"I won't tell anyone. I promise."

He took her hand. "I will tell you, but not right now. Can you give me more time?"

His eyes were pleading with her to accept, and Mey couldn't deny him. After all, she hadn't revealed everything either.

She still hadn't told him about her days in the Mossad, and she wasn't sure she could even if she wanted to. It had been drilled into her head so hard to keep it a secret that she doubted the words could leave her mouth.

And then there was Jin's paranormal talent, which she hadn't told Yamanu about yet...

Suddenly the pieces of the puzzle realigned themselves perfectly, and what had been a vague suspicion became a conviction.

Jin's talent, the Mossad, the American Secret Service, people following her around to see if she did anything unusual.

Damn, she was putting everyone in danger by being here. The immortals she'd been hanging with were a much bigger scoop than Jin and her paranormal abilities.

"I need to disappear," she whispered. "I'm putting all of you in danger."

"Are you talking about the detective following you?"

She nodded.

"I told my boss about him, and he said that we shouldn't worry about it. To the world, we are who we seem to be. A model and her entourage. You just happened to hook up with Arielle's business manager."

"Perhaps you are right. But I still need to disappear. I know now why they have Jin, and why they want me too."

"Jin shares your ability."

"How did you know?"

"It was a logical assumption. Talent usually runs in the family. Your mother must have had it too. It's a shame we don't know who she is. Although she is probably too old to transition safely anyway."

Mey sighed. "If she's alive. She might have died."

"That's possible. So, what's caused your sudden alarm? Was it fear of exposing us?"

"That too. But I just connected the dots. Jin's talent is more useful than mine. If she touches a person once, she can see what they are doing and hear what's going on around them."

"That's an amazing spying capability."

Her eyes widened as the implications sank in. "Oh my God. It's so much worse than I imagined just a moment ago. If Jin was tuned in to me while you told me your story, she saw and heard everything that you've told me. And since I think she's been recruited by the government for her spying ability, they can get the information out of her."

Yamanu's hold on her hand tightened. "Can she only see and hear in real time? Or can she see and hear past events?"

"Only in real time."

"So, if she wasn't tuned into you right now, she won't know what we've talked about."

"Correct." Mey let out a breath. "Sorry for panicking, but I just wasn't thinking straight. I always feel tingles when she does it to me, and I didn't feel a thing. So, she wasn't tuning in to me. Your secret is safe."

Yamanu didn't look convinced. "You were absorbed in my story. You might have missed it."

"It's not something mild. I get goose bumps all over my arms." She lifted them. "See? No goose bumps."

"Are you sure about that?"

"Positive. But I'm also sure that they are eventually going to get tired of waiting for me to manifest my talent and just take me forcibly."

"They didn't abduct your sister. She went willingly. Do you think she knew why she was being recruited?"

Mey nodded. "I went to her old dorm room and meditated there. I was hoping to find out more about her new employer, maybe overhear a phone conversation. But all I got was her breaking up with her boyfriend over the phone. When she was done, she cried a little, and then she murmured something about others who were going to be more like her."

"Do you think that she was referring to her paranormal talent?"

"What else? She surely wasn't referring to other Asians. There are plenty of us everywhere. In fact, her next comment was about her hair being exactly like that of two billion other Asian women, but that none of them could do what she could."

"So she knew."

"It would seem so. But I don't think she knew that they would be limiting her ability to get in touch with her family, or that they would be monitoring her communication with the outside world."

"It's not uncommon in special units, especially for new recruits. She might be allowed more freedoms once she goes through the training program."

"Perhaps I should let them take me? So, I could be with her?" Mey looked down at their joined hands. "It would solve your dilemma. Without me, you wouldn't need to break your vow."

Yamanu hooked a finger under her chin and lifted her head so she had to look into his eyes. "Do you think that I could survive without you? Or that you could survive without me? We are bonded, my lady Mey."

She knew he spoke the truth. When she'd suggested letting herself get taken, her gut had flipped frantically, twisting on itself and tying in knots within knots.

"So, what do we do?"

YAMANU

*Y*amanu pulled out his phone. "I have to call my boss again. I already spoke to him about bringing you in, but I thought there was no rush. We are getting reinforcements tomorrow, so I can leave and take you with me."

Mey shook her head. "I have a shoot on Monday."

"Can't you cancel?"

"I can ask Derek if he can work with what he has so far. If I drop the project a day before the end, I can kiss my career goodbye. Dalia is not going to take me back, and rightfully so."

Yamanu wanted to point out that once she transitioned, she wasn't going back anyway, but there was still a small chance that she wasn't a Dormant and that she would need her job back.

"Can you check with him while I talk to my boss?"

"Sure. Are you going to the executive lounge to make your call?"

"I'll call from here." He leaned and took Mey's lips in a quick kiss. "We shared our secrets, so I don't need to make it private, but I don't want to talk with Kian while you are on the phone.

There is a reason we put it in the safe. I told you that it's possible to eavesdrop on your conversations even when it's off."

Eyes widening in alarm, she put her hand on his arm. "What if the government is monitoring your phone as well?"

"First of all, we are not sure it's the government. And secondly, this is a special clan-issue phone. The communication is highly encrypted, and it goes through our own satellites."

"You have satellites?"

"Just one, but we rent space on a couple of others."

She looked at his phone for a long moment. "Aren't you worried about my phone being tapped? They know that I'm hanging out with you. If I suddenly disappear, they'll come looking for me here. Worse, they will follow the signal wherever I go, and I can't get rid of my phone because I'm waiting for a call or message from Jin."

Yamanu clapped a hand over his forehead. "That's why they are allowing her to communicate with you. To make sure that you don't dump the phone when you run."

Mey tilted her head. "That's a little farfetched. First of all, why would they think that I would run? And secondly why would they assume that I would get rid of my phone?"

The wheels in Yamanu's head were on overdrive. What Mey had said was true, but his gut was telling him that he was right, which meant that his subconscious had already processed information his conscious brain was still trying to figure out.

He got out of bed and started pacing back and forth in front of it. "They must know that you have a background in intelligence, and therefore you are more likely to notice someone following you around, like you did. And with the training you got, you would know to get rid of your phone and get a burner."

"That's possible..." Mey slapped a hand over her mouth.

"The messages are not from Jin. They are using her phone to keep me tethered. Oh my God, now I'm sure that they are holding her prisoner."

"Why? Was there something off about them?"

"Yes, and I wondered about it. I thought it was a hidden message to watch out, but it was the opposite. She, or rather whoever had her phone, told me to keep doing what I'm doing because modeling is a great job. Jin never thought that it was. She used to say that I have much more to offer than my looks. Whoever sent it wanted me to relax about Jin and to stay put."

As Mey started trembling, Yamanu sat on the bed and pulled her into his arms. "There is no need to jump to conclusions. She might still be in training and not allowed outside communication. Were you allowed to call home during your military training?"

Mey shook her head. "No cell phones were allowed. But at least we were told ahead of time, so we could warn our families that they were not going to hear from us for three whole months. It was supposedly done to encourage bonding within the unit, but I suspected that they wanted us to cut the umbilical cord."

"It's most likely the case here as well."

"I hope you are right. They probably collected the phones from all the new recruits." She pinched her forehead between her thumb and forefinger. "But what if the part about having no reception there was actually true? I found a West Virginia travel guide in Jin's room. One page looked like it had been earmarked, and it was about a National Radio Quiet Zone in West Virginia. I know it's not much of a clue, and I'm not even sure it was Jin who earmarked that page, but that combined with the no reception comment might be."

Yamanu picked up his phone. "On second thought, call Derek from my phone." He handed it to her.

"Good thinking. No reason to alert the snoopers that I might be going somewhere. I also need to call Dalia."

"Will she keep the job for you?"

"If I don't drop the ball on her in the middle of a project, then yeah. There are plenty of models she can use while I'm on vacation. I just hope she's not going to be too pissed off that I'm calling her on a Sunday."

"Tell her it's an emergency, and when she asks what sort, tell her that you are not free to talk about it."

Mey nodded. "That's close enough to the truth, which is good. I hate lying."

MEY

The irony wasn't lost on Mey. Her life was all about keeping secrets and that necessitated lying. Perhaps that was the reason she tried to stick as close to the truth as she could whenever she could.

She called Derek first. "How are you holding up? Did your nephews tie you up already?"

"How did you know?"

"That's what they did last time."

"How do you remember that? It was a year ago."

She remembered every personal story anyone had ever told her, especially when kids were involved, because she loved hearing about families.

"I just do. Listen, I need a favor. Is there a way you can work with what we shot already so I don't need to show up on Monday?"

He chuckled. "Why? Is your new boyfriend taking you somewhere special?"

And then some. She was still stunned that Yamanu was willing to take her to his people's secret hideout. It still needed his boss's approval, but Yamanu claimed that he'd gotten a tentative one already, so it shouldn't be a problem.

Except, she had to lie to Derek and make up a story.

Mey still wasn't clear about how Yamanu planned on sneaking her out of New York while she was being watched.

"No, I wish. Something came up, but I really can't talk about it."

"Don't tell me that you got an offer from another agency. Dalia will be crushed."

Mey rolled her eyes. The dragon lady would cuss and throw stuff at the walls and then start a search for a new, tall Asian model. To Dalia, Mey was just an asset. Dalia liked her, but they weren't friends. Still she could feed Derek's suspicions and reinforce them.

"Okay, I'm not telling you that I got another offer."

"You sly, sly girl. What are they paying you? Is it much more than you're getting now? Do they need an experienced and charming photographer?"

Mey laughed. "I can't tell you anything now. We will talk when I come back."

"And when is that?"

She had no idea.

Maybe never?

"A couple of weeks. I really need a break from New York."

"I know what you mean. So have fun and call me if you can. I won't survive two weeks without knowing."

"I guess that's your way of telling me that you can manage with what you have."

He sighed. "I'll make it work. But you owe me. This will take hours of fiddling on Photoshop."

He did that anyway.

"You are the best. And I owe you big time."

When she was done with Derek, Mey plopped down on the

bed. "That was the easy one. Now I need to call the dragon lady."

Yamanu leaned over her and brushed a strand of hair away from her forehead before kissing it. "Do you want me to get you a drink?"

"Don't be silly. It's too early for that. Besides, alcohol packs a lot of calories." Then she reconsidered. After the morning she'd had, she could use a drink. "On second thought, I'll have one after this call."

Yamanu grinned, looking happy to assist in any way he could.

Was he a keeper or what?

Definitely a keeper.

Even if he couldn't break his vow, they could make it work somehow. The clan's doctor could come up with a solution, something like artificial insemination and a simultaneous venom injection. It was a little gross, but women did that all the time, either because their husbands couldn't make them pregnant, or because they were single and didn't want to wait, or because they just decided that marriage was not for them.

Perhaps she could even get pregnant like that. Having Yamanu's children would be much better, but if that was not possible, then this was an option.

Except, unlike in the human world, Yamanu would know who the donor was, and that might be a problem for him.

Oh, well, they could adopt.

No, they couldn't.

Mey slapped her forehead. She was still thinking in human terms. If she turned immortal, she would outlive her adopted children and that was horrible. And besides, she and Yamanu couldn't stay with the clan if they were raising human children.

They had only two options. Either Yamanu broke his vow, or he agreed to her getting artificial insemination. It didn't have to be from an immortal, she could do it in a human clinic with a human's donated semen.

But wasn't she getting carried away?

They'd known each other for less than a week, and she was already planning the rest of their immortal lives together.

It was still possible that she wasn't a Dormant, she still needed to find her sister, and Yamanu's boss still had to approve her arrival as well as Yamanu's leave of absence.

Speaking of the handsome devil, Yamanu entered the room with a tall drink in hand. "We have the green light from Kian. Did you call Dalia?"

"Not yet. I was sitting here like a doofus and planning the rest of our lives." She shook her head. "Talk about getting carried away. I've known you for less than a week, and there are hurdles the size of Jupiter in our way to the happily ever after."

Sitting on the bed, Yamanu wrapped his arm around her shoulders. "When it feels right, it's right. You know what Kian told me? That's the name of my boss if you haven't figured it out yet. And just so you know, he is the most cynical dude, so don't think he's some diehard romantic." Yamanu chuckled.

"What?"

"He said that when he first met his future wife, he'd known right away that she was the one for him, but because he'd believed himself a realist and a logic-driven person, he'd refused to accept it. Then his sister had pointed out that he was lying to himself and hurting Syssi's feelings. And they lived happily ever after. The end."

"It's a nice story."

"Every word is true. Tomorrow, when we get to the village, you can hear her version of it, which I'm sure is much more detailed and interesting. We are flying out in the afternoon."

"How did you manage to convince your boss so quickly?

Didn't he tell you that he needed time to consult with someone?"

"I explained the situation, and Kian agreed that we need to get you out of here as soon as possible."

Mey reached for the glass, lifted it to her mouth and gulped a third at one go. "It's really happening, isn't it? I feel as if I'm going to jump through an inter-dimensional portal and land in an alien world."

"Yeah, that about sums it up. Unfortunately, it won't be as easy as stepping through a portal. It will take a six-hour flight. Fortunately, it's going to be on the clan's private jet."

COMING UP NEXT
The Children of the Gods Book 33
Dark Queen's Knight

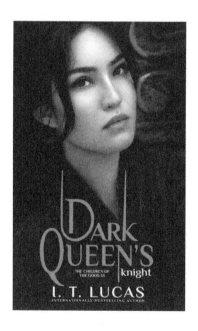

To read the first **3** chapters
JOIN THE VIP CLUB AT ITLUCAS.COM
and gain access to the **VIP** Portal

If you're already a subscriber and forgot the password to the VIP portal, you can find it at the

bottom of each of my emails. Or click **HERE** to retrieve it. You can also email me at

isabell@itlucas.com

Dear reader,

Thank you for reading the ***Children of the Gods***.

As an independent author, I rely on your support to spread the word. So if you enjoyed the story, please share your experience with others, and if it isn't too much trouble, I would greatly appreciate a brief review on Amazon.

Kind words will get good Karma sent your way -:)

Click here to leave a review

Love & happy reading,

Isabell

Find out more about Annani & Areana's past
The Children of the Goos Origins
1: Annani & Khiann's story
GODDESS'S CHOICE
2: Areana & Navuh's story
GODDESS'S HOPE

Don't miss out on
THE PERFECT MATCH SERIES
Perfect Match 1: Vampire's Consort
Perfect Match 2: King's Chosen
Perfect Match 3: Captain's Conquest

THE CHILDREN OF THE GODS SERIES

THE CHILDREN OF THE GODS ORIGINS

1: Goddess's Choice

When gods and immortals still ruled the ancient world, one young
goddess risked everything for love.

2: Goddess's Hope

Hungry for power and infatuated with the beautiful Areana, Navuh
plots his father's demise. After all, by getting rid of the insane god he
would be doing the world a favor. Except, when gods and immortals
conspire against each other, humanity pays the price.

But things are not what they seem, and prophecies should not to be
trusted...

THE CHILDREN OF THE GODS

1: Dark Stranger The Dream

Syssi's paranormal foresight lands her a job at Dr. Amanda Dokani's
neuroscience lab, but it fails to predict the thrilling yet terrifying turn
her life will take. Syssi has no clue that her boss is an immortal who'll
drag her into a secret, millennia-old battle over humanity's future. Nor
does she realize that the professor's imposing brother is the
mysterious stranger who's been starring in her dreams.

Since the dawn of human civilization, two warring factions of
immortals—the descendants of the gods of old—have been secretly
shaping its destiny. Leading the clandestine battle from his luxurious
Los Angeles high-rise, Kian is surrounded by his clan, yet alone.
Descending from a single goddess, clan members are forbidden to
each other. And as the only other immortals are their hated enemies,
Kian and his kin have been long resigned to a lonely existence of
fleeting trysts with human partners. That is, until his sister makes a
game-changing discovery—a mortal seeress who she believes is a
dormant carrier of their genes. Ever the realist, Kian is skeptical and

refuses Amanda's plea to attempt Syssi's activation. But when his enemies learn of the Dormant's existence, he's forced to rush her to the safety of his keep. Inexorably drawn to Syssi, Kian wrestles with his conscience as he is tempted to explore her budding interest in the darker shades of sensuality.

2: DARK STRANGER REVEALED

While sheltered in the clan's stronghold, Syssi is unaware that Kian and Amanda are not human, and neither are the supposedly religious fanatics that are after her. She feels a powerful connection to Kian, and as he introduces her to a world of pleasure she never dared imagine, his dominant sexuality is a revelation. Considering that she's completely out of her element, Syssi feels comfortable and safe letting go with him. That is, until she begins to suspect that all is not as it seems. Piecing the puzzle together, she draws a scary, yet wrong conclusion...

3: DARK STRANGER IMMORTAL

When Kian confesses his true nature, Syssi is not as much shocked by the revelation as she is wounded by what she perceives as his callous plans for her.

If she doesn't turn, he'll be forced to erase her memories and let her go. His family's safety demands secrecy – no one in the mortal world is allowed to know that immortals exist.

Resigned to the cruel reality that even if she stays on to never again leave the keep, she'll get old while Kian won't, Syssi is determined to enjoy what little time she has with him, one day at a time.

Can Kian let go of the mortal woman he loves? Will Syssi turn? And if she does, will she survive the dangerous transition?

4: DARK ENEMY TAKEN

Dalhu can't believe his luck when he stumbles upon the beautiful immortal professor. Presented with a once in a lifetime opportunity to grab an immortal female for himself, he kidnaps her and runs. If he ever gets caught, either by her people or his, his life is forfeit. But for a chance of a loving mate and a family of his own, Dalhu is prepared to do everything in his power to win Amanda's heart, and that includes leaving the Doom brotherhood and his old life behind.

Amanda soon discovers that there is more to the handsome Doomer than his dark past and a hulking, sexy body. But succumbing to her enemy's seduction, or worse, developing feelings for a ruthless killer is out of the question. No man is worth life on the run, not even the one and only immortal male she could claim as her own...

Her clan and her research must come first...

5: DARK ENEMY CAPTIVE

When the rescue team returns with Amanda and the chained Dalhu to the keep, Amanda is not as thrilled to be back as she thought she'd be. Between Kian's contempt for her and Dalhu's imprisonment, Amanda's budding relationship with Dalhu seems doomed. Things start to look up when Annani offers her help, and together with Syssi they resolve to find a way for Amanda to be with Dalhu. But will she still want him when she realizes that he is responsible for her nephew's murder? Could she? Will she take the easy way out and choose Andrew instead?

6: DARK ENEMY REDEEMED

Amanda suspects that something fishy is going on onboard the Anna. But when her investigation of the peculiar all-female Russian crew fails to uncover anything other than more speculation, she decides it's time to stop playing detective and face her real problem—a man she shouldn't want but can't live without.

6.5: MY DARK AMAZON

When Michael and Kri fight off a gang of humans, Michael gets stabbed. The injury to his immortal body recovers fast, but the one to his ego takes longer, putting a strain on his relationship with Kri.

7: DARK WARRIOR MINE

When Andrew is forced to retire from active duty, he believes that all he has to look forward to is a boring desk job. His glory days in special ops are over. But as it turns out, his thrill ride has just begun. Andrew discovers not only that immortals exist and have been manipulating global affairs since antiquity, but that he and his sister are rare possessors of the immortal genes.

Problem is, Andrew might be too old to attempt the activation process. His sister, who is fourteen years his junior, barely made it through the transition, so the odds of him coming out of it alive, let alone immortal, are slim.

But fate may force his hand.

Helping a friend find his long-lost daughter, Andrew finds a woman who's worth taking the risk for. Nathalie might be a Dormant, but the only way to find out for sure requires fangs and venom.

8: DARK WARRIOR'S PROMISE

Andrew and Nathalie's love flourishes, but the secrets they keep from each other taint their relationship with doubts and suspicions. In the meantime, Sebastian and his men are getting bolder, and the storm that's brewing will shift the balance of power in the millennia-old conflict between Annani's clan and its enemies.

9: DARK WARRIOR'S DESTINY

The new ghost in Nathalie's head remembers who he was in life, providing Andrew and her with indisputable proof that he is real and not a figment of her imagination.

Convinced that she is a Dormant, Andrew decides to go forward with his transition immediately after the rescue mission at the Doomers' HQ.

Fearing for his life, Nathalie pleads with him to reconsider. She'd rather spend the rest of her mortal days with Andrew than risk what they have for the fickle promise of immortality.

While the clan gets ready for battle, Carol gets help from an unlikely ally. Sebastian's second-in-command can no longer ignore the torment she suffers at the hands of his commander and offers to help her, but only if she agrees to his terms.

10: DARK WARRIOR'S LEGACY

Andrew's acclimation to his post-transition body isn't easy. His senses are sharper, he's bigger, stronger, and hungrier. Nathalie fears that the changes in the man she loves are more than physical. Measuring up to this new version of him is going to be a challenge.

Carol and Robert are disillusioned with each other. They are not destined mates, and love is not on the horizon. When Robert's three months are up, he might be left with nothing to show for his sacrifice.

Lana contacts Anandur with disturbing news; the yacht and its human cargo are in Mexico. Kian must find a way to apprehend Alex and rescue the women on board without causing an international incident.

11: Dark Guardian Found

What would you do if you stopped aging?

Eva runs. The ex-DEA agent doesn't know what caused her strange mutation, only that if discovered, she'll be dissected like a lab rat. What Eva doesn't know, though, is that she's a descendant of the gods, and that she is not alone. The man who rocked her world in one life-changing encounter over thirty years ago is an immortal as well.

To keep his people's existence secret, Bhathian was forced to turn his back on the only woman who ever captured his heart, but he's never forgotten and never stopped looking for her.

12: Dark Guardian Craved

Cautious after a lifetime of disappointments, Eva is mistrustful of Bhathian's professed feelings of love. She accepts him as a lover and a confidant but not as a life partner.

Jackson suspects that Tessa is his true love mate, but unless she overcomes her fears, he might never find out.

Carol gets an offer she can't refuse—a chance to prove that there is more to her than meets the eye. Robert believes she's about to commit a deadly mistake, but when he tries to dissuade her, she tells him to leave.

13: Dark Guardian's Mate

Prepare for the heart-warming culmination of Eva and Bhathian's story!

14: Dark Angel's Obsession

The cold and stoic warrior is an enigma even to those closest to him. His secrets are about to unravel...

15: Dark Angel's Seduction

Brundar is fighting a losing battle. Calypso is slowly chipping away his icy armor from the outside, while his need for her is melting it from the inside.

He can't allow it to happen. Calypso is a human with none of the Dormant indicators. There is no way he can keep her for more than a few weeks.

16: DARK ANGEL'S SURRENDER

Get ready for the heart pounding conclusion to Brundar and Calypso's story.

Callie still couldn't wrap her head around it, nor could she summon even a smidgen of sorrow or regret. After all, she had some memories with him that weren't horrible. She should've felt something. But there was nothing, not even shock. Not even horror at what had transpired over the last couple of hours.

Maybe it was a typical response for survivors--feeling euphoric for the simple reason that they were alive. Especially when that survival was nothing short of miraculous.

Brundar's cold hand closed around hers, reminding her that they weren't out of the woods yet. Her injuries were superficial, and the most she had to worry about was some scarring. But, despite his and Anandur's reassurances, Brundar might never walk again.

If he ended up crippled because of her, she would never forgive herself for getting him involved in her crap.

"Are you okay, sweetling? Are you in pain?" Brundar asked.

Her injuries were nothing compared to his, and yet he was concerned about her. God, she loved this man. The thing was, if she told him that, he would run off, or crawl away as was the case.

Hey, maybe this was the perfect opportunity to spring it on him.

17: DARK OPERATIVE: A SHADOW OF DEATH

As a brilliant strategist and the only human entrusted with the secret of immortals' existence, Turner is both an asset and a liability to the clan. His request to attempt transition into immortality as an alternative to cancer treatments cannot be denied without risking the clan's exposure. On the other hand, approving it means risking his premature death. In both scenarios, the clan will lose a valuable ally.

When the decision is left to the clan's physician, Turner makes plans to manipulate her by taking advantage of her interest in him.

Will Bridget fall for the cold, calculated operative? Or will Turner fall into his own trap?

18: Dark Operative: A Glimmer of Hope

As Turner and Bridget's relationship deepens, living together seems like the right move, but to make it work both need to make concessions.

Bridget is realistic and keeps her expectations low. Turner could never be the truelove mate she yearns for, but he is as good as she's going to get. Other than his emotional limitations, he's perfect in every way.

Turner's hard shell is starting to show cracks. He wants immortality, he wants to be part of the clan, and he wants Bridget, but he doesn't want to cause her pain.

His options are either abandon his quest for immortality and give Bridget his few remaining decades, or abandon Bridget by going for the transition and most likely dying. His rational mind dictates that he chooses the former, but his gut pulls him toward the latter. Which one is he going to trust?

19: Dark Operative: The Dawn of Love

Get ready for the exciting finale of Bridget and Turner's story!

20: Dark Survivor Awakened

This was a strange new world she had awakened to.

Her memory loss must have been catastrophic because almost nothing was familiar. The language was foreign to her, with only a few words bearing some similarity to the language she thought in. Still, a full moon cycle had passed since her awakening, and little by little she was gaining basic understanding of it--only a few words and phrases, but she was learning more each day.

A week or so ago, a little girl on the street had tugged on her mother's sleeve and pointed at her. "Look, Mama, Wonder Woman!"

The mother smiled apologetically, saying something in the language these people spoke, then scurried away with the child looking behind her shoulder and grinning.

When it happened again with another child on the same day, it was settled.

Wonder Woman must have been the name of someone important in this strange world she had awoken to, and since both times it had been said with a smile it must have been a good one.

Wonder had a nice ring to it.

She just wished she knew what it meant.

21: Dark Survivor Echoes of Love

Wonder's journey continues in *Dark Survivor Echoes of Love*.

22: Dark Survivor Reunited

The exciting finale of Wonder and Anandur's story.

23: Dark Widow's Secret

Vivian and her daughter share a powerful telepathic connection, so when Ella can't be reached by conventional or psychic means, her mother fears the worst.

Help arrives from an unexpected source when Vivian gets a call from the young doctor she met at a psychic convention. Turns out Julian belongs to a private organization specializing in retrieving missing girls.

As Julian's clan mobilizes its considerable resources to rescue the daughter, Magnus is charged with keeping the gorgeous young mother safe.

Worry for Ella and the secrets Vivian and Magnus keep from each other should be enough to prevent the sparks of attraction from kindling a blaze of desire. Except, these pesky sparks have a mind of their own.

24: Dark Widow's Curse

A simple rescue operation turns into mission impossible when the Russian mafia gets involved. Bad things are supposed to come in threes, but in Vivian's case, it seems like there is no limit to bad luck. Her family and everyone who gets close to her is affected by her curse.

Will Magnus and his people prove her wrong?

25: Dark Widow's Blessing

The thrilling finale of the Dark Widow trilogy!

26: DARK DREAM'S TEMPTATION

Julian has known Ella is the one for him from the moment he saw her picture, but when he finally frees her from captivity, she seems indifferent to him. Could he have been mistaken?

Ella's rescue should've ended that chapter in her life, but it seems like the road back to normalcy has just begun and it's full of obstacles. Between the pitying looks she gets and her mother's attempts to get her into therapy, Ella feels like she's typecast as a victim, when nothing could be further from the truth. She's a tough survivor, and she's going to prove it.

Strangely, the only one who seems to understand is Logan, who keeps popping up in her dreams. But then, he's a figment of her imagination —or is he?

27: DARK DREAM'S UNRAVELING

While trying to figure out a way around Logan's silencing compulsion, Ella concocts an ambitious plan. What if instead of trying to keep him out of her dreams, she could pretend to like him and lure him into a trap?

Catching Navuh's son would be a major boon for the clan, as well as for Ella. She will have her revenge, turning the tables on another scumbag out to get her.

28: DARK DREAM'S TRAP

The trap is set, but who is the hunter and who is the prey? Find out in this heart-pounding conclusion to the *Dark Dream* trilogy.

29: DARK PRINCE'S ENIGMA

As the son of the most dangerous male on the planet, Lokan lives by three rules:

Don't trust a soul.

Don't show emotions.

And don't get attached.

Will one extraordinary woman make him break all three?

30: DARK PRINCE'S DILEMMA

Will Kian decide that the benefits of trusting Lokan outweigh the risks?

Will Lokan betray his father and brothers for the greater good of his people?

Are Carol and Lokan true-love mates, or is one of them playing the other?

So many questions, the path ahead is anything but clear.

31: Dark Prince's Agenda

While Turner and Kian work out the details of Areana's rescue plan, Carol and Lokan's tumultuous relationship hits another snag. Is it a sign of things to come?

32 : Dark Queen's Quest

A former beauty queen, a retired undercover agent, and a successful model, Mey is not the typical damsel in distress. But when her sister drops off the radar and then someone starts following her around, she panics.

Following a vague clue that Kalugal might be in New York, Kian sends a team headed by Yamanu to search for him.

As Mey and Yamanu's paths cross, he offers her his help and protection, but will that be all?

33: Dark Queen's Knight

As the only member of his clan with a godlike power over human minds, Yamanu has been shielding his people for centuries, but that power comes at a steep price. When Mey enters his life, he's faced with the most difficult choice.

The safety of his clan or a future with his fated mate.

34: Dark Queen's Army

As Mey anxiously waits for her transition to begin and for Yamanu to test whether his godlike powers are gone, the clan sets out to solve two mysteries:

Where is Jin, and is she there voluntarily?

Where is Kalugal, and what is he up to?

35: Dark Spy Conscripted

Jin possesses a unique paranormal ability. Just by touching someone, she can insert a mental hook into their psyche and tie a string of her consciousness to it, creating a tether. That doesn't make her a spy, though, not unless her talent is discovered by those seeking to exploit it.

36: DARK SPY'S MISSION

Jin's first spying mission is supposed to be easy. Walk into the club, touch Kalugal to tether her consciousness to him, and walk out.

Except, they should have known better.

37: DARK SPY'S RESOLUTION

The best-laid plans often go awry...

38: DARK OVERLORD NEW HORIZON

Jacki has two talents that set her apart from the rest of the human race.

She has unpredictable glimpses of other people's futures, and she is immune to mind manipulation.

Unfortunately, both talents are pretty useless for finding a job other than the one she had in the government's paranormal division.

It seemed like a sweet deal, until she found out that the director planned on producing super babies by compelling the recruits into pairing up. When an opportunity to escape the program presented itself, she took it, only to find out that humans are not at the top of the food chain.

Immortals are real, and at the very top of the hierarchy is Kalugal, the most powerful, arrogant, and sexiest male she has ever met.

With one look, he sets her blood on fire, but Jacki is not a fool. A man like him will never think of her as anything more than a tasty snack, while she will never settle for anything less than his heart.

39: DARK OVERLORD'S WIFE

Jacki is still clinging to her all-or-nothing policy, but Kalugal is chipping away at her resistance. Perhaps it's time to ease up on her convictions. A little less than all is still much better than nothing, and a couple of decades with a demigod is probably worth more than a lifetime with a mere mortal.

40: Dark Overlord's Clan

As Jacki and Kalugal prepare to celebrate their union, Kian takes every precaution to safeguard his people. Except, Kalugal and his men are not his only potential adversaries, and compulsion is not the only power he should fear.

41: Dark Choices The Quandary

When Rufsur and Edna meet, the attraction is as unexpected as it is undeniable. Except, she's the clan's judge and councilwoman, and he's Kalugal's second-in-command. Will loyalty and duty to their people keep them apart?

42: Dark Choices Paradigm Shift

Edna and Rufsur are miserable without each other, and their two-week separation seems like an eternity. Long-distance relationships are difficult, but for immortal couples they are impossible. Unless one of them is willing to leave everything behind for the other, things are just going to get worse. Except, the cost of compromise is far greater than giving up their comfortable lives and hard-earned positions. The future of their people is on the line.

43: Dark Choices The Accord

The winds of change blowing over the village demand hard choices. For better or worse, Kian's decisions will alter the trajectory of the clan's future, and he is not ready to take the plunge. But as Edna and Rufsur's plight gains widespread support, his resistance slowly begins to erode.

44: Dark Secrets Resurgence

On a sabbatical from his Stanford teaching position, Professor David Levinson finally has time to write the sci-fi novel he's been thinking about for years.

The phenomena of past life memories and near-death experiences are too controversial to include in his formal psychiatric research, while fiction is the perfect outlet for his esoteric ideas.

Hoping that a change of pace will provide the inspiration he needs, David accepts a friend's invitation to an old Scottish castle.

45: Dark Secrets Unveiled

When Professor David Levinson accepts a friend's invitation to an old Scottish castle, what he finds there is more fantastical than his most outlandish theories. The castle is home to a clan of immortals, their leader is a stunning demigoddess, and even more shockingly, it might be precisely where he belongs.

Except, the clan founder is hiding a secret that might cast a dark shadow on David's relationship with her daughter.

Nevertheless, when offered a chance at immortality, he agrees to undergo the dangerous induction process.

Will David survive his transition into immortality? And if he does, will his relationship with Sari survive the unveiling of her mother's secret?

46: Dark Secrets Absolved

Absolution.

David had given and received it.

The few short hours since he'd emerged from the coma had felt incredible. He'd finally been free of the guilt and pain, and for the first time since Jonah's death, he had felt truly happy and optimistic about the future.

He'd survived the transition into immortality, had been accepted into the clan, and was about to marry the best woman on the face of the planet, his true love mate, his salvation, his everything.

What could have possibly gone wrong?

Just about everything.

47: Dark haven Illusion

Welcome to Safe Haven, where not everything is what it seems.

On a quest to process personal pain, Anastasia joins the Safe Haven Spiritual Retreat.

Through meditation, self-reflection, and hard work, she hopes to make peace with the voices in her head.

This is where she belongs.

Except, membership comes with a hefty price, doubts are sacrilege, and leaving is not as easy as walking out the front gate.

Is living in utopia worth the sacrifice?

Anastasia believes so until the arrival of a new acolyte changes everything.

Apparently, the gods of old were not a myth, their immortal descendants share the planet with humans, and she might be a carrier of their genes.

48: Dark Haven Unmasked

As Anastasia leaves Safe Haven for a week-long romantic vacation with Leon, she hopes to explore her newly discovered passionate side, their budding relationship, and perhaps also solve the mystery of the voices in her head. What she discovers exceeds her wildest expectations.

In the meantime, Eleanor and Peter hope to solve another mystery. Who is Emmett Haderech, and what is he up to?

THE PERFECT MATCH SERIES

PERFECT MATCH 1: VAMPIRE'S CONSORT

When Gabriel's company is ready to start beta testing, he invites his old crush to inspect its medical safety protocol.

Curious about the revolutionary technology of the *Perfect Match Virtual Fantasy-Fulfillment studios*, Brenna agrees.

Neither expects to end up partnering for its first fully immersive test run.

PERFECT MATCH 2: KING'S CHOSEN

When Lisa's nutty friends get her a gift certificate to *Perfect Match Virtual Fantasy Studios*, she has no intentions of using it. But since the only way to get a refund is if no partner can be found for her, she makes sure to request a fantasy so girly and over the top that no sane guy will pick it up.

Except, someone does.

Warning: This fantasy contains a hot, domineering crown prince, sweet insta-love, steamy love scenes painted with light shades of gray, a wedding, and a HEA in both the virtual and real worlds.

Intended for mature audience.

PERFECT MATCH 3: CAPTAIN'S CONQUEST

Working as a Starbucks barista, Alicia fends off flirting all day long, but none of the guys are as charming and sexy as Gregg. His frequent visits are the highlight of her day, but since he's never asked her out, she assumes he's taken. Besides, between a day job and a budding music career, she has no time to start a new relationship.

That is until Gregg makes her an offer she can't refuse—a gift certificate to the virtual fantasy fulfillment service everyone is talking about. As a huge Star Trek fan, Alicia has a perfect match in mind—the captain of the Starship Enterprise.

Also by I. T. Lucas

45: Dark Secrets Unveiled
46: Dark Secrets Absolved
Dark Haven
47: Dark haven Illusion
48: Dark Haven Unmasked

PERFECT MATCH

Perfect Match 1: Vampire's Consort
Perfect Match 2: King's Chosen
Perfect Match 3: Captain's Conquest

The Children of the Gods Series Sets

Books 1-3: Dark Stranger trilogy—Includes a bonus short story: **The Fates take a Vacation**
Books 4-6: Dark Enemy Trilogy —Includes a bonus short story—**The Fates' Post-Wedding Celebration**
Books 7-10: Dark Warrior Tetralogy
Books 11-13: Dark Guardian Trilogy
Books 14-16: Dark Angel Trilogy
Books 17-19: Dark Operative Trilogy
Books 20-22: Dark Survivor Trilogy
Books 23-25: Dark Widow Trilogy
Books 26-28: Dark Dream Trilogy
Books 29-31: Dark Prince Trilogy
Books 32-34: Dark Queen Trilogy
Books 35-37: Dark Spy Trilogy
Books 38-40: Dark Overlord Trilogy
Books 41-43: Dark Choices Trilogy

BOOKS 44-46: DARK SECRETS TRILOGY

MEGA SETS

THE CHILDREN OF THE GODS: BOOKS 1-6—INCLUDES CHARACTER LISTS

THE CHILDREN OF THE GODS: BOOKS 6.5-10—INCLUDES CHARACTER LISTS

TRY THE CHILDREN OF THE GODS SERIES ON AUDIBLE

2 FREE audiobooks with your new Audible subscription!

FOR EXCLUSIVE PEEKS AT UPCOMING RELEASES & A FREE COMPANION BOOK

JOIN MY *VIP CLUB* AND GAIN ACCESS TO THE VIP PORTAL AT
ITLUCAS.COM

CLICK HERE TO JOIN
(OR GO TO: http://eepurl.com/blMTpD)

INCLUDED IN YOUR FREE MEMBERSHIP:

- **FREE** CHILDREN OF THE GODS COMPANION BOOK 1
- **FREE** NARRATION OF GODDESS'S CHOICE—BOOK 1 IN THE CHILDREN OF THE GODS ORIGINS SERIES.
- PREVIEW CHAPTERS OF UPCOMING RELEASES.
- AND OTHER EXCLUSIVE CONTENT OFFERED ONLY TO MY VIPS.

Printed in Great Britain
by Amazon